'Whadda we do n

Shel Talmy was born in Chi
family to California when he
nationally networked teenage quiz programme – 'The Quiz Kids' – persuaded him that his future lay in the entertainments business. He became an international record producer, ultimately responsible for a sale of 85 million records, and amongst other groups he produced The Kinks, The Who and Manfred Mann.

Shel Talmy lives in London and is now devoting his career exclusively to writing. He has travelled the world in search of authentic material for his future books.

Shel Talmy

'Whadda we do now, Butch?'

Pan Original London and Sydney

For Steven and Jonna and special thanks to Anni

First published in Great Britain 1978 by Pan Books Ltd,
Cavaye Place, London SW10 9PG

ISBN 0 330 25672 2

Printed and bound in Great Britain by
Richard Clay (The Chaucer Press) Ltd, Bungay, Suffolk

Contents

1 Funeral in San Vincente 7
2 'What the hell are you doing on my ship?' 19
3 Pinkerton's leading agent 26
4 Walking-around money 32
5 Smash and grab in Old Burlington Street 39
6 Spending it 50
7 The proposition 62
8 Darts, a circus, and the Titan Crusher 71
9 Reconnaissance 90
10 Come with me, little girl 101
11 The Kaiser at Victoria station 109
12 Laughing gas 115
13 The big game at White's 121
14 Shootin' practice 138
15 'What the hell are we doing here?' 151
16 'Always leave 'em laughing' 179
17 Exit at eighty 187
18 Sylvia who? 198
19 'Whadda we do now, Butch?' 200

1 Funeral in San Vincente

The buzzing of the fly sounded loud in the stillness as it zeroed in on its target, the rump of one of a pair of animals that plodded along behind two dusty cowboys. The mule's tail swished in the hot air and squashed it flat.

For a mile or more Butch Cassidy had been watching his feet with fascination. There they went, one in front of the other, leaving a faint imprint of worn boots in the dusty road, each step a little closer to – where? He raised his eyes and squinted into the distance, and stopped.

The Sundance Kid, who had been busy watching his own feet, bumped in to him. 'What the hell are you stopping for, Butch?'

The smaller of the two mules used the halt to defecate noisily on to the baked earth.

Butch Cassidy pointed into the heat haze. 'Look, that must be San Vincente.'

Sundance shaded his eyes and peered down the narrow road. A huddle of small buildings, their white walls winking brightly in the glare of the midday sun, squatted on the parched plain like desiccated toadstools.

'Well, it sure as hell looks like somewhere.'

Twenty minutes later they entered the town through its one street, that meandered lazily between little adobe houses. A hot breeze stirred up dust devils at their feet that danced briefly and then collapsed.

'Looks dead as a cemetery,' Sundance grumbled.

'It's siesta time,' Butch said matter-of-factly.

'Let's see if we can rustle up some grub and a drink.'

'That sounds like one of your better ideas.'

They made a turn in the road and came to a low stone wall that bordered a wide strip of gravel-strewn ground and a shaded patio that led into a low-ceilinged adobe building. Over the door a faded and weathered sign read *Cantina*. Butch and Sundance tethered the mules to a hitching post and went in.

An old man lifted his white head from where it had been resting on his arms and looked blearily at the two strangers. '*Si,*' he greeted them without enthusiasm. The tips of his thick moustache swung pendulously with the effort of speech.

'Hi, *amigo,*' Butch said looking around the square room. The place was cool, protected from the sun by the thick walls, and was a carbon copy of dozens of other *cantinas* in Mexico and all through South America. 'We want a drink and some food.'

The old man looked at him without any sign of comprehension.

'Drink. *Copa.*' Butch snatched an imaginary glass out of the air and tilted it down his throat. 'And *comer.*' He mimed stuffing food in his mouth.

'Ah, *si si,*' the old man said, '*momento.*' He got up and shuffled through a doorway into a back room.

Sundance took off his hat, wiped the inside with his bandana and then mopped the perspiration off his face. 'It gives me a real good feelin' to know my pardner speaks such good Spanish.'

'It's nothin' Kid,' Butch said modestly. 'If you've got the knack you can do anything.'

The old man, busy in the kitchen preparing the food and drink for the two cowboys, looked idly out the window at the mules. The larger one was silver-grey and carried a pack covered by a blanket that was securely tied down, and it had a brand.

The old man, busy in the kitchen preparing the food and through rheumey eyes – three interlocked circles, the brand and trademark of the largest ranchero for hundreds of miles around. And it was only that morning that the policeman had stopped by and told him to watch for such an animal as it was stolen and the men who had stolen it had also, incidentally, robbed the payroll wagon, that was on its way to the mines, of *mucho dinero.* There would be a big reward.

The old man served the food and drink with trembling hands. Butch noticed and dismissed it as one of the penalties of old age.

The old man went back to the kitchen, paused long enough to jam a battered sombrero on his head, then shambled as quickly as his doddery legs would carry him out the back door, heading for the house where he knew the policeman was taking his siesta with an unmarried lady of the town.

Butch tilted his chair back and examined his half empty plate with a critical eye. 'Ya know somethin' Kid? Whatever that is we're eating, it hasn't stopped movin' yet.'

Sundance grunted. 'In that case you'd better hog-tie it before it gets away.'

'No, I think I'll just have myself another drink. Where's that old man gone?' Butch stood up and walked into the empty kitchen, spotted a jug and brought it back with him to the table. He filled the glasses and raised his in a toast. 'Here's to you, Kid.'

'I'll drink to that.' Sundance swallowed the contents of the glass thirstily and wiped his mouth on a dusty sleeve. 'Whadda you wanna do now, Butch? And if it's got anything to do with movin' I gotta tell ya, my feet are killing me.'

'I think we should stick around here until sundown and then travel through the night. I could use a couple of hours of shut-eye myself.'

Sundance put his hat back on and tilted it over his eyes. 'Suits me. See ya later.'

The sun was low in the west when the eight policemen reached the protection of the stone wall that marked the boundary of the *cantina*. They crawled on hands and knees to avoid being seen, stifling exclamations of pain all the way as one or another of them lowered his weight on to a sharp pebble. They used extreme caution when they peered over the top of the wall and into the dim interior of the building. The sign hanging from rusty bolts shivered in the light breeze, the leaves of the large shade tree rustled and sighed. Nothing else stirred.

The chair that was tipped precariously against the wall dropped to the floor with a bang. Butch woke with a start, rubbed his eyes, stood up and stretched and scratched, a vague thought going through his mind about fleas and how to get rid of them.

Sundance was still asleep, his hands folded in his lap. His hat covered his face and made his soft snores sound as though they had their origin in the depths of a cavern. Butch sauntered to the open door that led to the patio and leaned against the jamb.

As far as he could see almost nothing moved on the barren land that was so common to this part of Bolivia. The one exception was a buzzard that circled in lazy spirals in the distance, perhaps scouting for carrion or waiting with predatory patience until a sick animal breathed its last breath. The late afternoon sky was a deepening blue, melting into indigo, a few cirrus clouds like frisky lambs scudded along high overhead. Butch watched a scrap of paper that a sluggish breeze propelled along the ground at intervals. It was still hot and brought little relief. Off in the far distance the range of mountains was just a smudge on the horizon, an unbroken line too far off to discern individual peaks. It was very peaceful.

The shot that zinged past his ear and took a chink out of the wall only missed by a very little. 'Jee-sus.' Butch dived head first into the room.

Sundance jumped up, drew and cocked his gun in one motion. 'What the hell was that?'

'That,' said Butch from his position on the floor, 'was very close.'

Sundance dropped to a crouch and made for the window. 'Damn it,' he muttered, 'I always gotta find out things for myself.' He kept well out of the way of the line of fire, reached the side of the window and cautiously edged one eye around the frame. No one was in sight.

'Maybe it's a mistake,' Butch ventured hopefully.

Sundance grunted.

'All right, it isn't a mistake. Maybe there's only one of 'em.'

Sundance took off his stetson, draped it on top of his gun barrel and pushed it slowly into view. A barrage of shots ripped into the hat and pinged off the far wall. Sundance looked at the newly acquired holes. 'Butch, there's more than one of 'em.'

Butch scrambled up from the floor and drew his gun. Another volley of shots came through the open window.

'They're making me mad, Butch!'

'Just try to control yourself Kid. You know I warned you about your temper. Why don't you . . .'

Sundance jumped up and started blazing away with both his .45s. Yells, screams and several Spanish oaths could be heard clearly over the noise. Sundance stopped firing and gave a short mirthless laugh. 'That'll teach 'em to show us some respect!'

'That's right, Kid,' Butch soothed. 'You don't think that'll – ugh – get 'em mad at us, do you?'

'No. No I don't, Butch,' Sundance said with icy calm. 'I think they're gonna like it so much they're gonna invite us to a Saturday night hoedown. What else did ya have in mind?'

'Look, Kid, it's gonna be dark in about an hour and maybe we can slip outta here. After all.' he continued reasonably, 'we didn't steal all that money just to get shot fulla holes.'

'I remember the money. The money's on the mule, Butch.'

'I know, I know, but I'll go get it. I left it there, so it's up to me. You cover me and I'll go get it right now.'

Sundance stopped reloading, one bullet poised before an empty chamber and looked at Butch quizzically. 'Funny, I never figured you for a suicide.'

'C'mon, Kid. You know I got faith in you. You're not gonna let those *hombres* get me.'

Sundance considered the compliment and shrugged. 'Better go now before you change your mind.'

Butch drew his revolvers and held them out. 'You'd better take my guns in case you need 'em. I'll be too busy to do any shooting, and you know I couldn't hit the side of a barn anyway.'

Sundance stuck the extra guns in his belt and took up a position by the front door. 'Ready when you are, Butch. And don't be long.'

'Aren't you gonna wish me luck?'

Without turning Sundance lifted the revolvers and waggled them in Butch's direction. 'Your luck's right here, *amigo*.'

Sundance jumped out of the door firing as he went and Butch came right behind him sprinting for the mules. The policemen were taken by surprise and dived for the dubious cover of the low wall. They returned the fire wildly without getting close to either of the two targets.

Butch zigzagged his way to the smaller mule, tore at the straps restraining the saddlebags, broke the last one in his haste and slung them over his shoulder.

Sundance kept up a steady stream of fire. He bobbed and

weaved, and never presented a stationary target. He had already emptied his own guns and was halfway through the extra pair when, out of the corner of his eye, he saw Butch take off ten feet from the door and disappear into the restaurant sliding on his belly. Sundance backed up quickly, still shooting at the occasional head that was brave enough to show itself. Both hammers clicked on empty chambers just as he reached the safety of the thick walls of the *cantina.*

Butch, on his knees examining himself for holes and finding none, looked up cheerfully. 'We did it, Kid. With teamwork, we can do anything!'

Sundance was unsmiling. 'Yeah. Well, before you get too damned happy about what we can do next, take a look out of the window.'

Butch's smile disappeared. He crawled over to the window and looked out. 'Oh shit!' he said under his breath.

Off in the distance a troop of cavalry, at least fifty strong, were rapidly approaching. A standard bearer holding the Bolivian flag high rode alongside a magnificently dressed officer. The faint tinkle of harness and spurs drifted in through the open window. A cheer went up from the policemen and was promptly answered by the cavalry.

'Kid, I think we're in trouble.'

'We're in more trouble than you think. I'm almost out of ammunition.'

Butch and Sundance watched glumly as the troops rode up, dismounted, and, after a crisp order, deployed themselves around the house.

The officer handed his horse to a waiting soldier and strode towards the *cantina*, stopping just outside pistol range. '*Americanos!*' he shouted. 'Surrender, or we will be forced to kill you!'

'Well, at least he speaks English,' Sundance commented laconically.

'And he comes right to the point.'

'*Americanos!* What is your answer?' the officer bellowed.

'We're thinking!' Butch shouted back.

'Then here is something to help you with the speed of your

thoughts!' the officer yelled. He raised his arm and let it fall. A thunderclap of rifle fire exploded into the building and through the windows and door.

'Impatient little bastard, ain't he,' Butch said, then swallowed hard to stop his ears from ringing.

'And mean too,' Sundance agreed, shaking his head like a punchdrunk boxer. He sat on the floor and leaned his back against the wall. 'So, whadda we do now, Butch?'

'We could rush 'em.'

'Very funny.'

'I didn't think you'd like that much. I have another idea and I don't think you'll like that any better.'

'I don't think I wanna know.' Then with resignation, 'OK, tell me.'

Butch told him and the Sundance Kid sat bolt upright in indignation and then slumped in dejection.

Outside, the officer waited, resplendent in a spotlessly white uniform jacket that had a double row of shiny gold buttons and an array of rainbow-coloured medals pinned to his left breast. With care he had managed to retain the knife-edge creases on his breeches. They were sky blue and matched the broad brimmed hat from which a white plume protruded at a rakish angle. He decided that enough time had passed, filled his lungs and yelled, '*Americanos*, this is your ...'

He craned his neck forward to see what waved in the open window. It was certainly not a flag of surrender, but appeared to be a bundle of paper, green paper. The officer issued a curt command to his troops to stand down, but to be watchful and ready to fire at a moment's notice. He set his hat at a jaunty angle and strode with confident steps towards the *cantina*.

'Here he comes,' Sundance said in disgust. 'He looks like a goddamn Christmas tree.'

'That's good, Kid, 'cause he's about to meet Santa Claus.'

The officer came in and paused by the doorway, blinking to adjust his eyes to the dim light. He looked about him and took in at a glance the scarred wooden table, the uneaten food on tin plates, the dusty floor, and the unlit candle held in a bracket that trailed spindles of wax where it had melted. He turned to the two men, favoured them with a thin smile, swept off his hat with a flourish and made a slight bow. 'Capitan Rodriguez at your service, gentlemen. You are of course, Butch Cassidy and the Sundance Kid. I have heard much about you. I must confess I never thought I would meet you under such ... ideal circumstances.'

Sundance, hand on hip, looked at the captain mockingly. 'He's a real funny man, Butch.'

'Let me do the talking, Kid.' Butch twisted his face into a wide smile with an effort. 'It is our pleasure, Captain Rodriguez. You speak good English.'

'I was educated in your country, *Señor*. That is not, however, relevant to why we are here. You are notorious gunmen, two very bad *hombres*. To capture you ...' his black pencil-thin moustache twitched in a quick smile and he regarded them through eyes that resembled gleaming black marbles and hinted at Indian ancestry, '... dead or alive would be, as you say, a feather in my cap.'

'What's wrong with the damn feather you got in there now?' the Kid muttered.

'I was intrigued,' the captain continued, 'with what you were waving. It looked very like ...'

'It was money,' Butch cut in smoothly. 'Good old honest-to-God Yankee greenbacks. We thought you might accept them for the trouble you were put to – comin' all the way out here in this heat. I'll bet you had a lot better things to do, huh? Left a little woman at home, maybe? Card game with the boys?'

Rodriguez held them with a steady gaze. 'I assure you that no diversion would have prevented me from being here. I will savour this moment for a lifetime. As for the money,' Rodriguez tapped his chin thoughtfully with a forefinger, 'a more suspicious man than I could think that you were trying to bribe me.'

'Bribe you?' Butch echoed, his incredulity only partly feigned, as pay-offs to officials were a way of life out here.

Sundance looked up to the ceiling.

Rodriguez looked away and studied a spider in the corner that dangled at the end of a single thread. 'How much money is there, *Señor*?'

'Twenty thousand dollars, Captain – all for you.'

Rodriguez swivelled around to face them, his eyes narrowed, a glint of avarice just visible under the lowered lids. 'But,' he said pensively, 'there was forty thousand dollars on the payroll wagon, no?'

'Right again!' Butch agreed with enthusiasm. 'I knew you were a real smart fella. Didn't I say that, Kid? Half for you and half for us. What could be fairer?'

The captain caressed the polished black leather belt around his waist and fingered the holster that was attached to it. 'What, *Señor* Cassidy, is to stop me from killing you both and taking all the money?'

'How about this?' Sundance produced the revolver he held behind his back and levelled it at the captain's stomach. Rodriguez stared at the gun and spoke with indifference.

'If you kill me, *Señor* Sundance, you are both dead men.'

Butch forced a grin. 'What's all this talk of killing? He's only kidding, Kid. Aren't you, captain? You gotta watch what you're saying. My *amigo* don't have much of a sense of humour.'

'I understand completely. I too have a very little sense of humour. I want all the money,' the captain announced, 'and I will let you go free.'

Sundance growled deep in his throat and cocked the hammer on his Colt. Butch grabbed his arm. 'Hold it, Kid. Don't lose your temper.' He turned to Rodriguez. 'Now, just hang on a minute, don't go away. I gotta talk to my *compadre*.'

The gun Sundance held never wavered as he allowed himself to be hauled back into a far corner of the room.

'Listen, Kid,' Butch whispered, 'I know his type, he's a greedy bastard, but he'd rather be a dead hero than give in. You know how *macho* these South Americans think they are. I don't want to be a martyr over a few bucks.'

'It's twenty thousand bucks,' Sundance whispered fiercely, 'and it should be forty thousand. We risked our lives to get it, remember?'

'Oh, c'mon Kid, it wasn't that bad. Those guards started running the moment we showed ourselves. I don't think they had much stomach for *gringo* bandits.'

'Well, that don't matter none,' Sundance persisted with stubborn perversity. 'We still had to take the time to steal it, didn't we? And now you wanna give it away. I'd like to plug him just to wipe that smartass expression off his face.'

'C'mon Kid,' Butch pleaded. 'Do it my way. I never steered you wrong.'

'Ha!' Sundance spat it out like he'd found a live worm in a green apple. He thought about all the times he'd listened to Butch's ideas back in Wyoming, Colorado, their trip through Texas and the time he'd taken Etta Place to New York City and convinced her to go with him to South America. It was three years since she had left, and he wondered what happened to her. That was a weird thought to have now, when there was a great chance he was going to get his ass shot off at any moment. He tried to concentrate. On the whole he had to admit, Butch hadn't steered him too far wrong. And anyway, he could always have said no. Nobody had forced him to go along with all the crazy schemes. The tension drained out of his body at a slow trickle.

'Good boy,' Butch sighed with relief. He tugged at his sleeve and they moved back towards the captain. 'We've decided to accept your generous offer.' Butch was only able to muster a sick smile. 'But we want horses and some grub.'

Rodriguez was now sure of himself and sat down on a chair, casually crossing one leg over the other. 'I'm afraid that's impossible. What would dead men want with horses?' He held up his hand as Sundance reacted and drew a bead on the middle of the captain's forehead. 'A moment *Señor*. For the benefit of my men and the police, you must appear to die. After all, what would people think if it were to be known that Capitan Rodriguez from one of the oldest and most influential families in La Paz had cornered two famous outlaws with enough troops to start a small war, and then allowed them to go free? It would be the end of my career, and would bring lasting shame on my family. This, I am sure you understand, cannot be. So, as I said, as far as anyone knows, you must appear to die.'

Butch glanced out through the window, saw the soldiers spread out ready to fire and decided this was a good time to be agreeable. 'That's real smart, Captain. Isn't that smart Kid?'

Sundance said nothing.

'How you fixing to do that?'

Rodriguez had made some rapid calculations the moment the money had been offered. He had sifted through all the variables of this golden opportunity and arrived at a typically Latin solution. He related the story, taking pleasure in how glib he sounded. 'I will call my men in and tell them that two such desperate criminals deserve to be executed, and I will do it personally, as is only right. A leader of men does not ask them to do anything he will not himself do. They will accept this without question. I will say that you have buried the payroll somewhere and refuse to tell me where it is, so I have decided you must die. I will have them dig graves and then retire. Two shots, the graves are filled in and that is the end of Butch Cassidy and the Sundance Kid.'

'Very neat. And that way,' Sundance said with venom, 'you get away with the money and you go home looking like a goddamn hero! I bet ya they'll even give you another pretty medal to pin on your chest.'

Rodriguez touched the place on his chest where the new medal would go. It was a half unconscious gesture, but tangible enough for him to almost feel the hard outlines of the new decoration. 'As you say *Señor* Sundance, this exploit will not harm my reputation. I might even be promoted to Major.'

Sundance made a disgusted noise. 'Are we gonna let him get away with that, Butch?'

'Yeah, Kid, we are.'

An hour later, just as the sun dipped below the horizon in a final glorious burst that tinted the plain in hues of burnt orange, crimson and magenta, Captain Rodriguez led his troop of cavalry out of San Vincente with the police close behind. At the back of the *cantina* two fresh graves had been dug and filled in, and crude wooden crosses erected. Scratched on the crosses it said: *Butch Cassidy* and *The Sundance Kid – Died April 10, 1910.*

And so the story spread far and wide of how Butch and Sundance met their ignominious end at the hands of the Bolivian cavalry.

*

It had gone as smoothly as Rodriguez had predicted. When the soldiers came in, he held a gun on the two men, which Butch had taken the precaution of emptying. Sundance hid his fully loaded Colt behind his back – just in case the captain had delusions of being a real hero and decided to change his mind. The graves were dug by sweating troopers, and when they finished they laid down their spades and were ordered to go outside and stand to attention. They could hear the captain's clear ringing tones as he delivered the death sentence in Spanish, filled with phrases about the depravity of the human spirit and the depths to which misguided men, intent on wrecking their useless lives, could sink. It was a fine speech that would be told and retold around the barrack rooms and mess halls, and eventually filter into the better salons of La Paz, and echo down the marbled halls of the seat of Government. Captain Rodriguez would become a folk hero. Captain Rodriguez was destined for greater things.

There was a pause, a deathly hush, and the sound of two shots spaced closely together, richocheted off the walls and raced into the desert, dying away like distant thunder.

When the men were called back a few minutes later to fill in the graves, the sacks of potatoes that had been thrown in passed easily in the twilight for the huddled forms of dead men. The captain said a brief service over the souls of the departed, and the soldiers bowed their heads respectfully.

When the troops were lost to sight and only the dust cloud remained, Butch and Sundance came out of hiding. The Kid stood and glowered at what had been, for all practical purposes, their Waterloo. 'Laid it on pretty thick, didn't he?'

Butch moved around Sundance and over to the hitching post. 'You gotta look on the bright side, Kid. It was the best funeral we ever had!'

They straddled the mules that the captain in his generosity had left behind, and rode off into the night.

2 'What the hell are you doing on my ship?'

It took three days to traverse the mountainous region that was the border between Bolivia and Argentina and another four days and as many trains before Butch and Sundance reached the capital, Buenos Aires.

They never did find out the name of the small town where they made a brief stop, just a long enough pause in fact, to rob what passed for the bank.

The delapidated building, which had probably once been a stable, yielded as much as could be expected if looks were anything to go by. In this case they were, so in disgust they took the $688.42 and left with an admonition to the bank president that if he wanted to be a success in life, he would have to do a lot more business.

Butch shinned up a telegraph pole just outside of town and cut the wires that were the only link with the next town forty miles away, and they rode out a few miles to a point where they could catch a train for the long haul to Buenos Aires. They freed the mules with an affectionate pat and hid themselves behind a stand of trees that stood at the side of the railroad track. When the train came and slowed for the sharp curve, they jumped into an empty boxcar.

The next four days were a nightmare of getting off one train and on to another, all this accomplished while remaining undetected by the local Gendarmerie. By this time a fullscale alarm was out for the Yankee bank robbers, and a concerted effort was being made to find them.

They jumped off the train on the outskirts of Buenos Aires and walked in the rest of the way. They were dirty and dishevelled, but no more so than many of the city's inhabitants. They attracted no special attention as they ambled down one of the long roads leading to the port in the gloom of early evening.

It had started to drizzle when they reached Plaza de Mayo,

the main square near the port of Buenos Aires. They passed through it and on to Paseo Colon, a small street that bordered the port. The evening's activities were already in full swing, the bars and outside cafés jammed with sailors from all over the world. Blond-haired Swedes, fair skins flushed with drink, olive-skinned Portuguese and Italians, oily black hair glistening in the lamp glow, and yellow-skinned Asians, almond eyes as inscrutable as ever, vied for and almost tripped over each other in their eagerness to get to the solicitous young ladies who, for a few pennies or *pesos* or *kroners*, would grant any reasonable request, and, for an additional payment, a few that were less reasonable.

Sundance observed the activities on the street with a critical eye. 'That looks busy enough to lose ourselves in.'

Butch pulled his hat down further over his eyes. 'I wouldn't want to bet my life on it, Kid. The only smart thing to do is to get out of here fast. I reckon the quicker we get on a boat, the better I'm gonna like it.'

Sundance looked at the drunken lascar weaving aimlessly down the street, unaware of the dark-skinned tart tugging hopefully at his sleeve, and shrugged, 'Let's go find the boat.'

They squeezed into a space big enough for one person and propped their elbows on the wooden topped bar that was splintered and cracked from years of being pounded on for service, and greasy from the hundreds of drinks that got spilled on it. The fat bartender, hair parted in the middle, looked a lot like the bar he tended, and told them in halting English that the next ship out of Buenos Aires was bound for London.

'How do ya feel about goin' to England, Kid?'

'Will they understand us?'

'I guess so. They speak English.'

'Are the grub and the booze better than what we've been gettin' – and the women?'

'It's a big town.'

Sundance shrugged. 'So, let's go to London.'

When they located the boat, the tenth in line, they stopped dead in their tracks. Under the eerie light of the arc lamps the ship might have just possibly looked worse than it actually was, and then again, maybe not. The rust that covered her hull in leprous patches, ran all the way down to the waterline and there was no reason to suppose that it stopped there. The faded letters that were almost indiscernible, read *'BLACKPOOL P IN ESS'* It was some time later they discovered that it should have read *PRINCESS*. A worm-eaten plank that sagged precariously in the middle led up to a single deck that was littered with a jumble of rope, tarpaulins and an assortment of marine bric-à-brac. A single smoke-blackened stack stood between a couple of disused masts that were built into ships in the days when steam was less reliable.

'Think she'll float, Butch?' And then not waiting for an answer, 'Maybe we should wait for the next boat.'

Butch started to say something, then hesitated. He turned back and looked the way they'd come, then completed the circle and gazed at the old hulk reflectively. 'I think we'd better get on this old tub. I gotta feeling right down in my guts we can't take a chance on holing up for another day.'

'Shit!' Sundance said. 'Your feelings are gonna kill me yet.' He took off his hat and wiped away the misted rain from his face with the crook of his arm. 'OK,' he said with resignation, 'after you.'

Butch led the way as they climbed gingerly up the gangplank and on to the crowded deck. Close up it was even dirtier than it had looked from the dock and even worse now that they were no longer up-wind of the ship. A stench that seemed to rise in waves hit them full in the face.

'Goddam stinking hides!' Sundance spluttered, grabbed a handkerchief and covered his face with it.

'Yeah,' Butch agreed, his eyes watering.

A heavy, thickset man appeared from behind a bulkhead, saw the two strangers and headed for them with belligerent strides. The flaming red hair that grew in clumps on top of his head looked like a bird's nest with an absentee landlord; and a lower lip, pink and pugnacious, protruded from the foliage of a thick beard. More red hair sprouted on his chest covered only by a dirty undershirt, and brawny arms rippled with tattoos.

'What the hell are you doing on my ship?' he bellowed. The

Scottish accent was pronounced and Glaswegian in origin, and Butch and Sundance found themselves concentrating hard to understand it.

'Are you the captain?' Butch asked quickly after a sidelong glance at Sundance, whose short temper was about to erupt.

'What if I am, who are you?'

Butch ignored the question. 'We hear you're leaving tomorrow morning for England. If that's right, we wanna come along.'

The captain eyed them with suspicion, but not without a flicker of interest. He wiped his beefy hands on the sides of faded dungarees. 'Don't know why you'd want to come on this old barge, unless you're in a hurry to leave.'

Butch smiled easily. 'Hell, no. We're not in a hurry to leave. We picked this boat out particular 'cause we like the look of it.'

'It's not a boat, it's a *ship*,' the captain muttered. He looked at them knowingly and his lip curled to reveal teeth that were the same colour as the rust that covered his ship. 'It'll cost you 300 dollars apiece.'

'Three hundred dollars!' Sundance shouted. 'Why you ...'

Butch jabbed him hard in the ribs. 'That'll be fine, Captain.'

'That's practically all the money we got!' Sundance said in a fierce whisper.

'Just show us where we bunk, Captain,' Butch continued without a glance in the Kid's direction. 'You don't mind if we stay on board, do you? We had a hard day and we're gonna turn in.'

The captain held out a large hand. 'Cash in advance.'

Butch turned his back and took out six hundred dollars from his moneybelt. He turned back and handed it to the captain.

He snatched the money with greedy haste and counted it, licking a thumb every now and then to separate the bills. 'All right, it's correct.' He sounded almost disappointed. 'Come with me, and I'll show you your "State Room".' He guffawed loudly. 'My name's MacGregor,' he said over his shoulder as he led the way. 'Who are you?'

'I'm John Everett and my friend's Harry Lynch,' Butch supplied the names glibly, using the ones that were on their passports.

The 'State Room' was amidships, and in appearance not all

that dissimilar to a fair-sized closet, but for the double row of bunks that gave it a morguelike quality. Butch dropped their one valise on the floor and looked around morosely.

'Terrific Captain. It's everything we thought it would be.'

'And so that you won't get lonely, you're gonna have some more company,' the captain said with glee.

'You mean besides the cockroaches,' Sundance said. He squashed one with a vicious stamp of his heel.

The captain laughed again. 'You'll get used to them. Right friendly little beasts once you make their acquaintance. No, I mean another passenger. He'll be on board soon. He's a damned Sassenach.'

Sundance looked inquiringly at Butch. 'What's a Sassenach?'

Butch lifted a shoulder in a silent I don't know. 'I think it's some kind of religion, like Lutherans.'

'He's a damned Englishman.' The captain supplied the information with vehemence.

A short time later, a young man came aboard dragging two large and very battered cases with him. He was in his late twenties, very tall and stooped, the narrow frame of his body loose-jointed and awkward like that of a child who towers over his school-mates and is embarrassed by it. He had ash-blond hair that needed cutting, and a long thin nose that emphasized hollow cheeks. The sensitive face had a pinched look, along with the first ravages of dissipation that could be seen most clearly in his pale grey eyes. His clothes had once been fashionable, expensively cut, and were frayed around the edges.

Butch and Sundance watched from the rail as he had a short conversation with the captain and then looked their way. He came over with a smile on his thin lips and greeted them with boyish enthusiasm, a scraggly moustache wagging like the tail of a friendly dog.

'Hello chaps, I'm Reginald Ratlett, but don't let's stand on ceremony. I don't hold with addressing people by surname; please call me Reginald, or Reggie or anything else you think is suitable. I understand we're voyaging together. The captain tells me you're Americans. Lovely man, the captain, you know. It'll be jolly nice to have company. Sea voyages can be terribly tedious, nothing to do and all that, boring, you know. But not this time, what?' All this came out in one long stream of words unbroken by breath.

Butch and Sundance exchanged glances and then hearty handshakes as introductions were made. Ratlett prattled on late into the night, while Butch and Sundance, becoming progressively more silent under the torrent of words that flowed over them, watched the crew drift on board in ones and twos. Butch counted seventeen men of mixed nationalities and decided that the only common denominator was that he wouldn't turn his back on any of them.

Sundance spotted a pause for breath and jumped into the gap. 'That's real interestin' Reginald, but now I'm gonna get some sleep. See you in the morning.' He shot Butch a triumphant glance and left.

Butch yawned and stretched. 'Me too, Reginald.'

'Thank you for a most interesting conversation,' Reginald said politely. 'I look forward to the morning with anticipation, so that we may continue it. This will be a splendid trip.'

Butch groaned inwardly.

Butch and Sundance woke with a start as their little world started shaking with a violence reminiscent of a Californian earthquake. Sundance in the top bunk sat up and banged his head with a loud thump. 'Son of a bitch!' He rubbed the tender area with the palm of his hand. 'What the hell is that noise?' he grated between clenched teeth.

Butch's voice floated up from the lower bunk. 'It's the engine, Kid. I guess we're getting ready to leave.'

A few minutes later they came out on deck just as the ship weighed anchor and backed slowly into the channel. The ship creaked and groaned in protest when the engines were put full-ahead, but she held together and eventually gained momentum heading slowly up the River Plate.

The false dawn was just brightening into the real thing, the surrounding objects assuming tangible shapes, when the *Blackpool Princess* passed the last ship in line and settled down on her northerly course.

They stopped in Montevideo just long enough to take on extra coal and water, then proceeded to Santos in Brazil, where they loaded a last shipment of cargo and provisions and headed for the open sea.

Four weeks later, as the *Blackpool Princess* threaded her way into the Thames Estuary and made for the Port of London, Butch and Sundance, who were not religious men, had begun to believe in the existence of the Almighty. Frivolous and playful He might be, but ultimately He had delivered them, a little the worse for wear, but safely for all that. When the first storm had hit them with force nine winds and a driving rain that raised welts, Butch and Sundance had first thought the ship was going to founder – and when it didn't, wished that it would. Seasickness hit them like a buffalo stampede, and they heaved their guts out until they ached and were too weak to do anything but lie in their bunks and pray for an early demise to put them out of their misery.

But that storm had passed quickly. The next two were worse, and lasted longer.

Sundance reflected that one of the things that had helped pull him through was the hours he spent devising more and more bizarre ways to kill Reginald Ratlett, who was completely unaffected by the weather, the ship's motion, the stifling accommodation, or the cockroaches, and who chatted incessantly. He claimed only to be cheering them up.

Then there had been the time during a brief respite between storms when Butch and Sundance managed to drag themselves on deck (the smells of hide preferable to that of vomit), and when the captain had put in a sudden appearance. He was dressed in a kilt and a sporran that went beautifully with his salt-encrusted sea boots and ubiquitous dirty undershirt. He was shouting obscure Celtic oaths and waving a cutlass above his head, and drunk enough for five men. He chased several of the crew members around the ship, just narrowly missing chopping them to bits with the sharp blade, and it was only after they subdued him with a well placed bottle applied to the side of his head that they discovered it was a wake for the captain's pet pig, who had been tethered in the aft section. The line had parted during the storm and the pig had gone to porker's heaven by way of Davey Jones' Locker. On another occasion two days out of the Cape Verde Islands a sudden wind sprang up and shifted some of the cargo. A rooster and five chickens, kept for their fresh eggs, broke out of the coop and had the crew chasing after them all over the ship for the best part of a day.

But finally the *Blackpool Princess* waddled into London and dropped anchor.

3 Pinkerton's leading agent

Jonathan De Ford stood at the starboard rail of the ore freighter and glowered at the soot-stained buildings as they slowly passed. Viciously he bit off the end of a fat cigar and spat it into the murky waters of the Thames. He flicked a match into life with his thumbnail and thrust it at the end of the cigar as if it were a wild animal he held at bay. A cloud of smoke drifted up into the overcast London sky and merged with it.

Jonathan De Ford was angry. It seemed like he had been angry for years. In the rare moments he was able to examine his feelings with any kind of objectivity, he saw himself as a banked fire that could flare up in an instant and consume anything and anybody that stood in the way of the singleminded course he had set.

His thoughts were savage, veiled in a red mist that had begun to cloud his judgement. He had been trying for nine long years to catch Butch and Sundance and all he had to show for his pains were a dozen pairs of worn boots, an ulcer and an advanced case of obsession that bordered on insanity.

It had started out as a routine investigation of a couple of cheap hoodlums who were part of a gang that had romantically called themselves the 'Wild Bunch'. De Ford remembered when he had first heard the name and had laughed heartily at the time – dime novel stuff. Pinkerton's leading agent had pursued them methodically, for he was a methodical man, feared and respected by every crook he had ever trailed, and he had caught them one by one – Kid Curry, Harvey Logan, Elza Lay and several other members of the Hole-In-The-Wall Gang – all except for the ringleaders. But he wasn't worried then. It was said that if Jonathan De Ford was after you it didn't matter how fast or how far you ran, because eventually he would be there in his white hat, coming over the last hill or turning the final corner and you might as well stand there and hold your hands out politely for the cuffs. And so it had always been – until Butch Cassidy and the Sundance Kid.

He had followed them across five states through all kinds of weather and all manner of terrain. Three times he had gotten close enough to smell them and each time just as the long hunt should have ended they had slipped through his fingers, like trying to hold on to quicksilver. It was uncanny how they managed it, he had only missed by inches, but he had missed. Images of Butch and Sundance, distorted by time and paranoia, flashed into his mind and the bile rose in his throat. Violently he spat into the Thames for the second time, but the bad taste remained.

And now he was close again and this time ... they could not suspect that he was still on their trail. The corners of his mouth creased into a small tight smile that never stood a chance of melting the arctic blue of his eyes. They must be feeling very smug. As far as everyone was concerned they were dead and gone. He had not believed it, could not believe it. They couldn't get away from him that easily by just dying, it wouldn't be fair, after he had spent so much time coming after them. He had taken the long, dusty trail up to San Vincente and found the *cantina* where they were supposed to be buried. He had stared at the grave-markers with scorn, ripped them out in a fury and dug up the graves like a man possessed. It was with fierce joy that he discovered the remains of the rotting potatoes. Not a body in sight, as he expected.

And then he had made a beeline for Buenos Aires, because if he were them, that's where he would go as the quickest way off the continent. South America had become too hot. And of course, he was part of them, able to place himself inside their skins. After all that time it wasn't difficult.

And he was right again, and late as usual.

When he asked around the port, he heard that two men answering their descriptions, and who he felt sure had to be Butch and Sundance, had left on a ship bound for England the day before. There followed a week of impotent frustration, heavy drinking, desultory sex and more heavy drinking, before the next ship departed that had London for a destination.

De Ford fidgeted impatiently as the ship manoeuvred into its docking space. It seemed an eternity before all the lines were made secure and the engine finally shut down. De Ford was waiting at the top of the gangplank when the customs officers came on board and started asking questions as soon as their feet touched the deck. The *Blackpool Princess*, an even slower rust-bucket than the one on which he had arrived, he discovered to his delight, had docked a day earlier. The trail was not as cold as he had feared.

He lifted his valise and made his way on to the grimy pier. The docks were a hive of industry and grating and screeching discords. Boxes labelled *Tea from India* and *Wine – a Product of France* were mixed in with bales of jute and cotton and barrels of herring from Denmark. They were piled tree-top high, and a rusty crane, its winding mechanism howling in protest, industriously dipped into a ship's hold and added to the jumble.

De Ford stopped at the side of a warehouse and put his back against the rough stone wall and scanned the area. He wasn't going to waste any time finding Butch and Sundance.

He singled out a brawny docker who was bawling out orders in a thick Irish brogue to a small group of men. By the way they jumped to obey, De Ford guessed the foreman was able to back up his commands with his fists. De Ford pushed himself off the wall and went up to the man who stood with arms akimbo glaring after his crew. The man turned his red-rimmed eyes on De Ford and stared at him with hostility. 'And what might you be wantin'?'

'Information,' De Ford replied blandly. 'And I'm willing to pay for it.' The tip of an unhealthy looking tongue appeared in the corner of the man's mouth between wet, cracked lips.

'I'm thinkin' then that this be your lucky day. I'm full of information.'

'Were you here when the *Blackpool Princess* docked yesterday, and did you see the passengers that got off?'

'I was and I did. What is it you want to be knowin', and how much are you paying for it?'

'A guinea if it's what I want to know,' De Ford said with diffidence.

The foreman smiled, exposing a mouth half full of yellowing teeth. 'Done! For a guinea I'll even throw in the old woman.'

'I'm looking for two men,' De Ford said, stony-faced. 'One's about five-feet-nine with light brown hair, blue eyes and a sandy moustache, and a little scar just here—' De Ford indicated the place just under his left eye. 'The other man's about an inch taller, with brown hair and moustache, blue-grey eyes and a thin nose. You couldn't miss him if you saw him 'cause he's also very bow-legged.' De Ford illustrated this statement by bowing his legs.

The foreman gazed speculatively into the middle distance. 'What would you be wanting them for?'

'For the guinea I'm going to pay you I'd say that was my business.'

The foreman shrugged expressively. 'I remember them. They were with another gentleman and they all went off together. One of my boys found them a carriage and helped them with the cases.' He took a deep breath and bellowed, 'Mick!'

One of the dockers detached himself from the unloading party and came scurrying over. 'Yes sir,' he said nervously.

'This gentleman,' the foreman said indicating De Ford with a dirty thumb, 'is looking for two men who came off the *Blackpool Princess* and you loaded them on to a carriage. Would you be knowin' who the driver is?'

The man looked relieved at having committed no fresh transgression and relaxed visibly. 'That was Old Man Fletcher. He's here most every day, in fact I seen him this morning comin' in.'

'And don't just be astandin' there,' the foreman growled. 'Go find him and tell him there's a gentleman here that wants to talk to him.' With a look of instant fear the man took off running. The foreman sighed deeply 'I have to put the fear of God into these lazy buggers or they won't do a stroke of work.'

De Ford put a guinea into the outstretched palm. 'Thanks for your help.' He picked up his valise and followed the running man at a more leisurely pace.

Old Man Fletcher stood by his horse's head holding on to the bridle. De Ford had heard of an owner taking on the characteristics of his dog, but this was the first time, he decided, that he'd seen a man who looked like his horse, and the grey looked like a couple of hoofbeats away from the glue factory.

The old man alternated between being garrulous and unresponsive to De Ford's questions. Yes, he finally agreed, he had taken three men into town and yes, he would take De Ford there also – for a price.

The financial arrangement completed, De Ford climbed into the battered carriage and settled himself gingerly on to the cracked leather seat. With considerable urging the horse was persuaded away from the furrow in the ground at which he had been staring with concentration, and the carriage lurched away.

De Ford peered through the dusty window at his first sight of London, but very little registered. He was vaguely aware of Old Man Fletcher, in a voice like a cracked banjo, pointing out the prominent landmarks, but the first one he heard was when the carriage stopped in Sloane Street.

'That's it,' Old Man Fletcher said, pointing at the Cadogan Hotel. 'That's where I let 'em off, guv. Did you know Oscar Wilde used to stay there? Dirty old poof!' he cackled.

De Ford paid him off and watched as he turned the carriage around and headed back towards the East End. He approached the entrance with caution, outwardly a picture of icy calm but at the same time acutely aware of his pounding heart. He peeked through the glass door into the lobby. Empty. He pushed the door open and entered slowly, observing at a glance the squashy maroon velvet settees and chairs, the magazine stand jammed with periodicals, the ornate crystal chandelier with dozens of teardrop-shaped glass baubles, a combined hat and umbrella stand in one corner and an aspidistra in another. The lone clerk looked up from behind a counter with an obsequious smile. 'Yes sir, can I help you?'

De Ford walked over to the man passing on the way a painting of an indeterminate landscape in faded watercolours. 'I'm looking for a couple of friends of mine ... fellow Americans,' he added as an afterthought. 'They arrived in the country yesterday and I understand they checked in here. I think they were with a third man.'

The clerk smiled and nodded and De Ford was fascinated to see his adams-apple duck in and out of his stiff collar. 'Oh, Mr Lynch and Mr Everett.' De Ford made a mental note of yet another set of aliases. 'And,' the clerk's voice lowered with a touch of reverence, 'Lord Ratlett. I'm afraid you just missed 'em. They left this morning sir.'

De Ford sagged, placed his elbows on the marble-topped counter and buried his head in his hands. His voice came out hoarse and muffled through his fingers. 'Did they leave a forwarding address?'

'No sir,' the clerk said brightly.

De Ford turned his back on the man and leaned against the counter, his face working with unconcealed emotion. He passed a hand over his eyes and took a deep breath. He seemed in need of more oxygen.

'But,' the clerk continued as if he hadn't noticed, 'I believe they've gone to take up residence in Lord Ratlett's house. It's in Mayfair, you know.'

De Ford turned so quickly that he almost lost his balance. 'Where in Mayfair?' he demanded.

The clerk's face closed up tightly. Obstinacy descended like a veil.

De Ford realized his mistake at once and lowered his voice. 'It's very important I see them,' he said. 'You see, I've come a long way to complete our uh ... business. And, of course,' watching the clerk beginning to unbend, 'I will need a room while I'm here in London.'

The clerk's smile magically reappeared. 'Of course, sir. If

you'll just sign the register I will attempt to get Lord Ratlett's address for you.'

De Ford was shown to a room which he hardly glanced at, did some minimal unpacking – his Smith and Wesson revolver – and fidgeted on the edge of the bed, his Derby pushed well back on his head, until a tap at the door produced the clerk with Lord Ratlett's address. He left the hotel at once.

4 Walking-around money

Butch and Sundance were like a couple of *rubes* on their first visit to the big city. They tried to see everything as their carriage passed St Paul's Cathedral and clattered on to the woodblocks of Fleet Street, under which flowed the river Fleet. They stared in open-mouthed fascination at Buckingham Palace which was, as their carriage pulled up, undergoing a Changing of the Guard. The soldiers in their scarlet tunics, dark blue breeches, shiny boots and tall black bearskin hats, were the Coldstream Guards, Reginald explained. One could tell by the white plumes.

Reginald took his new role as tour guide and royal genealogist with serious pedantry. He pointed out the flags flying at half-mast. News had reached them at sea of the death of Edward VII on 6 May. Reginald launched into a potted history of the Kings and Queens of England, culminating in how the former Prince of Wales had succeeded his father and was now George V, King of Great Britain and Ireland and Protector of all the dominions on which the sun never set.

They reached the Cadogan Hotel where Reginald assured them only gentlemen stayed, especially when they couldn't afford the Savoy. Sundance pointed out that he and Butch could afford the Savoy, and a few other things, just as soon as Reginald paid over the $2,500 that he had lost to them at poker.

'Ah yes,' Reginald murmured with a vague wave of his hand.

'I must rush over to see Father. I'm sure he'll lend it to me.' He didn't sound too convinced, a fact that Butch and Sundance had already guessed was the case.

Although it seemed to have conveniently slipped Reginald's memory, they recalled the evening on board the *Blackpool Princess* when the foul weather had broken just before sunset, and the sun blazed through the clouds and lay on the pewter sea like a huge red eye, that Reginald in one unbroken hour-long recitation had told them the story of his life, and why he was now returning to England.

A persistent telegraph company had followed him from one temporary residence to another and had finally traced him in Buenos Aires where he eked out a meagre existence, tutoring spoiled brats of the Argentine aristocracy to speak the King's English. The telegram was from his family and had stated in flat, unemotional words that his father was ill and that his presence in London was advisable. As this was the first communication in the three years he had been away, Reginald had concluded that the matter was serious and started back immediately. He confided to Butch and Sundance that his family was not terribly happy with him. As an only son of a British lord who would inherit the title one day, certain proprieties were expected of him, which Reginald had found difficult to observe, or to be more correct, impossible. He explained how he had been 'sent down' from university, expelled without a degree, for transgressions upon which the university frowned. He had been caught with a girl in his rooms, a serious enough offence in itself, but made worse by the discovery that she was two months pregnant and was threatening to blow it up into a huge scandal unless Reginald married her. Reginald, a gentleman to the end, was willing, but his father flatly refused to let such a union take place. After all, she was just a scullery maid seeking to better herself at the expense of the aristocracy. And expense it was; as she took leave of Reginald, clutching a fistful of money that his father had given her, the flood of crocodile tears barely disguised the smile of triumph.

Reginald was scarcely out of the jaws of one disaster before he blithely jumped into the teeth of another. He sought solace among the more sordid elements of London and became heavily involved in gambling – inevitably he lost, and even more inevitably, was unable to pay his debts. His father bailed him out the first few times and then made a forceful suggestion that the best thing Reginald could do for everyone concerned was absent himself from the country until he came to his senses.

And so Reginald began his odyssey, landing first in New York and then drifting down through the southern states from where it was a short hop to Havana, where he acquired a taste for rum and native girls, and the torpor that results from long periods of indolence. When his money got so low that he couldn't raise the price of a secondhand *taco*, he talked himself into the job of a fishing guide, of which he knew nothing. He was thrown off at the first port of call, Montego Bay.

Like a leaf floating free he eased his way through the islands and eventually wound up in South America, and the ignominious tutoring job. But even that couldn't dampen his spirits. Somehow he had always managed to retain his boyish enthusiasm and his passion for communicating. Butch and Sundance as the recipients felt like the resident experts.

'We sure hope your Pappy's gonna be glad to see you,' Sundance said with just the slightest hint of a threat. 'How much we got left, Butch?'

'Twenty-seven dollars and 42 cents,' Butch answered promptly.

'How much is that in pounds?' Sundance asked.

Reginald screwed up his face in concentration trying to work it out and finally gave up. 'Not much,' he admitted.

'Goodbye, Reginald,' Sundance said in a stern monotone. 'You'd better hightail it over there and start talking to your old Dad about some cash, and don't forget to come back!'

Reginald looked deeply hurt. 'I wouldn't leave you chaps in the lurch. After our voyage I feel we're like – blood-brothers.'

Sundance shuddered.

Reginald pointed them in the direction of the West End while he went off to see what reception his father would give him. They turned into Knightsbridge and, as they had no idea of what lay ahead, followed their noses, neither one of which was exactly straight. They walked through Park Lane and stared at the uniformed Major Domos, as haughty and magnificent as the hotels and blocks of flats they attended. Liveried chauffeurs waited patiently by immaculate automobiles. Four-wheeled carriages, spruce in new lacquered paint, trimmed in silver and gold, were poised at the kerbside to wait upon the foreign-looking ladies and gentlemen.

They turned again at Marble Arch and entered the wide cobbled expanse of Oxford Street. The road bustled with carriages, delivery wagons, omnibuses and motorcars, the astringent smell of horse manure wafted on the breeze and mingled with the pungent odour of tar and petrol fumes. They stopped and peered into the windows of Selfridges department store (which had opened a year earlier), Peter Robinson and Marshall & Snelgrove at Oxford Circus. They passed hoardings that advertised *Allen and Ginters Richmond Gem Cigarettes*, *Rowntrees Chocolates*, *Cerebos Table Salt* and *Sanitas Disinfectant*. They resolved to change their luck and their clothes at the first opportunity. They were acutely embarrassed by the suits they wore, salvaged from a trip to New York several years earlier and carried through all the days of ranching and riding the trail in preparation for their next appearance in the city. They received disapproving glances from the passers-by who were more fashionably attired, and struck off into the side roads to escape them, scuffed boots ringing on the pavement as they sought out a shelter. They found a café that had the dual appeal of being secluded and modest in price. Their bellies fortified, if not their spirits, they set off again.

They found the Biograph tucked away discreetly between an Italian bakery and a corset shop that brazenly displayed foundation garments in the window. Neither one of them had ever seen a moving picture and they entered the cinema eagerly. The new-fangled medium was showing a flickering film billed as the 'Melodrama Of The Age' and entitled *The Great Train Robbery* made by the *genius* Edwin S. Porter. They were entranced, and when they left the theatre Sundance commented – 'It would be really great if someone did a film about our great train robberies. I can see it now,' he announced. 'They could call it:

The Daring Robbery Of The Overland Flyer In 1897 (or was it '98, Butch?) *And the Further Audacious Exploits Of The Infamous Butch Cassidy and The Sundance Kid.'*

'Sure, Kid,' Butch replied.

Back at the hotel, they waited, pacing the marble floor and leafing through periodicals when they got tired. When the magazines held no further attraction they just sat in silence. Reginald came falteringly through the door, his face a peculiar mixture of awe and elation, sadness and distress. He motioned for them to follow, and the three of them trooped upstairs to his room.

Sundance broke the silence. 'Well,' he began, 'what about it?'

Reginald took a deep breath and hiccuped. 'My father died three weeks ago while we were at sea.'

Butch and Sundance had simultaneous visions of their money on silvery wings retreating at speed into the distance. 'That's too bad, Reginald,' they said in unison.

'My father's title passes to me and I'm now Lord Ratlett.'

Butch and Sundance looked at each other. 'That's real good, Reginald!' they said in unison.

'Does that mean you inherit his money also?' Butch asked with renewed hope.

'Oh yes!' Reginald bobbed his head with the vigour meant to convey a valuable piece of information.

Butch beamed. 'Well, that's all right then.'

'But I won't get it for six months—'

Butch's face fell and Sundance made a disgusted noise.

'—and,' he hesitated, like a doctor who has to tell a patient he has three months to live, 'I don't think there'll be very much then. I saw my solicitor and he tells me that Father made some, er, rather indiscreet investments in his last days. Father,' he said delicately, 'shall we say, *over-committed* himself.'

'Weren't you able to get *any* money?' Sundance asked, not wanting to believe this was the case.

'Frankly chaps, not a *sou*. I'm afraid my family is stony-broke. But of course,' he brightened, 'we still have the house in town and the one in the country, the cars, and an excellent wine cellar.'

'Hey, Reginald,' Butch cupped his chin in his hand, 'this might sound like a real dumb question, but how you gonna keep all them things goin' if you don't have any money?'

'Oh, that's not a problem. Our solicitor has been taking care of our affairs for the last twenty years. He's an old and dear friend of the family, a marvellous chap. Said he thought it was his duty to support the estate until we could see in which direction the wind was blowing, and all he took as collateral were some worthless shares that my father had invested a fortune in. A diamond mine in South Africa, called *Kimberley*. Can you imagine that? As if one expects to pluck diamonds out of the ground as the Irish do potatoes. I wish there were more honest people in the world, willing to help their friends.'

'Well, you can just sell one of those, Reginald,' Sundance flared, 'and get some cash money and pay your blood-brothers what you owe them.'

Lord Ratlett looked crestfallen. He intertwined his long thin fingers and fidgeted nervously. 'I'm afraid I can't do that, Mother wouldn't let me. She says we must keep up appearances. And then, of course, there's the matter of a dowry for my sister. She couldn't possibly marry anyone of our class without one.'

Sundance rolled his eyes heavenwards and clapped himself on the forehead. 'Oh my God! It gets worse and worse.'

'Uh, Reginald,' Butch asked, 'you got any good ideas how we're gonna live while you keep up appearances?'

'On credit?' Reginald said doubtfully. 'Yes, on credit,' he confirmed with decision. 'The aristocracy never pay bills with money, it's *vulgar*. Why, I wouldn't dream of paying my tailor for at least a twelve-month after I receive my suits, and my clubs just send bills. I remember seeing some once ...' he reflected. Then with mounting excitement, his face lighting up like a small boy's: 'The same holds true for the wine merchants, and *Fortnum and Mason* and ...'

'What about walking-around money?' Butch asked gently.

Reginald considered the question. 'I admit that does present a slight problem.'

Butch looked over at Sundance. 'What ya think, Kid? I was kinda hopin' we wouldn't have to get back to our old habits.'

The Kid sighed and nodded. 'Don't see any other way out.'

Butch shrugged. 'Ah shit! Beats the hell outta working for a living.' He turned back to Reginald. 'What are the banks like around here?'

Reginald looked puzzled. 'The banks? They're like ... banks. They take people's money and they allow one to have an overdraft, and ... they're everywhere.'

'Sit down, Reginald. I think it's time we told you the facts of life as accordin' to Butch Cassidy and the Sundance Kid.'

Lord Ratlett's eyes grew wider and wider as Butch told him of their exploits with and without the Wild Bunch, embellishing only a little. He was finally unable to contain himself any longer. 'That's capital, chaps! Like Rob Roy and Robin Hood and Raffles, all rolled into one! I'm your man. When do we start?'

'Just hold on there, big fella,' Butch said straight-faced. 'It's not quite that easy. We wanna make sure we get away after we rob them 'cause we wanna stay free to spend the money. So, we gotta case the place first. You gotta find us the right bank.'

Reginald straightened, puffed up his chest and looked very important. 'I'll start looking at once, I know where all of them are.' Butch held up a restraining hand.

'Not so fast. We gotta find a place to operate from first. We can't afford to stay here.'

Reginald clapped his hands. 'I forgot to tell you. Mother and my sister have just left for the country house, and we're going to move into the house in Mayfair tomorrow. I've instructed the servants to prepare for our arrival in the morning.'

'Servants?' Sundance inquired.

'Oh, just ten of them,' Reginald said with diffidence. 'We're badly understaffed, but you just can't get good help these days.'

5 Smash and grab in Old Burlington Street

Jonathan De Ford hurried out of the hotel and flagged down a hansom on Sloane Street. He gave the driver the address he had been given of Lord Ratlett's house in Hill Street, and the cab took off in a cloud of dust. De Ford watched the traffic ahead of him with unseeing eyes. He was getting closer and his excitement mounted. A gnawing in his stomach reminded him that his ulcer was clamouring for attention, and that he hadn't eaten since the previous evening. He put it out of his mind.

The cab entered Park Lane, turned right at the Dorchester, crossed South Audley Street and entered Hill Street, slowing up at the address he had been given.

De Ford banged on the roof and when the trap opened he told the driver to go another six houses further on. The hansom skirted a road-sweeper and stopped. He paid off the driver and crossed over to the other side of the street from the house.

The house, the second from the corner, was a large, handsome red-bricked affair of five storeys. Four windows faced the street at ground level, all heavily curtained. Freshly whitened steps led up to an ornately carved oak door with a dome-shaped transom set in the stone facing. The newly polished brass knocker and fittings sparkled brightly.

De Ford pushed past a crowd of servants, averting his face, and turned the corner. He leaned against an iron railing and watched the house with an intensity born of years of longing. His hands twitched in sympathy as he thought of each of them surrounding a familiar neck. Now that he was here, what was he going to do? *They* – he couldn't even bear to repeat their names – if he'd been told the truth, were in that house. He had not stopped to consider what he was going to do when he finally found them. He patted the Smith and Wesson in his pocket for inspiration and found none. He was in a foreign country where the rules were different, and this wasn't a South American banana republic where you could pay an official to look the other way. It was England, the cornerstone of freedom, where corruption among the police was unthinkable and a bribe inconceivable. Short of Shanghai-ing them (and he dismissed that idea as impossible as soon as it entered his head), the only alternative left was to report their presence to Scotland Yard and apply for extradition. He chewed that over for an hour, and finally decided that it was, unfortunately, the only way. But first he had to make sure they were actually there.

Three hours later, shifting his weight from one foot to another in an attempt to ease his aching back, he suddenly stiffened. The door was opening, and yes, there they were.

Butch, Sundance and Lord Ratlett came out into the street laughing and joking. They paused by the iron railing that guarded the steps that led down to the servants' entrance. A butcher's wagon was parked by the kerb and a grizzled man in a greasy apron was delivering a parcel of meat to a teenage scullery-maid who stood at the top of the steps. She blushed at the sight of Lord Ratlett and his two American friends, grabbed the package and ran down the steps, skirt trailing.

When they had taken up residence that morning Sundance's eyes had bugged out at what Reginald had casually called 'trinkets that Father had collected over the years'. A tall, glass-fronted mahogany cabinet stood against one wall of the main drawing room and was crowded with jade and ivory figurines. They stood in groups and looked unblinkingly at Sundance with eyes made of diamonds, or rubies, or sapphires. Against another wall a rosewood armoire contained a collection of several dozen gold and silver snuffboxes, all of them intricately filigreed and some of them encrusted with gems. Three of the walls were lined with paintings rendered in vivid primary colours, the figures depicted twisted into grotesque shapes. It was a new school of painting called *Impressionism*, Reginald informed them, that Father had fancied. Butch read the artists' signatures – *Degas*, *Monet*, and *Van Gogh*; *Toulouse-Lautrec* and *Picasso* – and decided they'd never make it.

'Butch,' Sundance whispered, 'we don't have to look for a bank. Let's just knock off this place.'

'Not so fast, Kid,' Butch whispered back. 'I'm beginning to

like the idea of living like a gentleman and besides,' he said with a sweet smile, 'that would be bad manners!'

The three of them strolled slowly towards Park Lane, Reginald as usual doing most of the chatting. He pointed to each house in turn and in a voice that carried only half a block told Butch and Sundance what he remembered about the occupants – who had done what to whom, and with whom, and listed several generations of family skeletons. He nodded with familiar ease to the long-serving retainers of the other houses on the block, as they dashed in and out of doorways to attend to chores or errands. They saluted him respectfully and smiled. The black sheep of the Ratlett family was well liked. They didn't notice De Ford following them at a discreet distance.

De Ford left them as they reached the top of Park Lane and passed beneath Marble Arch. He found another hansom and directed the driver to take him to Scotland Yard. Big Ben was just striking the hour for four o'clock as they pulled into Whitehall.

The desk sergeant sat behind a dark-wood counter that was pitted with age. Shadows darted in the far recesses of the high-ceilinged interior, and the musty odour that must have contained the smell of fear from long-dead miscreants entered De Ford's nostrils in gentle waves. He wrinkled his nose.

De Ford marched up to the counter and planted himself in front of the sergeant. The man looked up from his racing form incuriously.

'I want to report two American criminals who have arrived in England. They're roaming the streets and nobody's safe while they're out there!'

'Oh yes, sir?' the sergeant said.

'Let me speak to whoever is in charge here!'

The sergeant stared at him blankly for a few long moments. He saw a man with craggy brows and a wild light in his blue eyes, a nose that had once been broken and never set properly, a mouth compressed into a thin line accentuated by a cleft chin that was deep enough to fall into and break a leg. The man's tall, raw-boned frame was bent over the counter, and the large hands that gripped the stained wood were white with strain. A nutter, the sergeant thought, as sure as a London fog. It would be too much trouble to deal with him, he was going off-duty. He picked up the telephone receiver and cranked it noisily.

De Ford was shown into a small cubicle of an office and was introduced to a detective inspector whose name he didn't catch. The man listened patiently, albeit with a bored expression on his bland face.

'Very interesting, sir,' he commented at the end of the long recital. He thought of his dinner and escorted De Ford to his superior, a chief inspector whose name De Ford promptly forgot.

A half hour later the process was repeated and a now agitated De Ford sat in front of a superintendent whose name he didn't even bother to remember.

The superintendent, only half listening as he persisted in trying to work out the answer to a crossword clue in *The Times* that had eluded him, finally left the office at the end of the exposition and nobbled the chief superintendent. He testily agreed to see De Ford for a few minutes, but he had no intention of being late for dinner at his club.

De Ford yet again went through his story from start to finish, his voice rising a little more in pitch each time the chief superintendent extracted his pocket-watch and glanced pointedly at the time. At the end of the tale De Ford received the same comment to which he had now become accustomed.

'Very interesting, sir.'

The chief superintendent looked at his watch again, replaced it with finality and rose. 'You are staying at the Cadogan Hotel, sir?' he monotoned. It was more of a statement than a question. 'We will be in contact with you as soon as we make our inquiries.'

Colour defused De Ford's angular face. He tugged viciously at one end of his handlebar moustache, managing to detach a few hairs in the process, and bit off an angry outburst before it escaped his lips. With effort he managed to relax and with exaggerated calm said, 'Please don't take too long Chief Superintendent. These are desperate men.'

'Of course, sir.'

The chief superintendent reached his club ten minutes late for his appointment. He spotted Geoffrey Martinette propped up against the bar with a whiskey in one hand and a cheroot in the other, the lazy swirls of smoke complementing his dreamy reverie. The chief superintendent made his way through the crowd, nodding to acquaintances as he went. 'Sorry I'm late, old boy. Some damned Yank detective held me up with a story about some other damned Yanks. *Desperadoes*, he called them.' He guffawed at the memory.

'Oh?' Martinette looked mildly interested.

'Yes, some damned nonsense about a couple of small-time crooks with the improbable names of Butch Cassidy and the Sundance Kid.'

'Oh?' Martinett's interest became more pronounced. 'Tell me about it.'

The chief superintendent looked surprised. 'I can't imagine why you'd want to know, old boy. They're certainly of no interest to MI5.' Martinette's dark eyes crinkled slightly.

'Humour me.'

Martinette went back to his office after dinner, and seated himself behind a large mahogany desk with papers and files piled neatly on one end. He lit a cheroot and stared blankly into space for a long while. Then he picked up the receiver of his brass telephone and placed a call.

The following morning a black Daimler Landaulette chugged into Hill Street and came to a stop across the road from Lord Ratlett's house. It was similar to a half dozen other limousines that were parked on both sides of the street, waiting to be used. Three of the chauffeurs stood in a semi-circle speaking together in low tones. The man who looked like a carbon copy in peaked cap and uniform lit a cheroot and leaned back against the seat idly watching the house on the other side of the road.

Geoffrey Martinette inhaled on his cheroot, his first of the day, enjoying the taste of the smoke as it filtered into his lungs. He had borrowed the car from a high official at the Home Office and, in the uniform that he had used before as a disguise, he was prepared for a long period of surveillance, confident in the knowledge that the uniform rendered him almost invisible.

He looked about him and spotted the man he expected to find lurking around the corner. Going by the chief superintendent's description Jonathan De Ford was already on duty, watching.

As on the previous day, Butch, Sundance and Lord Ratlett came out of the house laughing and joking and strolled off in the direction of Park Lane.

Martinette, lounging on a fender, started the car with the hand crank, drove off in the opposite direction, then turned the car around and stayed about 200 yards behind the trio. De Ford on the opposite side of the road was the middle-man in this game of follow-the-leader.

Reginald hailed a motor taxi with an imperious wave, and the three men piled in and set off in the direction of Hyde Park Corner. Martinette followed close behind, and smiled to himself as he passed De Ford whose anger was evident as he vainly tried to find a cab in which to follow.

The taxi containing Reginald, Butch and Sundance retraced part of the route by which they had arrived from the docks and finally stopped at the beginning of Lombard Street, the financial district of the City. Martinette parked his Daimler and followed them on foot. Today, it seemed, they were very interested in banks. They paused and peered into the interior of the Midland Bank, Barclays, Lloyds, Coutts and half a dozen others. Each time, Martinette observed that they huddled in deep conversation, then shook their collective heads and moved on.

The next four hours provided a lot more of the same, in different parts of the City. At last they were back in Park Lane, where they entered a tea shop and sat in weary silence. Reginald sipped his tea, a dainty pinkie finger poised in the air. Sundance sampled his and made a face. Butch left his steaming cup where it was. 'These banks sure ain't like the ones we got back home.'

'They sure ain't,' Sundance agreed.

'They sure ain't,' Reginald said, hating to be left out.

'When we decided to *get back to work* I didn't guess it would be this tough to earn a few honest dollars!' Butch picked up his newly acquired bowler and twirled it experimentally on one finger. Satisfied that the spin was true, he stopped it before the inertia shot the hat off into a far corner. 'I think we're gonna have to try somethin' else.'

'Don't forget them figurines,' Sundance said out of the side of his mouth. Butch ignored him and stared off into the distance.

'Excuse me chaps,' Reginald started. 'What do you think about jewellery shops?'

Butch shifted his eyes from a spot on the wall and looked at Reginald between lowered lids. 'Why?'

Reginald straightened up and fidgeted. 'Well, you see chaps, it just occurred to me that a jewellery shop might be a nice place to rob. We can do what is called in England a smash-and-grab. One simply breaks the window with a brick and scoops up handfuls of jewellery and runs off even before the Bobbies know the crime's been committed.'

'And what do we do then?' Sundance asked with scorn. 'How do we get rid of it? Advertise in the papers for people to buy hot jewellery? We don't know nobody here, remember?'

'Oh, no chaps,' Reginald broke into a high pitched giggle. 'We sell it to what I believe one calls a *fence*. I met two such gentlemen when I last lived here. I was doing some extensive gambling at the time and they frequented the same places. I became rather friendly with them. They had very peculiar names: Patrick McGnaw and Weasel Wilkinson.'

Butch looked at the Kid and laughed. 'Well, don't suppose it's any stranger than Butch and Sundance. We might as well take a look.'

Martinette kept up his steady surveillance for the next three days, following them on forays to the East End and on other occasions on foot, as they walked about Piccadilly Circus, Regent Street, Bond Street and all the intervening roads.

He made a note of all the addresses at which they stopped and on checking with Scotland Yard discovered that two of the locations in the East End were of known fences. At the other end of town they now seemed preoccupied with jewellery shops instead of banks.

One source of amusement for Martinette was that De Ford,

who was at his observation post bright and early each morning, failed miserably every time he attempted to follow them. Once he had engaged a hansom in advance which was unable to keep up with their motor-taxi; and on the following day the motor-taxi engaged broke down in a huge cloud of steam just as the trio started off in a healthy motorcar of their own.

On the third day Butch, Sundance and Reginald finally confined their interest to a particular jewellery shop on Old Burlington Street. The road ran parallel to Bond Street and Regent Street, and was about equidistant between the two. Martinette noted with a keen interest of his own that there were several ways of getting out of Old Burlington Street quickly.

When they returned to Hill Street late that afternoon Martinette saw a car in British racing green parked outside the door. He identified it as an Itala. A chauffeur dressed similarly to himself was waiting near it for Lord Ratlett. He touched his cap deferentially, said a few words to Lord Ratlett and followed the trio into the house.

At seven-thirty in the deepening twilight the three men re-emerged and headed for the car. Reginald eased his lanky frame into the driver's seat, with Butch alongside him and Sundance in the one seat just behind. Reginald's chauffeur, who had followed at a discreet distance, cranked the car for his lord and master. A deep throated roar filled the street as Reginald stepped on the accelerator and pinned it to the floor. The car took off in a billowing cloud of exhaust fumes. Martinette followed in the Daimler and De Ford started running like a wild man, looking for transportation.

They drove to St James's Street where most of the well known gentlemen's clubs were situated, and they stopped outside Boodles. Martinette parked behind one of several chauffeur-driven cars and became part of the scenery. He tipped his hat back and rubbed his red-rimmed eyes. His lone vigil was beginning to take its toll. On the two previous evenings Reginald, Butch and Sundance had gone on a pub crawl of the East End and had not called it quits until after three a.m. Martinette was slightly puzzled as to why on each of these occasions the three men sought no feminine companionship. The simple explanation, that they couldn't afford to, never crossed his mind.

The threesome alighted from the car and went into the club. They were outfitted in evening clothes, black coats that tapered to mid-thigh, black trousers, spats, braided waistcoats, stiff collars and white ties, silk top hats and a carnation in their buttonholes. They each wore a cloak lined in red silk and carried a gold headed walking stick in kidgloved hands. Butch and Sundance looked slightly ill at ease, and not only for the reason that this manner of dress was foreign to them. Their two suits of clothes had belonged to Reginald's father and the hurried alterations left something to be desired; in any event, Sundance's bow legs would have made the best tailored pair of evening trousers look misshapen.

Butch, Sundance and Lord Ratlett emerged from Boodles several hours later with the exaggerated stiff-legged gait of men who had had too much to drink and were holding themselves in readiness in case they'd be asked to walk a straight line. From his vantage point inside his car, Martinette watched the commissionaire help them into their vehicle. He looked at his fob-watch. It was two-thirty a.m.

The Itala started with a roar, backfired once, and with a clashing of gears wove down the road.

'I think we had maybe one little drink too many,' Butch mumbled.

Lord Ratlett giggled and hiccuped. 'Nonsense, old boy.'

Butch straightened up with an effort. 'Reggie, old bean, you're right as usual,' he slurred. 'I feel great.' He slapped Sundance on the knee. 'Do you feel great?'

Sundance's head was slumped on his chest. He opened one bleary eye. 'I feel great.'

The car swung around a corner precariously. 'Me too,' Reginald echoed.

'That's great,' Butch intoned with alcoholic gravity. 'Let's go ahead with the job. Did you bring the brick, Reggie old chap.'

Lord Ratlett clapped himself on the forehead and the car swerved dangerously towards the kerb. He yanked it back, missing the kerb by an inch. 'Oh, my Lord, I forgot the brick,' he wailed.

'The damned Limey forget the brick,' Sundance muttered.

'Now, Reginald,' Butch reasoned, 'how can we break a window with a brick, if we don't have a brick?'

'Perhaps we can buy one,' Reginald suggested.

Sundance snorted in disgust and mumbled something incoherent.

Butch thought about it, then shook his head with deliberation. 'No, I don't think so, Reginald, I don't think it's right to buy a brick you're gonna rob a store with, and besides,' he added craftily, 'where do we find a brick store that's open this time of night?'

The car had entered Regent Street from Piccadilly Circus as Butch was speaking. Dead ahead a red lantern suspended from a wooden trestle, warned of road construction in progress. 'Stop!' Butch yelled, and banged the side of the car for emphasis. 'This is our lucky night,' he chortled. 'There's a brick.'

And indeed a whole pile of bricks were stacked neatly to one side of a gaping hole in the roadway. Butch jumped out as the car rolled to a stop, lifted one from the pile and got back in.

'Tally-ho!' Reginald shouted as they roared off down Regent Street.

The car turned into Old Burlington Street and stopped with a jerk, the engine idling in a low snarl. The street was deserted for its entire length, all the shops dark and shuttered. The only light was the steady glow of the gas lamps that lined the road. Butch put his finger to his lips. 'Shhh,' he whispered, 'let's go, Reggie.'

The car lurched ahead and then stopped halfway down the street next to a jewellers whose gold-lettered sign proclaimed *Whorley and Whorley – Established 1731*. Butch hefted the brick palm up, jiggling it in his hand. He satisfied himself that it was heavy enough and stepped out of the car. Sundance stumbled after him. Reginald started to follow but Butch stopped him with an upraised hand. 'Now you just wait there, big fella,' he whispered. 'We wanna make a quick getaway.' Reginald subsided back into his seat and having completed this dangerous manoeuvre signalled his success to Butch with a thumbs up sign.

Butch and Sundance walked over to the shop window and looked up and down the street – still no one in sight. Butch lifted the brick and was about to throw it, when a thought struck him and he lowered his arm. He swung his arm back and forth, testing the underhand delivery. He turned back to Reginald. 'Hey,' he called softly. 'Is there any special way you're supposed to throw this brick?'

Lord Ratlett looked chagrined. 'Gosh, I never thought to find out.'

Butch shrugged. 'Never mind, I'll give it the old *curveball.*' He lifted the brick and flung it at the window. It shattered with a loud crash and set off an alarm bell that clanged with a furious ring.

'Jesus Christ!' Sundance shouted. 'Let's get the hell outta here!'

Butch tugged at his sleeve. 'Get the jewellery, Kid.' Reluctantly Sundance reached into the broken window and scooped up a double handful of rings, watches and pendants and stuffed them in his pockets. Butch did the same. Heads poked out of windows and cries of 'Police!' and 'Stop thief!' could be heard clearly over the clanging bell.

'Let's go, Butch,' Sundance said urgently. Butch took one more handful of jewellery and they ran for the car. They jumped in just as the engine roared and the Itala jerked away from the kerb, heading for Piccadilly.

Around the far corner Martinette stepped out from where he had been watching, with a satisfied smile on his sallow face. He watched the Itala disappear round the corner. He put his hands in his pockets and whistling a passable version of 'Ride a Cock Horse to Banbury Cross', walked slowly back to his own car.

6 Spending it

Butch woke up with the worst hangover that he remembered having since the time he'd tied one arm and tried to teach a bunch of Argentine *gauchos* how to do the square dance. The copy of the *Daily Mirror* that the upstairs maid had left on his bedside table made him smile, and that in turn made him wince. The story on the front page, accompanied by a picture of the jeweller's shop with shattered windows, talked of daring masked raiders who had accomplished a smash-and-grab with verve and dash, and who had escaped in a foreign racing car.

When Butch made his way downstairs, walking cautiously to prevent his head from wobbling, he found that Sundance and Reginald were in similar straits. A gallon of coffee and several aspirins later the three of them managed to pile into the Itala and head for the East End.

Patrick McGnaw, it seemed, had not merely come by his name by acquisitiveness alone. He looked like a rat, and a cornered one at that. Narrowed eyes darted everywhere keeping a constant vigil for whatever represented the tomcat in his existence. They displayed the loot and the negotiations began.

'Five hundred pounds!' Reginald exclaimed as they reached the narrow, dirty street. 'That's absolutely first class.'

'We was robbed,' Sundance muttered. 'That stuff was worth about five times that.' He turned to Butch and asked petulantly, 'Why don't you let me wring that little runt's neck?'

Butch patted him on the shoulder. 'Take it easy, Kid, we may wanna do some more *business* in this town. It wouldn't look so good if we started leaving a string of bodies and anyways,' he added with philosophical detachment, 'I'm looking on it as a stake. Now you can sit down and win us some more, just as soon as Reginald can find us a poker game.'

They drove back towards Mayfair, paused at the Dorchester to buy cigars, and then on to Hill Street.

'Sweet Jesus!' Butch looked up sharply at Sundance who had gone deathly pale.

'What's the matter?' he asked anxiously.

'I think I just seen a ghost.'

Butch looked around but no spirits were immediately apparent. 'Where?'

Sundance pointed at the corner. 'He was there but now he's gone.'

'Who?'

'Jonathan De Ford.'

Butch looked sick. 'You're kidding?'

'I swear to you I saw him. I'm not likely to forget him in a hurry.'

Butch scanned the street intently. All he could see was a crowd of people going about their lawful business. 'Well,' he said finally, 'he's not there now. You're sure?'

The kid looked stubborn and nodded once.

'You don't think it's just what you get when you've had a little too much to drink? *Delirium* something?'

Sundance's face looked stormy enough for lightning to flash. Butch shrugged. 'Let's go in the house.'

Reginald followed them, looking puzzled. He had watched the exchanges with birdlike interest and was still none the wiser. 'Who's Jonathan De Ford, chaps?'

Butch sighed. 'That's a long story.'

The celebration of their successful endeavour must be held, Lord Ratlett told them, at the Savoy. He'd thought about Chathams, and the Globe, and Romano's, but decided that it had to be the Savoy. All the best people went there, he informed them, and it was an excellent place to re-establish links with the society from which he had made a forced withdrawal three years ago.

'Now that we have money, how about women?' Sundance said. 'I'm beginning to feel like one of them guys they stick in a harem because he can't do anything about it.'

Reginald made a dismissive gesture. 'Some of the most beautiful women in England come to the Savoy.'

'And the most expensive, I'll bet,' Butch said to nobody in particular.

They made their grand entrance on the stroke of eight in

their freshly cleaned and pressed evening clothes, and paused in the doorway looking and being looked at, until the *maitre d'* approached. Reginald smiled and raised his hand in greeting to a foppishly dressed young man whom they passed on the way to their table. He received a wintry smile in return. 'That's an old friend of mine from university.' Reginald proclaimed.

Butch shook his head. 'I don't think so, Reginald.'

They were seated at a table at the edge of the dining room and Butch and Sundance looked about them with unconcealed interest.

'This place makes me feel like a real country-boy,' Sundance whispered to Butch.

'I know what you mean, Kid,' Butch murmured. They stared at everything, and marvelled at the whiter-than-white tablecloths, the napkins in sterling silver rings, the crystal goblets, the chandeliers and candelabra, the deep-pile carpets; at the women bejewelled and bedecked in long evening gowns and gloves, the gentlemen in white ties and dinner jackets, and even at the uniformed waiters.

The menus were produced and Butch and Sundance stared at them. 'This ain't in English,' Sundance accused.

'Oh, no. Of course not. The cuisine here is French.'

Sundance stabbed at an entry with his index finger. 'What's this? Rog-nons sought aw vinn rouge-ce?'

Lord Ratlett looked to where he was pointing. 'Oh. *Rognons sautés au vin rouge* – kidneys cooked in red wine.'

Sundance made a face. 'And what's this, gren-oils?'

Lord Ratlett looked and tittered, 'Oh, *grenouilles*, that's frogs' legs.'

'Ugh!' Sundance said.

'Perhaps,' Lord Ratlett suggested, 'you will allow me to order for you.'

Sundance sat back in his chair, folded his arms and looked resigned.

'Good idea,' Butch agreed.

The *maitre d'* approached and asked with a deference reserved for the aristocracy if the gentlemen were ready to order. 'Ah, yes, my good man,' said Reginald haughtily. 'Would you summon the wine waiter so we may order at the same time.' The waiter turned and signalled to a red-coated man, with the badge of a *sommelier*, a shallow silver cup on a chain around his neck.

'I believe we'll start with the *Fonds d'Artichauts au Foie Gras La Mère Brazier*, and a bottle of the 1901 Meursault.'

'Excellent,' the *sommelier* said. 'It has a quiet luxuriousness and a lasting and marvellous aftertaste. It's soft, round and feminine in texture, with a bouquet that eludes description.'

'Quite so,' Lord Ratlett huffed. 'And to follow we'll have the *La Bourride Raphaeloise à La Rouille de La Voile d'Or*, and a bottle of Madeira, the Sercial I think.'

'What's that?' Sundance asked out of the side of this mouth.

Reginald covered his own mouth with his hand. 'Fish soup,' he whispered. 'And after that I believe we'll have the *Maquereaux au vin blanc Le Petit St Benoit*.'

'What the hell's that?' Sundance said a little louder.

'Mackerel in white wine. And a bottle of the 1876 Corton-Charlemagne,' continued Reginald.

'A truly great wine,' the *sommelier* murmured.

Reginald turned back to the waiter. 'And after that, the *Chateaubriand à Maitre d'Hotel avec petit pois, pommes de terre Duchesse*, and the *champignons en brochette*.'

Reginald leaned over to Sundance. 'That's steak with peas, potatoes and mushrooms.' Sundance looked happier. 'And we'll have a bottle of the Chambertin 1890 with that course. It has a wonderful austere masculinity, don't you agree?' The *sommelier* did, and wrote it down. Reginald continued, 'And for dessert we'll have *Gâteau de pommes à la crème* and a bottle of your 1865 Château d'Yquem.'

Sundance opened his mouth to ask the inevitable question. 'Apple pie,' Reginald said quickly.

'Afterwards a selection of cheeses, some English Cheddar perhaps, some Brie and some Port Salut; and a bottle of Chateau Margaux, 1887.'

'Oui, Monsieur,' the waiter beamed and went to place the order. The *sommelier* headed in the other direction.

Butch looking thoughtful and ever practical asked, 'How much is this going to cost, Reginald?'

Reginald looked blank. 'I really don't know, old boy. I never thought to look at the prices, but I wouldn't think it would be any more than a hundred pounds.'

'A hundred pounds?' Butch and Sundance said simultaneously. Heads turned at some of the other tables.

'It's only money,' Reginald said with inescapable logic.

'Oh well,' Butch sighed. 'I suppose we'd better enjoy it,' he said to the Kid, who was looking thunderous.

The food and the wine arrived . . . and arrived . . . and arrived. Butch and Sundance watched Reginald closely for a lead to his choice of cutlery as the courses progressed. Toasts were exchanged as each new wine was poured with a flourish into a fresh crystal goblet.

'Great grub,' Sundance said. He burped softly.

The food had finally stopped coming and a bottle of 1878 Dow and boxes of cigars were produced along with a silver salver of *petits fours.*

Sundance fixed Lord Ratlett with a baleful stare. 'You know somethin', old boy, this is the best hundred pounds I ever spent.'

'Oh, jolly good,' Reginald said, his attention elsewhere. He was staring across the room at a muscular grey-haired man whose dinner companion was a slim olive-skinned woman in her early thirties, with strikingly large dark eyes. 'There's a friend of my father's that I've known since I was a boy.' They followed his gaze and Sundance's eyes opened wide.

'You knew her when you were a kid? She doesn't look that old.'

'Not her, him.'

'Oh,' Sundance said with obvious disappointment.

'He's something hush-hush in the Navy, an admiral, you know. I must go over and say hello.'

'We'll come with you,' they chorused, rising quickly and almost knocking over their chairs.

They trooped over in Indian file and hovered expectantly at the table. Sundance leered. The man and the woman, deep in conversation, broke off and looked up.

'Ah, Reginald Ratlett,' the man said, as recognition came. He smiled. 'Or should I now say *Lord* Ratlett? I was profoundly sorry to hear about your father.' He extended a hand and Reginald shook it.

'Thank you, sir. It was a great shock to me. May I introduce my two friends. This is Bu— I mean this is Mr John Everett and Mr Harry Lynch from America. This is Admiral Sir Godfrey Hall.'

'Howdy,' Sundance said. Butch nodded affably.

The Admiral turned to his companion. 'And this exquisite creature is the greate artiste who has stolen all the hearts in Paris. Gentlemen, may I present Mademoiselle Mata Hari.' She lowered her eyes demurely in acknowledgement.

The Admiral turned his attention back to Reginald. 'Won't you join us for a brandy, old chap?'

'We'd be honoured sir, if we're not intruding.'

'Thanks Admiral,' Sundance cut in, seating himself at once next to Mata Hari.

The Admiral signalled to the waiter. 'Bring us some cognac. The 1883 Exshaw will be splendid.'

'Hi, darling,' Sundance tried as an opening gambit. He kept his voice low. 'What sort of an artiste are you?'

Mata Hari turned her remarkable eyes on him and replied in a husky tone that made Sundance tingle, 'I'm a temple dancer. I perform the sacred dances of Java.' Her accent had more of the soft sibilants of the Far East than the harsh gutterals of her Dutch ancestry.

'Oh yeah? Where can I catch your act?'

Mata Hari smiled invitingly. 'I'm afraid I'm just passing through London.' Then with a long practised coquettish look, 'You'll have to come to Paris to see me, as the Englanders will not allow me to perform. You see, as the temple decrees, I dance in the nude.'

Sundance began to sweat. 'Oh yeah?' He looked surreptitiously over to where the Admiral was engaged in conversation with Lord Ratlett, and then back at Mata Hari. 'I don't suppose you put on any private shows?' he asked softly. 'I mean, are you with the old boy?'

'The Admiral and I are just good friends, he's telling me all his secrets.' A dimple appeared with the delicious smile and the double entendre. She reached for his hand and squeezed it lightly. 'I might be persuaded to do a private showing for the right man.'

Sundance took a deep breath and expanded his chest. 'Honey, me and you's gotta lot of talkin' to do.'

'Are you still with the Navy, sir?' Reginald was asking.

'Oh yes. They have me advising on matters to do with intelligence,' the Admiral replied vaguely. He chose that moment to glance towards the door, and said, 'Ah, damn me, if this isn't my night for running into people I haven't seen for a while. There's an old colleague of mine.' He waved and the man waved back in recognition and came towards the table. The man was small and wiry and walked with quick, athletic steps. Bright intelligent eyes that appeared to glint with sardonic amusement looked out from a sallow face. His white scalp gleamed where a parting cleaved a dead-straight passage through dark brown hair that was greying at the temples, betraying the man's age. Contrary to the fashion of the day, he was clean shaven and it drew attention to the long thin nose and thin-lipped mouth.

The Admiral stood to greet him. '*Mademoiselle* and Gentlemen, I would like you to meet Mr Geoffrey Martinette.'

Martinette bowed to Mata Hari and shook the others by the hand.

'Do join us, Geoffrey, it appears we're having a party. These gentlemen,' indicating Butch and Sundance, 'are from the Colonies,' he guffawed.

'Oh?' Martinette raised an eyebrow. 'Have you been here long?'

'We just got here a few days ago,' Butch said.

'You sure got yourself a great little ol' town here,' Sundance added.

'Have you seen much of it?' Martinette inquired with bland understatement. 'Did you know that London is famous for its banks, and has some of the finest jewellers' shops in Europe? You really should see them. And then, of course, there's the Tower of London. Anne Boleyn's head was chopped off there and they did worse things to thieves.'

Butch glanced at Sundance for a lead, but the Kid was looking bemused. Butch produced a weak laugh. 'You sure gotta great sense of humour.'

'You're in a terribly macabre mood tonight, Geoffrey,' the Admiral chided. 'We have a lady present, do think of her delicate feelings.'

Martinette bowed his head to Mata Hari. 'My most humble apologies, *Mademoiselle*.'

He turned his attention to Lord Ratlett. 'I believe you've just returned after a long absence, m'Lord.'

'By God, you're well informed,' the Admiral burst out. A mischievous smile creased his face into weathered lines. 'You cloak and dagger boys keep up with everything, eh what?'

'*Cloak and dagger boys?*' Mata Hari inquired with practised innocence.

'A rather dramatic expression for a boring civil service job, *Mademoiselle*.'

'Oh, I'm sure you're not boring, Mr Martinette.'

The cognac arrived and was duly poured into brandy snifters, followed by a toast to everyone's good health and an appreciation of the rare vintage.

A half hour later they left the dining room, the Admiral to escort Mata Hari to her room in the hotel, Martinette, he claimed, to a late appointment, and Reginald, Butch and Sundance to find their car. They lingered in the foyer while the commissionaire went to get it, and Sundance took the opportunity to saunter off to a corner and glance at the piece of paper Mata Hari had slipped into his hand. It read 'Suite 259 in an hour'. The car had arrived when Sundance rejoined the group. He inhaled, sampling the air with apparent relish. 'Tell you what, boys, the night's young and it's fine weather out. I think I'm gonna go for a walk.'

'Jolly good idea,' Reginald said, 'I'll join you.'

Butch with a sardonic smile on his face took him by the arm. 'No, you come with me, Reginald. There's some things I wanna ask you.'

Sundance looked relieved, and winked in gratitude.

He waved to Reginald and Butch as they drove away, strode out into the Strand and turned left towards Trafalgar Square. A long line of four-wheeled carriages, hansoms, and one elegant Rolls Royce Silver Ghost with a basketwork roof, were drawn up in a neat line close to the kerb, waiting varying degrees of patience for the theatregoers to emerge from the Adelphi where they would go on to their next destination. Simpson's-in-the-Strand next door to the Savoy and famous for its roast beef and Yorkshire pudding, was doing a brisk trade in late suppers, two noisy parties converging on the doorway at the same time, going through an elaborate ritual of forced politeness: 'After you, sir,' – 'No, after *you*, sir.'

Sundance checked the time on a jewellers' clock as he passed it by – it read two minutes to eleven. Sundance estimated that he had another half hour to kill before he could keep his appointment with Mata Hari, and slowed his pace to a crawl. He paused on the kerb to let a hansom go by, then started to cross to Trafalgar Square, peering through Admiralty Arch, down the gaslit Mall to where Buckingham Palace sat solidly at the other end. He almost jumped out of his skin as a four-wheeler nearly ran him down, the driver turning in his seat to let loose a voluble string of curses. For a moment, Sundance thought about running after the carriage and strangling the driver, but gritted his teeth instead and worked out his aggression on his open left hand with the clenched fist of his right. Pretty damned quick, he thought savagely. He'd better learn which goddam way this goddam English traffic went or he was going to wind up as a basket-case in some goddamn funeral parlour. And that would be a hell of a way to go when he'd spent a fair amount of time successfully dodging bullets!

He reached the comparative safety of the central square without further mishap and stopped to light the Havana cigar that the Admiral had thrust upon him earlier. His hand still shook with a slight tremor. He looked up from the cigar as a Bobby passed by; the policeman touched his helmet in recognition of a *gentleman*, then quickened his pace as he spotted a couple of vagrants at the far side of the square. Sundance watched with passive interest as the constable hustled them away. He puffed hard on the cigar, creating a miniature snowstorm with the smoke and glanced around the square. He nodded to himself with tacit approval for the bronze lions on sentry duty, then craned his neck to see Admiral Lord Nelson standing forlornly on top of his column. He ambled towards the fountain and did three slow circuits, taking a perverse pleasure in dislodging pigeons with a wave of his hand. Then he headed back to the Savoy.

Sundance made his way through the long hallways, going up and down stairs and losing himself twice before he found Suite 259. He raised a fist to knock and froze, hand poised six inches from the door. His heart was beating wildly and droplets of sweat appeared as if by magic on his forehead; one slithered down the side of his nose, poised at the tip and dropped on to the thick carpet. 'This is really goddamn silly,' Sundance muttered to himself in an undertone. 'I'm acting like a virgin on her weddin' night.' He took out a handkerchief and wiped his forehead. 'What the hell's wrong with me?' he thought. 'It's just another woman who wants the same thing any of 'em want. And I'm gonna give it to her.' He felt better when he'd decided that, but then a doubt crept in. She wasn't any other woman: a lot more exotic than anyone he'd ever known. A picture of Etta Place formed in his mind. Funny, he hadn't thought about Etta in a long time. He grinned as the high points of their affair flashed through his mind – Etta was a good sport, Etta was a comfortable woman. He wondered what she was doing now ... how she was getting on. Like his quicksilver temper, his mood changed abruptly and he shook his head with an angry jerk. To hell with Etta, she was gone and might as well be dead. He raised his fist again and pounded the door harder than he intended.

A smiling Mata Hari opened the door and found the Sundance Kid standing on the threshold with his hands on his hips. He glared at her. Her smile disappeared and was replaced by a tentative expression that was half fearful. She looked down at the silk robe she had changed into, a delicate shade of primrose with a dragon embroidered in gold on the front, that undulated gently with the rise and fall of her bosom. Everything seemed to be in its proper place; the dragon was sleeping peacefully.

'Mr Lynch—' she hesitated. 'Is there something wrong? Are you angry about something?'

Sundance looked surprised. 'Who? Me? Angry? No, Ma'am.' He looked down at himself and realized the aggressive stance he had adopted. He blushed and forced a nervous laugh. His hands slid from his hips and he fumbled with them like a bashful schoolboy. 'Pardon me, Ma'am, I was just thinkin' some bad thoughts. And then, I couldn't hardly wait to see you,' he finished smoothly.

Mata Hari's smile reappeared. 'And here I am, kind sir.' She opened the door wider and Sundance stepped into the suite.

He took off his hat, handed it to her and looked around while she placed it on the side table. Heavy dark furniture dominated the rectangular room, a long four-seater sofa covered in bottle-green velvet sat on one side of the fireplace along the wall, and two massive chairs in the same material faced the sofa on the other side of the hearth. A coffee table with a thick veined marble top rested in between, allowing for only narrow aisles of passage. The wall above the sofa held a neat row of hunting prints of horses leaping and hounds in full cry.

Mata Hari went over to the drinks cabinet that was sandwiched in the far corner and fussed with the decanters and glasses. She looked inquiringly at Sundance.

'Whiskey, please Ma'am, neat.'

Mata Hari poured a liberal portion into a tumbler. 'I wish you'd call me Mata, it sounds so formal when you say *Ma'am*. I'm Mata to my friends – we are going to be friends, aren't we Mr Lynch?'

'Well, I surely do hope so. And we can't have you calling me Mr Lynch. I'd be obliged if you'd use ma first name, it's Harry. Or you could call me Kid if you like.'

Mata Hari glided, smiling, from the drinks cabinet and handed Sundance his drink. 'Kid? That's very unusual for such a big, strong man.'

Sundance blushed again. He had a fleeting thought that this was getting to be a habit. 'Oh, yeah, well, that's a long story.'

'But Harry,' she purred, 'there's plenty of time. We have all night.'

Sundance stared at her; hastily he swallowed half his drink in a gulp. The whiskey plummetted to the bottom of his stomach and finally settled after a couple of bounces. Sundance laughed; it sounded very loud in the quiet of the room. 'Well, that sure is nice to hear, Mata. I got me a powerful lot of talkin' to do. Ya know, I haven't talked to a woman in a real long spell.'

'Really?' she said with disbelief. 'You're teasing me, aren't you, Harry? An attractive man like you and no woman to talk to?'

'Well, it weren't out of choice, Ma'am, I mean, Mata. You see, where I've bin, there weren't a whole lot of womenfolk around.'

Mata Hari patted him on the cheek. 'Poor darling. Come, sit down next to me and tell me all about it.' She led him by the arm over to the sofa and pushed him gently down on to the cushion. Sundance polished off the rest of his drink on the way. Without asking, Mata Hari went to get the whiskey decanter from the drinks cabinet and brought it back to the table. She sat down with a graceful motion and arranged the silk robe about her. She looked at him contemplatively through the huge, dark eyes that had mesmerized many a man before Sundance. She tapped small, white teeth with a polished red nail. 'You interest me, darling. I've not met many men like you. I have a thousand questions to ask you.'

Sundance reached for the decanter and refilled his glass. 'Ask away, I'll tell you anythin' you wanna know.'

'Oh, good,' she said.

'And then it'll be my turn, huh? 'Cause I sure never met anybody like you before.'

The dimple showed for an instant. 'There are not many like me, Harry.'

'I'll drink to that.'

7 The proposition

At eleven o'clock the following morning, a fine sunny day, Geoffrey Martinette pulled up in his civil service issue Wolseley and stopped in front of Lord Ratlett's house in Hill Street. He had traded in the chauffeur's uniform for his own morning coat, striped trousers, stiff white collar and tie, and bowler hat, and carried a black rolled umbrella with a carved oak handle. He glanced over his shoulder as he reached the steps of the house and caught a glimpse of De Ford lurking around the corner. He smiled to himself. He pulled the bell handle and when the door opened he presented his card to the butler, along with his request to see Mr Everett and Mr Lynch. He was relieved of his umbrella and bowler and shown into the library which was at the far end of the long, marbled hallway. He interested himself in the books that lined three walls of the room. The butler reappeared and requested Martinette to follow him into the drawing room.

Butch stood hands in pockets with his back to the window. A haggard-looking Sundance was flopped on a chair. A maid glided silently in, set down a silver tray with the coffee, and left as quietly as she had come.

Martinette's opening gambit was a benign smile. He made an exaggerated bow. 'Gentlemen.'

Butch extracted a cigarillo from a breast pocket, one of the last few from South America that he had hoarded, lit it carefully and examined Martinette through the smoke as if he were an insect at the other end of a microscope. 'I kinda thought we might see you again,' he drawled. 'It was one of my feelin's.'

Sundance looked up sharply. 'Whadda ya mean, Butch? Ya never said nothin' to me.'

Butch rolled his eyes heavenwards. 'You mean *John*,' he corrected.

'On the contrary,' Martinette contradicted. 'He means *Butch* as in Cassidy and,' turning to the chair, '*Sundance*, as in Kid.'

Sundance looked startled and turned to Butch for a lead. His expression remained unchanged. Finally he shrugged and went to sit down on the edge of an antimacassar covered armchair. He took a deep drag on the cigarillo, held it for a few moments and then allowed a twin stream of smoke to trickle from his nostrils. 'So what?' he said nonchalantly. 'So, we're Butch Cassidy and the Sundance Kid. There's no law against it – here.'

Martinette's smile exposed a double row of perfect white teeth. 'Generally speaking, I would agree with you. If one observes the rules and regulations of the country, the law of the land so to speak, one shouldn't be persecuted for past – indiscretions,' he paused for emphasis. 'This, however, isn't really the case, is it?'

Sundance looked sullen. 'What do you mean?' Martinette ignored the comment.

'Allow me to show you something.' He walked over to the heavily curtained window and tipped the velvet drapes back a fraction. Sundance ran a hand through his hair, caught Butch's eye and shrugged. He heaved himself out of the chair and went over to the window. Butch joined him there and they peered over Martinette's shoulder.

'Son-of-a-bitch!' Sundance exclaimed. He turned to Butch. 'I told you I saw that bastard De Ford.'

Butch's eyes narrowed as he watched their nemesis at his vigil around the corner. 'Right again, Kid.'

Martinette let the curtain fall back into place, blocking the view from the street. 'Shall we sit, gentlemen, this may take a while?'

Resignedly Butch and Sundance followed him back to the chairs where they sat facing Martinette and watched him, tense and wary. Martinette helped himself to a cup of coffee, stirring in the milk and sugar with deliberate slowness. The tension mounted. Martinette took an exploratory sip and leaned back with a smile of satisfaction. 'You see,' he began, 'Jonathan De Ford followed you over here, I fancy you would say *trailed*, and realizing that you were indeed in a foreign country, and that he was therefore powerless to apprehend you, he informed Scotland Yard of your presence, hoping, I imagine, that His Majesty's Government would place you in his hands for extradition. This information reached me by chance; and after thinking on it, I took the liberty of checking your *careers*.' He shook his head sorrowfully. 'You are two very naughty boys. You robbed the First National Bank of Winnemucca, Nevada in 1900,' he ticked it off on a finger. 'Is there really such a place as Winnemucca?' He tapped a second finger, 'Then you robbed the Great Northern train near Wagner, Montana in 1901 of $40,000.'

'The dirty liars!' Sundance muttered. 'There was only $25,000.'

'Then as part of your good neighbour policy, there were several other banks and trains all over South America. You realize I'm not detailing the complete list of your escapades or we might be here all day.'

'So, what's your point?' Butch drawled languidly. 'None of that happened here.'

Martinette took another sip of coffee and smacked his lips in appreciation. 'A very astute observation. We shall now come to the present. You see, when I learned of your existence I decided to watch you. Can you guess what I observed?'

Butch, who by now had a fair inkling of what Martinette had observed, wasn't about to aid him in his revelations. He busied himself with a smoke-ring.

'There is a little matter of a certain jeweller's shop in Old Burlington Street. Tsk. Tsk. Tsk. And in company with a Peer of the Realm! What a scandal that would create.'

The door to the drawing room burst open and Lord Ratlett came running in. 'Take me! It's all my fault. They're just innocent babes in the woods!'

'For God's sake,' Butch moaned. 'Sit down Reginald.'

'Yes,' Martinette commented dryly. 'Martyrs are rather out of fashion this year m'Lord.'

'Is he going to put us in prison?' Reginald asked, anxiety puckering his face as if he were about to cry. 'Mother would think that was terribly *non-de rigueur*.'

'No Reginald,' Butch replied with shrewd insight. 'He's not gonna put us in jail, otherwise he would have come with a squad of coppers. He's got something else in mind for us. Ain't that right, Martinette?'

Martinette replaced his cup and saucer on the table. 'It's always a pleasure to deal with intelligent people. It makes life so much easier.'

'Well,' Butch demanded, 'what's your proposition?'

'Hmm,' Martinette mused, 'I wouldn't actually have classed it as a proposition. I see it more in the nature of an offer you will find difficulty in refusing. It is quite simple. I've got a job that needs doing – an urgent job. I've been casting about for a solution and I think you've provided it for me. Do it successfully and I guarantee you will stay out of the tender embraces of Jonathan De Ford.'

'What kind of a job?' Sundance growled.

'A simple one, or it should be, for the two of you. After all, it is your speciality. I want you to rob a train.'

'*Rob a train?*' Butch repeated, the words sinking in with difficulty. 'For you?'

'No, not exactly for me. For the British Government. I assure you it's in a good cause.'

'That's the craziest thing I ever heard,' Butch stated in a flat monotone.

'Yeah,' Sundance said leaning forward. 'What are you, some kind of pervert?'

'If you don't do the job,' Martinette said staring at Sundance with a look cold enough to freeze him into a popsicle, 'I will make sure you're on the next boat for New York with Jonathan De Ford as your nursemaid. I believe making the trip across in irons is not the most pleasant way to travel.'

Butch leaned back in his chair. He fiddled with his cravat, bunching the folds between his fingers. The silence in the room stretched into the distance, the ticking of the grandfather clock became an ear-splitting rhythmic clunk; tick-tock, tick-tock. A horse neighed in the street and the crack of the whip from the driver sounded like a pistol shot. Butch's face wreathed in smiles, he slapped his knee. 'Congratulations, Mr Martinette, you just hired the two best damned train robbers west of Jesse James.'

'I'm so glad we finally understand each other, Mr Cassidy.' He paused to light a cheroot.

'What you want us to steal?' Butch asked.

'As you heard last night, I am a civil servant, in fact I'm deputy head of a department called MI5.'

'Oh, gosh,' Reginald breathed, 'secret agents.'

'That,' Martinette continued, making a point of ignoring Lord Ratlett, 'is a Government organization whose dual purposes are internal security and counter-espionage. We learned through one of our agents in Berlin, that the Germans are sending an envoy to their ambassador in London. He will be carrying a pouch containing papers of the utmost interest to the British Government. According to our agent, there will be a full report on the state of German preparedness in the event of war in the near future. In addition, there are special instructions to the ambassador on how he should handle German policy, or more accurately, duplicity, in the Court of St James. And finally, and certainly no less important, there is a list of German spies living in England, poised to do their worst in a crisis, and who would be activated on a signal from the ambassador. This envoy will be coming over in a private train from the Hook of Holland and landing in Harwich, where his special carriages will be attached to a British locomotive, then proceed to London.'

'So what do ya need us for?' Sundance asked. 'Why don't you just stop the train and take the papers?'

Martinette looked at him pityingly. 'That is what we obviously cannot do. I see that Mr Cassidy understands the problem.'

Butch nodded wisely. 'You can't afford to get involved.'

'Precisely. It would be the biggest diplomatic blunder of the century. It would create an international incident of the highest magnitude, and might even touch off hostilities between our two countries. I will tell you in confidence that England is not prepared for war at present. We need time to convince various *politicians*—' the thought of the elected officials for whom he had such little regard and yet was obliged to report made him wince, and his nose wrinkled in distaste, '—that appeasement is the road to disaster. As your own Teddy Roosevelt said, *speak softly and carry a big stick*. Your procurement of the documents will provide us with the ammunition with which we may observe that maxim.'

Butch leaned forward and placed his hands on the table.

'Lemme get this straight. You want us to rob a train for you because England can't get involved. But you don't mind involving a couple of Americans. You don't mind throwing us to the wolves if it goes wrong. How about the good old US of A? They might not take too kindly to having a couple of their native sons getting tossed right in the middle of your hornets nest. We're patriots, ain't we Kid?' Butch placed his hand on his heart. The gossamer outlines of the stars and stripes fluttering proudly in the breeze could almost be seen, and if you listened hard enough you could hear the faint strains of a fife and drum playing 'Yankee Doodle Dandy'.

'A very stirring speech, Mr Cassidy. You've missed your calling. You're as long-winded and say as little as any politician I've ever met.'

'Now now, Mr Martinette, no call for you to be rude. I was just telling you how we feel. You're not interested, huh? You still want us to rob this train, or we're off to the *hoose-gow*, right?'

'An excellent appreciation of the situation.'

'We've never robbed a moving train before, they've always been standing still.'

'I don't see the difference.'

'You ain't robbin' the train. What happens if we get caught?'

'Ah!' Martinette said. 'That *would* present a problem. You understand of course that we would have to disavow any knowledge of your activities.'

'I was afraid of that.'

'I don't like it,' Sundance muttered.

Martinette raised an eyebrow. 'At the risk of being boring, you know what the alternative is.'

Sundance shot him a venomous look, then turned to Butch. 'He's playing this game with a stacked deck.'

'I know, Kid, so why don't you just shut up and lemme figure how we're gonna come out with our pants, and maybe our scalps.' He stood up, paced back and forth and then turned to Martinette who was sitting quietly watching him. 'What about men, we can't pull this job off by ourselves, and how much time we got?'

'You have ten days. The train will commence its journey to London at two a.m. on the morning of 25th May, and as to men,' he shrugged, 'officially we can't assign anyone to you, but we might be able to enlist—'

'I know some,' Reginald interrupted. They all turned to look at him.

'Reginald,' Butch said kindly, 'we need professionals. This ain't no tea party.'

'Well, you have me for starters,' Reginald replied brightly; then, speaking in staccato as the protests began, 'You'll need a driver, and I,' he looked at them with modest assurance, 'am the best driver in southern England.'

Sundance glared. 'I had a taste of your driving. I hate to think what the others are like.'

'And besides that.' Reginald continued blithely, 'I know several professionals like those two gentlemen in the East End.' He looked at Martinette and blushed. 'Yes,' Martinette confirmed, 'Lord Ratlett does have a reputation for being well known to the criminal element in this city.'

Butch looked thoughtfully at Reginald and turning to Martinette he asked, 'Where will the papers be kept?'

'My agent tells me they will be in a safe,' he said. 'I can arrange for you to see a replica.'

'So, we need someone who can break it open.'

Reginald bounced up and down in his chair in excitement. 'I know one, I know one!'

'Great, Reginald. Tell me later. How about guards?'

'Ah, yes. The envoy will be in a carriage by himself. However, the carriages on either side of him will contain guards. Ten men in each and, I'm afraid, they will be armed.'

'Shit, it can't be done! We'll need a goddamn army to get in there,' Sundance growled. 'Or do you expect us to sing them a lullaby and just sashay in while they're snoozing peacefully?'

Martinette examined his manicured nails, wiping away an invisible smudge from the index finger. 'I was rather hoping you'd think out a way to do it with something less than that, and to devise a method by which gunfire would not be required. According to the dossier I have on you, you have never felt obliged to kill anyone in pursuit of your goals, a philosophy of which I approve, and one that is doubly important in Great Britain. Our police, you know, do not carry guns and therefore neither do the criminals.'

Butch stopped by the cabinet with the snuffboxes, picked one at random and tossed it absently into the air. He missed the catch and it clattered to the carpet. He stopped to retrieve it. 'Do the Germans know the rules of the games you guys play here?'

Martinette took a handkerchief from his breast pocket, dabbed at his lips and returned it. 'I admit that the Germans, with their Teutonic visions of grandeur, are barbaric when it comes to the sanctity of human life. They don't play cricket in Germany. They will have no compunction about firing their weapons; they will shoot to kill.'

Butch slammed the snuffbox back on to the shelf. 'Well, that's just great. If you think we're gonna get our asses shot off for you, you're crazy.'

'Mr Cassidy,' Martinette's reply was deceptively mild, 'certainly there must be a way to immobilize the guards that will not put you at risk. All you have to do is find the way. After all, you are the expert.'

'Yeah sure,' Butch agreed, thinking about the expert way that he, Deaf Charlie Hanks and Sundance had blown off the side of the Adams Express car near Malta, Montana, and wound up with $50,000 in bank notes, mostly shredded. He still had nightmares about the ashes drifting on the wind.

Butch came to a painful decision, the only one under the circumstances that he could make. 'OK, Martinette, we do it. We'll need money and equipment.'

'The Government will provide the money you need for the operation, for which,' Martinette said stiffly, 'I shall want an exact account.'

Sundance stuck out a belligerent lower lip. 'What about us, how much are we gettin' paid?'

Martinette's reply was bland and urbane. 'How much value do you place upon your liberty?'

Butch decided on another tack. 'But we'll need walking-around money.'

'The Government is prepared to overlook your illgotten gains; you should be able to walk several miles on those.'

'OK, OK, what do we tell the guys we get – what we're robbing?'

'I'm sure your genius for invention will come to the fore. Just don't tell them that it's secret papers for the British Government. As far as the world is concerned, and the Germans in particular, at the proper time we shall start a rumour to the effect that the train was carrying the Kaiser's personal gem collection, or the combined treasury of Frankfurt and Munich.' He waved a hand in dismissal. 'Don't worry about it, it will be something credible.'

Butch looked over at Sundance, who answered him with a reluctant nod. 'OK, my pardner and I will go along with you. Now, there's a little matter of Jonathan De Ford. We can't operate with him doggin' our trail.'

'We will restrain Mr De Ford if he becames too persistent. You have nothing to worry about.'

'I worry, I worry. You've never had him comin' after you. He sticks closer than an Injun to a jug of whiskey.'

Butch started pacing again. 'You haven't given us much time for this kind of a job,' he grumbled.

Martinette stood up and straightened his jacket. 'In that case, I suggest you don't waste any of it.' He took a notepad and a pen out of his pocket, wrote on it, tore off the sheet and left it on the table. 'That's my private number at my department, and my home number. Call any time, I like to be informed. In fact, I insist upon it.' He headed for the door. 'Don't bother to see me out.'

The three of them sat despondently, not speaking for a long time after he was gone. Sundance finally broke the silence. 'Whadda we do now, Butch?'

8 Darts, a circus, and the Titan Crusher

'How come,' Butch asked Reginald as they were driving towards the East End in a Rolls Silver Ghost, another one of the cars that Mother couldn't bear to part with, 'that you know all these crooks?'

'Father used to ask me the same thing,' Reginald replied sadly. 'He couldn't bear me consorting with these *low lifes*, as he called them. It was one of the reasons he asked me to leave the country, you know.' Reginald sighed with wistful memories. 'And I have missed my friends, very genuine people. On the whole far more interesting than the people with whom I was forced to associate – in my class. They work for a living, stealing, gambling; there's not a dilettante among them.'

'That's what I like about you,' Butch asserted, 'you're no snob.'

It had taken Reginald two days to find the man he wanted. He left early in the morning on both days and plunged into the depths of the East End to seek out former acquaintances in clubs, pubs and betting shops, to ask questions about the most famous cracksman in London, who was also proving to be the most elusive.

Butch and Sundance did a lot of sitting around, mainly in dejection, until a message arrived with a note for Sundance. He cheered up immediately but remained mysterious about its contents, and when Reginald returned, tired and hungry from his day's quest, Sundance begged off accompanying them for supper. He declared that he had so enjoyed his evening constitutional that he was going to make it a regular habit.

Butch casually pointed out the direction of the Savoy, and added that he wouldn't want Sundance to get lost. 'Kid, satisfy my curiosity, whadda you find to talk about to that lady?'

Sundance grinned, 'Between you and me, Butch, we don't do a hell of a lot of talking.' He paused. 'Well, she don't anyhow. She's real interested in what we done out West, so I made up some stories 'bout how we struck it rich out Colorado way.'

Butch thought it over. 'Well, I guess that won't do us no harm.'

Almost as an afterthought, Sundance mumbled, 'She's real interested in what we're doin' here, too.'

Butch caught the tone of voice and gave Sundance a penetrating look. 'And whadda ya tell her?'

Sundance turned away and fiddled with his belt buckle. 'I didn't tell her nothing.' He turned defiant eyes on Butch, daring him to disagree.

Butch shrugged, a corner of his mouth lifting in a half smile. 'If you say so, Kid. Does she give you much to drink?'

Sundance became animated, choosing to misinterpret Butch's question. 'Oh, yeah, she's got some real fancy hooch, somethin' called *Chartreuse*, some green stuff that the monks make and somethin' else called *Aquavit*. I wanna tell ya, that's like liquid dynamite!'

'Hope it don't make ya mouth explode, we got enough problems.'

Sundance huffed, 'What the hell you take me for, Butch? I know when to keep my lip buttoned.'

'OK, Kid, calm down. No harm in asking.'

Sundance set his mouth in a tight line, an expression that Butch wouldn't find out of the ordinary; in this case it served a double purpose. It disguised the self-doubts Sundance had about how much he'd actually shot his mouth off. He reviewed the second night he'd seen Mata Hari, the night of the day Martinette had unloaded his bombshell. He'd used the Savoy, in a strange way, like he'd used the Hole-In-The-Wall – somewhere to run when the heat was on. He sought solace like a wounded animal hiding in the safety of a warm den. The enveloping arms of Mata Hari had accomplished that purpose. He remembered her scent: exotic, mysterious, musky, sensual. And he remembered the heat of her breasts, the smoothness of her skin, and the penetration and the climax that had left him breathless. And the hypnotic eyes – always the hypnotic eyes. But he couldn't damned-well remember what he'd told her.

He had a hazy recollection that he'd told her about the one-roomed cabin where he had been born – part of what was laughingly called a 'town'. There were four other houses that made up Moosetrail, in the northern part of Minnesota. Mata Hari had held him especially tight and stroked his hair when he told her that he'd never known his mother. She had died of pneumonia when he was only two weeks old, as his father never ceased to remind him. It was his fault she'd died, because of her lowered resistance due to the exertions of childbirth.

Nils Longbaugh was a dour man at the best of times, a dark-haired Swede who had come over from the old country with his child bride to start a new life in the 'wondrous land of opportunity', and settled in an area that was remarkably like his village in Sweden.

Young Harry's memories of his father were sharp-etched but in the way an old tintype was, flat and two-dimensional. Nils Longbaugh never spoke unless he had to, in fact never really mastered the English language. He never exhibited any warmth for his son and never forgave him for surviving his mother.

Harry hit the trail at fourteen without a goodbye and without regrets. He drifted aimlessly for a while, cadging meals when he could and working at anything if he couldn't. He was a skinny, half-starved kid when he wound up in the Texas Panhandle and met the man who changed the course of his life. John Clayton was a grizzled cowboy who'd knocked around all over the West, one of the breed of drifters that was as stable as tumbleweed. There was a rumour that he was half Cherokee, an item that he never bothered to deny, or for that matter, confirm. His face was like weathered rawhide and his body as sinewy. He took a shine to the kid from Minnesota, probably in the same way one picks up a stray dog. He'd sit around the campfire at night and shake his head in sorrow – how a kid as green as he was had survived this long was a miracle. He fondled the well-worn Colt he wore high on his hip and lectured Harry long into the night about how everyone needed an edge, and this was the way to get one.

Young Harry showed a startling aptitude for shooting quick and straight and in a short time surpassed his teacher. Clayton also showed him how to do other things, like rustling, at which

Harry proved to be just as talented. It was on one of these forays that Clayton's string ran out – a watchful cowboy plugged him between the eyes and with the briefest of whispered goodbyes, Harry Longbaugh melted into the darkness.

He headed north, practising his new-found profession as he went. He was cocky and overconfident; and was caught, at the age of seventeen, horse stealing in a little town outside Wyoming. When he was taken to jail a humorous Sheriff said, 'Welcome to Sundance, Kid, you're gonna learn to love it here.' A prophecy that, as it turned out, was untrue, but after eighteen months Harry decided that the name suited him.

Sundance could not remember on which night he'd let slip to Mata Hari that there was just the smallest possibility he'd continued his criminal activities, escalating them to banks and trains. He had a vague memory of telling her about the time he and Harvey Logan had robbed the bank in Belle Bourche, South Dakota, been captured, and had escaped from Deadwood Jail, just before the trial. The booze had kept coming just around that time and Mata Hari had provided him with alternatives to whiskey. Sundance knew from past experience that he should never mix his drinks. He knew he'd told her how he'd met up with Butch at the Hole-In-The-Wall and how they'd become fast friends; and he'd craftily deviated from their actual exploits to tell her about a fictitious gold mine in Colorado. Mata Hari was fascinated, wheedling, cajoling and demanding more detail, which all seemed to have one purpose – what were he and Butch doing in England? He thought he'd explained about the hasty exit from Bolivia, but what drove him wild was that he couldn't remember if he'd said anything about De Ford and how Martinette came into the picture. He sure needed to tell someone. He wanted to explain how, at another time in another place, he would take a runt like Martinette and string him up by the thumbs, but the warning bells always went off when he was about to indulge in loose talk ... he hoped.

As Reginald, Butch and Sundance drove deeper into the East End they passed identical rows of grimy, brick buildings, which stood tall and menacing and appeared to lean into the narrow streets. Each building had its own pocket of urchins who observed their territorial imperative and played whatever game it is that kids play. Street vendors selling jellied eels, posies of flowers, cockles and mussels and hot chestnuts, lined the pavements, keeping up a steady stream of bantering chat to attract the customers.

They entered the Mile End Road, turned off about midway down and stopped opposite a pub called the Cock and Monkey. This was where Reginald had assured them they would find his friend, the famous cracksman Jimmy Trewe, known to all the police in the Home Counties for his expertise in opening safes. No man, Reginald asserted, would be more qualified to engage in this 'secret, dangerous mission'. Butch and Sundance, although dubious, thought they'd at least go along for the ride and take a look at him. They entered the pub and paused in the doorway adjusting their eyes to the dim interior. Patrons at beer-stained tables on both sides of the door looked at them with curiosity; the buzz of conversation descended to a murmur. At one end of the room a small man in mis-matching tweeds had just aimed a dart at the board. 'Triple twenty!' he shouted gleefully, then noticing the quiet he turned round to see what caused the lack of commotion. His bird-like features lit up in a smile exposing a missing front tooth. He waved. 'Reggie, me ol' China. C'mon over 'ere.'

The strangers, now obviously known by one of the regulars, ceased to be of interest, and the conversation level returned to normal. They made their way across the sawdust-strewn floor to where Jimmy Trewe took Reginald's hand in both of his and greeted him like a favourite uncle with one foot in the grave, who had just made him the main beneficiary. Reginald made the introductions, and Jimmy examined them with shrewd eyes that missed little, and commented that Yanks sure had funny names.

Armed with pints of the warm bitter which Americans usually find particularly distasteful (Butch and Sundance being no exception), they made their way to an empty table in the corner. Jimmy Trewe inspected Reginald from top to bottom, noting the new Savile Row suit, a homburg from a famous Jermyn

Street haberdasher, the walking stick that could only be found in Harrods, the hand-made shoes from Tuezek's the society bootmakers, and commented that it looked as if he'd come into some money. Reginald blushed, thinking of the unpaid bills that would remain unpaid for quite a while, and informed Jimmy of his father's recent demise and his new status in life because of it. Jimmy touched his forelock cheekily. 'Nice of ya to come down and take a butcha's at yer old mates, m'Lord.'

Sundance looked at Reginald inquiringly.

'That's cockney rhyming slang,' Reginald explained. 'They have expressions for practically everything. They use only the first word of the expression so that if you don't know it, it's almost unintelligible. Butcha's is for *butcher's hook* – look. Get it?'

Sundance nodded and continued to look mystified. Jimmy watched them with bright intense interest during the explanation, then turned to Reginald.

'Slummin' are they, guv?'

'Oh, no, not at all. In fact,' he looked around conspiratorially, 'they have a proposition for you. Absolutely in your line. I recommended you,' he said with pride.

'A couple of tea leafs are they, then?'

'In a manner of speaking,' Reginald confirmed. He leaned over to Butch and Sundance. 'He's inquiring as to whether you are in the same line of work as he is.'

Sundance looked at Jimmy. 'We,' he indicated Butch, 'me and my pard,' he said slowly and deliberately as you would talk to a foreigner, 'we rob trains, you know, choo-choo?' He sat back looking very pleased with himself.

Jimmy looked over to Reginald and said in a low voice, 'What is he, a nutter?' He tapped his head significantly.

Butch decided it was time he took over before things got out of hand. 'My friend and I might have a deal for you. We hear it's right up your alley, breaking open a safe. Savvy?'

Jimmy sniffed. 'Sure, mate. I speak English don't I?'

Butch looked relieved. 'Good. We gotta real juicy job coming up in a few days and old Reginald here tells me you're the best safe cracker in town.'

'Oh, I don't know about that,' Jimmy said modestly. 'Old Alf Grimes is as good as me. 'Corse, he's brown bread now – that's dead, mate. What's this job all about then?'

Butch took a sip of his beer to give him time to think. He almost gagged on the tepid brew, but swallowed it with a gulp that left him coughing. He pounded himself on the chest. Jimmy Trewe just sat and waited with an enigmatic smile. Butch considered the little man. He acted smart enough and might be as competent. Butch felt hampered by his lack of knowledge of the protocol for interviewing English crooks. Jimmy Trewe might take offence if asked to list his top ten safe openings. Butch decided to risk it, and anyway he didn't know where else to go on such short notice.

He explained about the train coming from Germany, using Martinette's suggestion that it was carrying jewels and money to the German ambassador, and carefully omitted any mention of secret papers. Jimmy had given the entire discourse his complete attention and looked thoughtful at the end of it.

'Dunno mate,' he mused. 'Don't really like the sound of it, moving train an' all. I get seasick when I step in a puddle. You see, I'm used to nice safe jobs, climbing up four or five storeys of a building that stands still, and crackin' open a safe that ain't jigglin' about.'

'What if your share were ten thousand pounds,' Butch asked in a stagewhisper, crossing his fingers behind his back.

Jimmy took a long swallow of his beer and wiped his mouth with the back of his hand. He grinned. 'Do you know anythin' I can take for seasickness?'

They left the pub, after arranging to meet Jimmy again in three days time to explain the job in detail. Jimmy suggested that the meeting take place in the backroom of another public house in Chelsea which a friend of his owned. They agreed readily. Reginald inquired where to go next, and Butch, looking worried, said he had to think, and he did that best on his feet, so they should go somewhere where he could take a long walk.

Reginald found a parking space for the Silver Ghost in Knightsbridge and they walked through the passageway that led to Hyde

Park. The London season had begun in earnest and the 'gay blades' were out in force. An unbroken line of broughams, open victorias, landaus, shrewsburys and talbots drove back and forth between Hyde Park Corner and Rutland Gate. High stepping pairs of matched horses in handsome trappings, sleek drivers and powdered lackeys were the order of the day. Each of the young aristocrats was accompanied by a gorgeously gowned and bejewelled lady, the majority of them resistered 'blue-bloods'; but the most beautiful women on display, whom the more daring of the 'bloods' had on their arms, were from the Gaiety and the other West End music halls. Reginald noted monograms on the coach doors and recited them like a litany – The Duke of Newcastle, The Marquis of Headford, The Count of Ostheim, The Count of Torrington, The Count of Dudley and The Count of Suffolk. There was also Baron de Clifford, Lord Cholmeley, Lord Churston, Lord Paget and Lord Dromlandrigg.

They steered a course across the grass, making for the path that bordered the Serpentine. The spell of fine weather had continued to hold and the park was full of uniformed nannies in starched dresses and caps, who marshalled their charges in prams or at the end of harnesses, or in stern commanding voices. The swings and sandboxes were full, and over to the left as they passed by, a group of boys were kicking around a football. They paused on the path when they reached it and watched in silence as the sailboats criss-crossed each other on the Serpentine, and the ducks swam in close to shore, quacking loudly for stale bread.

'Let's walk,' Butch muttered, and they followed him as he turned towards the bandstand, stepping over a golden Labrador who'd picked that moment to lie down in his path. He rapped his knuckles on his temple. 'I've been racking my brains and I can't think of a way to get on that train while it's moving.'

'Yeah,' Sundance agreed. 'This ain't the prairie so we can't use horses, and even if we could you'd have to be a goddamn trick rider to get on the train, and then there's all them guards.'

Reginald giggled. 'It would be helpful if one was an acrobat, eh chaps?'

'What did you say?' Butch asked distractedly.

'An acrobat.'

Butch refocused his attention on Reginald. An acrobat, he mused. 'What made you think of that?'

'I received a letter in the morning post from a former girl-friend of mine who heard I was back in town. She's an acrobat and a trapeze artist.'

Butch thought about it and the revelation took root and grew into a towering sequoia in a matter of seconds. 'Now just hold on a moment.' He pounded a fist into his other hand several times as if his thoughts would congeal by main force. 'An acrobat could swing on the train and throw us a rope,' he muttered, 'and we could climb it to the top of the cars.'

'You're crazy,' Sundance said with absolute certainty. 'What are we supposed to be doing, running alongside?'

'No. No wait,' Butch insisted. 'Old Reginald here tells us what a great driver he is. He's gonna get a chance to prove it. He's gonna have to steer that car right alongside the train so that we can jump on to it. Can you do it?'

Lord Ratlett lit up with excitement. 'Yes, yes, chaps, splendid idea.' He reached for and grabbed an imaginary steering wheel and hunching his shoulders, aimed his narrowed eyes down the roadway, turning this way and that to avoid potholes, outhouses, fences and maybe the odd hedgehog. He braked to a stop and looked up with a smile. 'Don't worry, I'll simply scorch down the road to keep up with the train.'

Butch gave him an affectionate pat on the shoulder. 'Good boy. Where do we find her?'

'Oh, she's performing in a carnival not too far from here.'

'You're gonna get us killed, Butch,' Sundance stated with conviction.

They drove out of Hyde Park and turned the car due north with Barnet as a destination. There, Reginald told them, was where the annual Barnet Fair was being held, and where he had once run the carousel and got to know all the carnival people, including a troupe of acrobats and trapeze artists who appeared there every year, and he had had a little *romantic* fling with the girl in the troupe.

They parked the car on the edge of the common and strolled

into the fair. Crowds milled around the food stalls and the beer stalls, the coconut shies and the hoopla. A long line of people, the men in straw boaters and the women in summery frocks, holding on to excited children, waited patiently to ride the merry-go-round and the whirligig.

The music of a steam-calliope contrasted sharply with that of an organ grinder whose cute little monkey grabbed a handful of hair and didn't let go until a coin was put into its paw. A squad of dark-skinned gipsy women filtered through the crowd with handfuls of heather for luck, and a string of curses if you didn't pay for it. The three men passed the fenced-off area where dozens of ponies were on display for sale, and finally stopped in front of the big top.

They paid their admission, armed themselves with bags of peanuts and sat down to watch the clowns go through their paces. Soon the ringmaster announced *The Flying Bertoluccis* and the crowd hushed in expectation. Three men and a girl in spangled costumes entered to an instant ovation and climbed quickly up the trailing ropes to the trapeze perch. The brawny 'catcher' swung himself out into his position to receive the 'flyers'. The two remaining men and the girl went into a series of somersaults and leaps with precision timing that had the audience gasping. The act concluded with a drum roll and a death-defying triple somersault which was accomplished with ease. The Flying Bertoluccis dropped gracefully into the net, bowed deeply to the prolonged applause, and left the arena.

Reginald, Butch and Sundance went after them. They weaved their way through the staging area, bypassing the animal cages, the trick riders astride their horses, and an elephant with one massive foot held in the air, whose trainer was examining it for ingrown toenails. The elephant deposited his dinner on the ground with a plop, in gratitude.

They arrived at a caravan with *The Flying Bertoluccis* painted on it in bright red letters. The slim, dark girl who had flown through the air with the greatest of ease had not gone unnoticed by Butch and Sundance, and when she answered Reginald's knock they were delighted to see that she looked even better close up.

'*Mi amore,*' she greeted Reginald effusively. 'It hasa been a longa time since I seena you. Come in, come in.' She eyed Butch and Sundance with a smile, '... Anda your friends.'

They entered the caravan which was lit by a couple of gas lamps, and seated themselves on cushioned benches. The girl shut the door with a bang and turned back to her guests. 'Phew! Good, I can drop that phony Italian accent now. My public,' she apologized to Butch and Sundance.

They looked surprised. 'You're not Italian?' Butch ventured.

'Oh, no,' she laughed. 'Welsh. My real name is Sylvia Jones, but can you imagine that in lights? The Flying Bertoluccis featuring *Sylvia Jones*. The ticket-buying public would feel cheated.'

Butch and Sundance examined her with frank admiration as she sat down at the dressing table. She had an oval face that wasn't beautiful by classical standards, but which would still make men catch their breath. Her mobile mouth was a shade too wide; her upturned nose a shade too small; gracefully arched eyebrows framed large, expressive, hazel eyes with golden flecks. She filled out the spangled leotard in all the right places and her long, well-shaped legs were encased in black net stockings. She was unembarrassed by their examination and watched with a glint of amusement. It deepened. 'You two are looking at me like you've been marooned on a desert island and haven't seen a girl for years.'

They blushed and mumbled, 'Pardon Ma'am,' and 'Sorry Ma'am.'

She laughed again at their embarrassment. 'That's all right, I don't mind being looked at. I'd start worrying if you didn't. And Reginald, where have you been for so long? I know that you left the country suddenly, but what have you been doing?'

Reginald told her in his usual long-winded way; Butch and Sundance had become used to it by now. He related anecdotes about strange customs, climatic conditions, bizarre foods, thieves and blaggards, and angry fathers, that made her laugh. Eventually he worked up to the meeting on the boat, the rediscovery of London, his new title, and here they were. 'And now you; I was delighted and surprised to receive a note from you. How did you find out I had returned?'

'Oh, you silly boy,' she laughed coyly. 'You can't hide your light under a bushel. When the famous Reginald Ratlett comes back to claim his title, simply everybody knows. They're all talking about it.'

Reginald blushed with pleasure.

Butch took the lull in conversation as his cue. 'We were watching your act Ma'am. Did it take long to learn all those fancy tricks?'

Sylvia shrugged her bare shoulders with a very feminine gesture. 'Oh, it took time.'

'I reckon that's right. You must have been *born* in the centre-ring to get that good.'

'Not quite. I was born in a mining village in Wales and I couldn't imagine staying there the rest of my life, so I ran away and joined a circus when I was fourteen. We travelled all over Europe and I did everything: fed the animals, mended costumes, did some bareback riding, and finally, when the girl who was with the Flying Bertoluccis left to get married, I begged for the chance to join them.' She smiled. 'They trained me and here I am.'

She picked up a brush from the dresser and ran it absently through her chestnut hair that fell to her shoulders in gentle waves. 'What about you two gentlemen. Are you here on holiday?'

Butch thought over his answer. 'Not exactly. We kinda thought a change of scene would be healthy for us.'

'Yeah,' Sundance confirmed with feeling.

'Will you be here long?'

Butch replied in an offhand manner, 'Looks like we'll be here for a time. We ran into a business deal.'

'More like stumbled,' Sundance said.

Sylvia's eyebrows arched inquiringly. 'Oh?'

'Yes, Ma'am.'

'Please call me Sylvia.'

Butch smiled. 'Sure, Sylvia. This business deal I was talking about, we kinda thought—' he hesitated, 'that is, Reginald kinda thought – I mean, you see, there's something we gotta do and

Reginald thinks you might be able to help us do it. He says you got real high spirits and he reckons that you might be interested in doin' something that you, us . . . don't usually do.'

Sylvia looked interested. 'Me? I'm afraid you're not making yourself very clear. What could I do?'

'Well, it's like this. There's this train . . .' He took the plunge and explained about the train and how they wanted to get on it while it was moving. Ergo, the trapeze artist. He told her the prepared story about the jewels and the money and the German ambassador.

She listened attentively, her expression changing slowly to surprise, and said nothing for some time after he had finished. 'You know I've never done anything like that before, break the law I mean.'

'Oh,' Butch said in a small voice. 'I never thought about that. I just reckoned that if Reginald brought us here you . . .'

'My dear Butch,' Reginald declared stoutly. 'Not all my friends are crooks.'

'Will it be dangerous?' Sylvia asked.

Butch shrugged. 'Don't know for sure. It's not as dangerous as doin' that act of yours. All we want you to do is get us on that train, and then your part's finished.'

'Will there be men with guns?'

'Yes Ma'am, Sylvia. But I wouldn't let a little thing like that worry you. They ain't gonna use them because *we'll* be there.' He put every ounce of confidence into his voice and left the cupboard bare for his own feelings. It was a large hollow space, and very uncomfortable.

Her brow furrowed in concentration. 'I'll do it,' she said firmly. 'My horoscope said I should look for some excitement in my life.'

They left after agreeing on the time and place of the next meeting at the pub in Chelsea. Butch and Sundance kept looking back at the caravan and waving to Sylvia who was standing in the doorway, both privately thinking identical thoughts.

'What a game girl!' Reginald enthused as they walked towards their car.

Butch nodded in agreement. 'Yep,' he said in admiration. 'It didn't take her hardly anytime at all to make up her mind.' A shadow crossed his face. 'But I feel kinda bad about it now that she's agreed, turning that sweet lady to a life of crime.'

'But you're not, dear boy,' Reginald objected. 'She's doing it for King and Country.'

'But she don't know that,' Sundance said.

Reginald sobered with the presentation of that single fact. 'Hmm, true. Can't we tell her?'

'No, Reginald,' Butch declared with finality. 'Just keep in mind that your good buddies, Butch and Sundance, have got their asses on the line, and we're not going to give Martinette any reason to think we're double-crossing him. He's one mean son-of-a-bitch.'

'I'm sure she'll be marvellous,' Reginald said.

Martinette answered his telephone on the first ring and listened in silence when Butch identified himself as the caller. He told Martinette what progress they'd made in assembling a team without being specific – Martinette gave an approving grunt – and that they were now ready for more details. They arranged to meet the next day for a complete briefing on the projected route.

Butch put the telephone down in the hallway and went into the drawing room and sank into a chair. 'We're meeting him tomorrow.'

Reginald nodded and took another delicate sip of tea, his pinkie finger extended as usual. Sundance bolted down his whiskey in a gulp. 'Now what?'

Butch contemplated his steepled fingers, moving them backwards and forwards like a spider doing push-ups on a mirror. 'Now we work out who else we need. I've been giving it a lot of thought, and I think we need some muscle. Someone who's big enough and strong enough to handle any of the heavy work, and who could double as a pacifier, just in case. Reginald, any of your funny friends fit that bill?'

Reginald, caught in the middle of a sip by the question, gulped it down the wrong pipe and went into a spasm of coughing.

Sundance leaned over and pounded him on the back. The coughing stopped abruptly, punctuated by a burp. 'Thank you,' he said weakly, then in a stronger voice, his old enthusiasm returning, 'I know just the man.'

'I thought you might,' Butch said with resignation.

'The Titan Crusher.'

'The Titan Crusher,' Butch repeated. 'No, Reginald, I don't think you understand. I want to know about a guy, not a machine for making cement.'

'But he is a man, old boy. That's the name under which he wrestles. He's an awfully nice Australian chap, helped me out of a spot of bother once when I was being pressed to pay a gambling debt. Two of the three chaps sent to collect it ended up in hospital, and the third must have set a new record for the hundred-yards dash.'

'Sounds like a nice fella,' Butch said deadpan.

'Oh, he's just the ticket. What recalled him to mind was an advertisement in today's newspaper. He's wrestling in the main event tonight in Hammersmith.'

Butch got up and walked over to the window and peeked through the curtain. 'OK,' he said without turning, 'we'll go see him.'

Sundance went over to the sideboard and poured himself another whiskey. Butch continued to watch. 'Ya know what I'm gonna do, Kid? I got me this powerful urge.'

'What?'

'I'm gonna have a little talk with Jonathan De Ford.'

Sundance sprayed his whiskey all over Reginald. Determinedly Butch turned away from the window and went for the door. Sundance finally found his voice when Butch had his hand on the knob. 'Hold it, Butch, is that a smart thing to do?'

'Why not? He can't touch us in this town, and besides,' he pulled the door open, 'we're the good guys this time.'

'I forgot.'

'Yeah,' Butch agreed with a grin. 'So did I. It ain't somethin' I'm used to. Coming?'

Sundance put his glass down and a mischievous smile lit up his face. 'I wouldn't miss it for the world.'

They started out of the front door with Reginald following but Butch stopped and pushed him firmly back into the hallway. 'This is between him and us.'

They strode across the street and up to the corner, where they paused. De Ford had his back to them, leaning on the car with one hand and stuffing a sandwich into his face with the other. Butch signalled Sundance to silence with a finger to his lips and motioned for him to follow. They walked quietly up to De Ford and Butch tapped him on the back. 'Traded your white hat in for a Derby, I see.'

De Ford whipped round in surprise and his sandwich went flying across the bonnet of the car. His face convulsed in anger and the blood rose like a geyser to his hairline, 'Um, um, um, um!' he shouted, doing a fair imitation of a Gatling gun with a mouthful of sandwich. Butch and Sundance ducked to miss the flying bits. De Ford spluttered, 'You dirty . . . !'

'Temper, temper,' Butch cut in and chucked him under the chin.

De Ford hunched his shoulders and looked like he was about to charge. He rocked on the balls of his feet and then with a herculean effort of his iron will he forced himself to remain where he was. His voice was a hoarse whisper. 'Very good boys, you almost got me to attack you, and then it would be me who wound up in jail, but that's not gonna happen, 'cause I can wait. I've waited nine years, and a little while longer ain't gonna kill me. I'm gonna see you rot in the darkest dungeon I can find.'

Sundance stuck out his tongue and gave him a prolonged Bronx cheer.

'Why don't you stop bothering us,' Butch drawled. 'Why don't you show your ugly face to someone else for a change? You got nothin' on us, we're clean here.'

De Ford flushed a deeper scarlet and clenched his teeth. 'You couldn't stay within the law if your life depended on it. You'll step out of line, and when you do . . . I'll be there.'

'I wouldn't hold my breath,' Butch said equably. 'We kinda like being gentlemen.'

'Ha!'

'And if you don't leave us alone,' Butch warned, 'we're gonna pin that tin star to your backside and kick you outta the country. We got influence. C'mon Kid.' He turned, and they walked away leaving De Ford speechless.

Later that evening they set out for Hammersmith; catching a glimpse of De Ford as they passed the corner, they waved to him. He cranked his car furiously, then jumped in and started to follow them.

'Shall I lose him, chaps?' Reginald asked, watching De Ford in the wing mirror.

Butch slumped down in his seat and pulled his hat over his eyes. 'Nah, why bother? We're only going to a wrestling match. Wake me when we get there.'

They entered the arena which looked like a disused warehouse, and picked their way through to the front row. The ring, covered with well-worn and patched matting, stood empty, and the impatient crowd stamped and clapped, whistled and catcalled. The din was just reaching its crescendo when the promoter stepped into the ring and raised his arms for silence. The spontaneous applause at his appearance died away.

'And now, ladies and gentlemen, the main event of the evening. The Brighton Rock versus the Titan Crusher!'

'That's him,' Reginald pointed as the Titan Crusher stepped into the ring. Butch and Sundance had to admit they were impressed. A crop of curly yellow hair topped his six-and-a-half-foot frame and he looked almost as wide. He posed for the crowd, bending his arms in the classic fashion, and his biceps rippled. He glared at the crowd and gnashed his teeth hard enough to make his thick blond moustache whip about. They booed him heartily. 'He likes to play the bad chap,' Reginald shouted above the noise. 'He's really a very gentle person.'

'Ah huh?' Butch said. He looked at the Brighton Rock. 'But I still feel sorry for the other guy.' The 'other guy' was hardly insignificant at a brawny six-foot-two, but looked small by comparison.

The match lasted for twenty minutes amid a chorus of grunts

and groans and a series of agonized expressions. It ended when the Titan Crusher placed the Brighton Rock's head in a vice-like grip between his thighs and dropped on to the mat like a piledriver, not once but half a dozen times. It was then a simple matter of rolling him over and falling on top of him until he was counted out. Then the Titan Crusher leaped up and strode around the ring, holding his hands high in a victory salute. The chorus of boos doubled in intensity. The Crusher collected his robe, stepped out of the ring and headed for the dressing room. Reginald, Butch and Sundance followed, pushing their way through the crowd.

The voice that said 'Come in' in answer to their knock came from deep down in the belly. When they entered, the Crusher had his back to them and was buttoning his shirt. He turned and looked at the three of them, then stared at Reginald in disbelief.

'Well, I'll be a dingo's daddy if it ain't Reginald Ratlett. I thought you was long gone.'

'I was away for a while, Crusher,' Reginald replied primly.

'Ah, c'mon mate, don't call me that, you know I'm Basa to my friends.'

Reginald introduced Butch and Sundance, and Basa commented on what funny names Yanks had. As the situation was different from Jimmy Trewe who made the same comment they decided not to argue the point.

'We saw the match,' Sundance said almost bashfully. 'You handled that guy like he was a baby.'

The Crusher turned mild blue eyes on Sundance and smiled shyly. 'Oh, it wasn't nothing, mate, it was my turn to win.'

'Do you mean the fights are fixed?' Butch inquired.

'I wouldn't exactly say that. Me an' the boys are good friends outside the ring. We wouldn't want anyone to get hurt.'

'Coulda fooled me,' Butch mumbled under his breath.

'... so we kinda decide who's gonna win, and then we put on a little show for the folks. Gotta give the people their money's worth. A lot of the boys earn their living out of it.'

'Don't you?'

'Me? Oh, no. I just do it for fun, and I like to stay in shape. I'm a dentist,' he announced with pride. 'Old Basa Billington, the painless dentist. Fillings, five shillings; yank 'em out, five shillings; clean 'em up, five shillings. In fact, everything's five shillings. Ya see, I'm what's called the five-shilling dentist.' He turned back to Reginald and clapped a friendly hand on his shoulder that made Reginald stagger. The Crusher pulled him erect again. 'Sorry mate, I forgot you were a puny little fella.'

Reginald stretched to his full six-feet-four with dignity. 'Not so much of the *puny* if you don't mind. Now, Basa, I must tell you why we're here.'

'Ya need some protecting again, mate?'

'On the contrary. My friends and I are going to rob a train and if you are not otherwise gainfully employed, we thought you'd like to come along for the ride.'

The Crusher looked shocked and backed away. 'Rob a train? I couldn't do that, that's dishonest.'

Butch covered his face with his hands. 'Reginald, let me tell him. You know we agreed that I should do the talking.'

'Sorry old boy, lost my head.'

'Now, ya see Basa, it's not like you think.' He paused, his mind racing furiously to find a plausible story. Then, with a flash of inspiration, 'You see, this train's coming over from Germany, it's a special train that was hired by the Baron Von Glockenspeil. Now, he's kidnapped a beautiful young girl right from out her daddy's castle, and he's bringing her into England against her will, and he's gonna force her to marry him.'

'No kidding?'

'Really.'

'And the other Germans couldn't stop him?'

Butch gave his head a slow, lugubrious shake. 'Oh, no, Basa, he's rich and powerful and they're afraid of him.'

'Can't her daddy do anything about it?'

'Oh, didn't I tell you? Her daddy would go after him if he could, but he's a cripple, all he can do is just lie there. That's why he got in touch with us.'

The giant's face took on a look of concern, and then anger, his hands balled into huge fists. 'That dirty dog, if I get my hands on him I'll squeeze him up smaller than a koala bear's nostril.'

'Then you'll come?'

'Try and stop me mate. When do we go?'

Butch calmed him down sufficiently to tell him it would be soon and he would be contacted shortly. He had the presence of mind not to mention the meeting, where the Crusher would find out that he was being hoodwinked; the consequences of that were too painful to contemplate.

Then they left.

9 Reconnaissance

Martinette had told Butch that they should all be at the Regent Street entrance of the Piccadilly underground at precisely noon, and that they should be driven there by Reginald's chauffeur. They arrived only five minutes late, and when they reached the top of the steps they saw Martinette standing on the next level down, hidden from the street.

He beckoned to them. 'Quickly,' he called. They ran down the steps, catching a glimpse of De Ford, who was looking around in vain for a place to park his car. They ran after Martinette, who led them through a maze of tunnels to the Bakerloo line. A train was just pulling in as they arrived on the platform.

'Why all the running?' Sundance puffed as they got into the train. 'Who are we hiding from?'

'There's no point,' Martinette replied coldly, 'in De Ford knowing who I am or where I am. He saw me once for a moment when I came to the house. That's enough.'

Butch decided this was not the time to tell Martinette about their confrontation with De Ford the day before. He winked at Sundance, the Kid stifled a smile.

They took the train one stop to Trafalgar Square, re-emerged into the street and followed Martinette through Whitehall, past

Scotland Yard and Downing Street and into King Charles Street. They entered the Foreign Office, went up two flights of stairs, down a long corridor and stopped at a plain wooden door with just a number on it.

Martinette's office was a spartan affair – that of a compulsively neat man. The large desk was bare except for two telephones and a spotless blotter that was lined up at precise right-angles to the desk. The only other furniture in the room consisted of three straight-backed visitors' chairs. Three of the pale green walls were bare, the fourth covered with maps on rollers. Martinette indicated the chairs and sat down behind his desk. He took a notepad from a drawer and a pen from his pocket and uncapped it. 'Tell me about the people you've recruited.'

Butch told him about Jimmy Trewe, and he made notes, nodding in approval.

'I've heard of him. He's a good choice. It will be nice to see that he's on our side for a change, even if he doesn't know it.'

Butch told him about Sylvia Jones, alias Louisa Bertolucci.

Martinette frowned and laid his pen down. 'A girl in this operation? I don't like it.'

'Well, that's too damn bad,' Butch contested hotly. 'Who's robbing this train, anyways, you or us? I need her.'

Martinette's voice was steely hard. 'For what? One of your amorous escapades?'

Butch was half out of his chair when Reginald cut in. 'My dear Mr Martinette, we need her skills and I assure you, she's completely reliable.'

'Why can't you get a man? This could be very dangerous for the young lady.'

'How about us,' Butch retorted, 'or don't we count?'

'That's different.'

'The hell it is. We die just as easily. I don't know what kind of shit you read when you checked on us but we're not . . .' he turned to Reginald, 'what's the word?'

'Invincible?' Reginald offered.

'That's it. We're not that. We stop lead just like anybody else. You came after me and the Kid 'cause we're supposed to be the goddam experts. That means we pull this job the way we want to, start to finish, and don't forget it. The fact is we need her to get on this train because I don't have any better ideas, and I know damned well you don't. Take it or leave it.'

'Gentlemen, gentlemen,' Reginald pleaded, 'can't we put aside this rancour.'

Martinette glared at Butch and picked up his pen. 'And who else have you recruited?'

Reginald, with a quick glance at Butch, told him about the Titan Crusher, limiting the details to the Australian's dimensions and avoiding any mention of his peculiarities.

Martinette accepted it without demur. He completed his notes and looked up. 'Are there any others?'

'That's it for now.'

'Will there be more?'

'I haven't decided yet. When I go over the ground I'll let you know, and speaking of that—'

'I've anticipated that.' Martinette stood up, went over to the wall and pulled down a map from its roller. He picked a pointer that leaned against the wall and touched the tip to the map. 'This is the county map of Essex. The Germans will send their train from Berlin to the Hook of Holland and ferry the carriages over to Harwich.' He pointed to the north-east corner of the map. 'There the carriages will be adjusted to our railway gauge and attached to one of our locomotives.'

'Just the three carriages?' Butch asked.

'A good question. We insisted upon placing a guard's van of our own at the end of the train, I believe you'd call it a *caboose.* The Germans objected, but we quoted British safety regulations at them.'

'Are there any?'

Martinette shrugged. 'There are now. Now, as I told you the train will leave at two o'clock in the morning and make a non-stop run, theoretically arriving at Liverpool Street station eighty-four minutes later.' He traced the route with his pointer, following the undulating line that represented the railway track. 'It is extremely important that the engine driver knows nothing of what is going on and that he completes his journey in the prescribed time. He must appear blameless for what is to transpire, and in keeping with that philosophy he will not be taken into our confidence.'

'What about the guard in the caboose?' Sundance asked.

Martinette permitted himself a smug smile. 'He will be one of my men, and will be there for two reasons. To assist you in any way he can, and to make sure you get the right papers. When you procure the documents you are to take them to the guard's van for him to look at. You leave only after he certifies their authenticity. As no hint of suspicion is to be attached to this operative, you will bind and gag him before you go.'

'What if the papers are phonies?'

Martinette showed his teeth in a smile devoid of mirth. 'Then you go back and shake the real ones out of the envoy. And I don't care how you do it.'

'You're asking a hell of a lot.'

'There's a hell of a lot at stake – for everyone.'

Butch cupped his chin in his hands and looked thoughtful. 'Eighty-four minutes, huh? That doesn't give us much time to get on, find the papers and get off again.'

'It gives you the best part of an hour.' Martinette turned back to the map again. 'I've been over the route myself and there was one area about fifteen minutes out of Harwich that looked a reasonable place to board.' The pointer rested at a spot on the map that had an 'X' pencilled on it. 'It's just outside a town called Manningtree. The train has to pass through the station and then slow down for a sharp curve. The spot is quite isolated, and the next town, Colchester, is a further eight miles.'

'I'll have to see it for myself,' Butch interjected.

'I know that, and I've booked tickets for the four of us. The train leaves in,' Martinette took out his fob watch and checked the time, 'exactly thirty-three minutes, and we have just enough time to make it comfortably.'

They found a four-wheeler in Whitehall and Martinette instructed the driver to take them to Liverpool Street station.

They passed through the high-ceilinged Victorian building and found the platform from which their train departed.

'Hey, that's real cute,' Sundance said, pointing at the engine. 'They don't have them like that back in America.'

The locomotive was royal blue, lined in red and black with blue wheels and red coupling rods, and a highly-polished brass chimney cap. Large gold letters on the tender proudly proclaimed THE GREAT EASTERN.

They located their compartment in the First Class carriage and settled themselves in red velvet seats, pushing the curtains back to watch late arrivals scurrying for the train. The whistle blew, doors slammed and the train slowly chugged out of the station. They passed through Shoreditch and Bethnal Green, and into the outskirts of London. They made several stops along the way at tiny stations like South Weald and Ingatestone, each of them spotlessly clean, painted in the same royal blue motif and surrounded by flowerbeds.

Butch paid special attention to the stretch between Colchester and Manningtree, getting up several times to look through the window at the retreating landscape. Three stops later they pulled into Parkstone Quay, the station for the boats to the Hook of Holland.

They disembarked and walked the hundred yards down the quayside where an engine was backing up to couple on to the carriages that had just been ferried across the Channel. Martinette told them to watch carefully as that was how it would be done with the German train. They inspected the surrounding area, found nothing more of interest and walked down into the seaside resort of Dovercourt, where they stopped for tea at a little shop.

A half hour later, after devouring scones, jam tarts, a selection of cakes, lashings of Devonshire cream and at least a gallon of tea, they strolled back to the station to await the train back to London. Butch took great pleasure in insisting that Martinette pay the bill, as their little outing was Government inspired. Martinette did, reluctantly, and made a meticulous entry in his notebook.

On the trip back Butch again took special note of the area between Manningtree and Colchester, attempting to fix every detail in his mind. He told Martinette that he wanted to go over every inch of the ground himself. He would need some form of transportation that would allow him the flexibility to search off the road if necessary. A motorcycle, he suggested, would suit him down to the ground.

'Do you know how to ride one?' Martinette asked.

'Never been on one in my life, but I can ride the hell out of a bicycle. It oughtta be easy.'

Martinette looked sceptical but Butch insisted, and grudgingly he agreed to provide a motorcycle. He made another meticulous note in his little black book.

They parted outside Liverpool Street station, Martinette walking briskly in the direction of his office, and the other three to find a taxi for Hill Street.

At just before eight the next morning Butch was summoned to the telephone. He answered in a voice heavy with sleep, and an obviously wide-awake Martinette informed him that a motorcycle was awaiting his pleasure at a garage in Fulham; he gave him the address. Butch muttered that he could have called at a decent time of the day because he had no intention of running out of the house at this hour; but Martinette had already hung up. Butch subscribed wholeheartedly to the theory that if he was rudely awakened, then everyone else would be, and took malicious delight in pulling Sundance and Reginald out of bed.

The three of them arrived at the garage by nine-thirty. The proprietor displayed the motorcycle with the pride of a mother hen over one of her precious chicks. The machine stood in the middle of the forecourt, its brightwork gleaming, its tank filled. They crowded around the machine, poked and prodded it, worked the brake and gear levers and tested the comfort of the leather seat.

'How fast does she go?' Butch asked.

'Oh, it's the new Triumph, she'll do seventy miles an hour,' the proprietor said.

'No kidding.'

'Beats walking,' Sundance said, impressed.

Butch eased himself on to the seat and took hold of the handlebars. 'How does it work?'

The proprietor motioned Butch off the bike and took his place, first making a cursory attempt to push his beer belly into his trousers; he gave it up as a lost cause. He kicked the machine into life and showed Butch how to use the gears. He rode slowly around the forecourt, explaining as he went.

'Ah, that's easy,' Butch smiled. 'Let me at it.' Butch seated himself and waved to his two friends. The engine roared, the bike lurched and then fell in slow motion as the motor cut off with an abrupt cough. There was silence for a time.

'My brand new motorcycle!' the proprietor wailed.

'Screw your motorcycle,' Butch yelled. 'Get me outta here!'

Reginald and Sundance rushed over and lifted the bike from where it had Butch pinned like a fly in a spider's web.

'Look, you've scratched the paintwork,' the proprietor moaned.

Butch examined himself for broken bones and looked surprised when he didn't find any. He stood up gingerly and brushed off his clothes. 'Kid,' he said through clenched teeth, 'get this guy outta here before I murder him.'

Sundance took the man by the arm and walked him, protesting, around the corner and out of sight.

With a look of determination, Butch got back on the motorcycle, started the engine again and tried his luck for the second time. The bike jerked, slowed, and jerked again but continued to run, and Butch made a wobbly circuit of the forecourt. In another half hour he had got the knack of it, and stopped the bike in front of Reginald with a triumphant look on his face. 'I'm ready, big fella, where the hell do I find the road to Harwich?'

'There's a packet of maps in the office.'

Butch whistled for Sundance who appeared in a few moments with the proprietor, who was still grumbling. They went into his office and spread out the maps on his battered desk. The three men pored over a map that terminated at the outer limits of London, Reginald pointing out the route through the East End. They exchanged it for another map that ended at Chelmsford and a third that continued on to Harwich.

'It looks easy,' Butch commented, 'once I get to the Mile End Road. Why don't you lead me there with the car, Reginald?'

And so the little convoy set out from the garage, leaving the proprietor standing on the forecourt, shaking his fist after them.

Butch braked alongside Reginald in the Mile End Road and grinned. 'Guess I'll mosey along.'

'Sure you don't want us to accompany you?'

'Yeah, I'm sure. It'll be easier to do the scouting on my own. I'll see ya back at the house, I hope,' he said under his breath. Butch found his way out of London without difficulty, which wasn't surprising as the road was almost completely straight. He reached Chelmsford around lunchtime and stopped the bike at the kerb by a workmen's café. He was hungry and thirsty, dusty and sore from all the jolting on the uneven road. The greasy egg, sausages and chips reminded him of nights on the trail with the same kind of fare. They weren't his fondest memories.

He got back on the road, and twenty miles later reached Colchester, passed through the town and slowly rode the eight miles to Manningtree. He stopped the bike with a half a mile still to go. Manningtree, not much more than a village, could be seen in the distance and all the rest of the surrounding area was, in the main, flat and featureless farm and pastureland. The railway line which bordered the road to Butch's left was between it and the River Stour that flowed sluggishly to the north-east. A few poplar trees grew irregularly on the other side of the road providing just enough cover to hide a car if you didn't look too hard. Butch used a handkerchief on his dirt-streaked face and managed to leave a ring that framed the clean spots. He patted his moustache, and the dust that had collected flew off in wispy clouds. Butch walked up the railway line to where the track diverged in two directions. One set of tracks headed north towards Ipswich and the other branch, the one in which he was interested, curved away at about a forty-five-degree angle south-west to Colchester.

The train indeed would have to slow down considerably to make the curve, perhaps to as little as ten miles an hour. He looked back up the line, and then down it. About three-quarters of a mile to a mile, he estimated, where the train would run at reduced speed – if they were lucky. They would have to be very quick boarding the train, or do themselves permanent injuries.

Butch had a queasy feeling in the pit of his stomach when he thought about it. The problem was, there were so many imponderables. Sylvia would have to get on the caboose further up the line and, assuming she could accomplish that in the dark, she would then have to tie the rope ladder securely to something on top of the swaying car, and drop it in time for them to climb on when the train slowed down. And Reginald would have to steer the car without the benefit of headlamps, close enough to the train for them to do it. Butch was beginning to doubt that any of it was possible.

Dejectedly he walked back to the bike and rode into Manningtree. He might as well go through the motions. He passed through the village and counted eleven houses, one combination general store and post office, and a church with a needle spire that leaned into the road and looked like it would wind up there one day. He came to a bridge about three miles outside the village, spanning a narrow stream; one that the train would have to cross.

Butch stopped the motorcycle, sat back in the saddle and gazed at the bridge with interest. It wasn't a very large bridge and he estimated that the girders that supported it weren't much higher than the train would be itself; still, it was a possibility. Someone with guts could flatten himself, or in this case herself, on top of the horizontal girder and remain hidden from the approaching train, then jump on to it as it passed underneath. Risky as hell. Butch decided that anyone who would do that would have to have an advanced case of the suicide compulsions.

He revved up the engine and continued on the road to Harwich. He passed through Wrabness and Strandlands and into Parkstone Quay without seeing anywhere more suitable to board the train. He turned the bike around and drove back even more slowly. About the only thing he could say in favour of the bridge idea was that the approach to it ran in an elongated 'S' curve, the top of the 'S' flattening out just as it reached the bridge. Would the train have to slow down enough? He didn't know. Would the train slow down in any case to cross the bridge? He didn't know that either. Questions for Martinette. He compiled a mental list.

He went back through Manningtree and stopped again where the line branched to London. He sat down on a little hillock at the side of the track, drew his legs up with his arms wrapped around them and rested his chin on his knees. He looked up from under lowered lids, quartering every section within his field of vision, without turning his head. He shut his eyes and tried to relate what he had just seen to past experiences. Memories of other trains and other places, jumbled by time, resurrected themselves in his mind's eye. There was a time in '98, or was it '97 that he had robbed the Union Pacific's Overland Flyer with George Curry, Harvey Logan – crazy old Kid Curry himself – and Elza Lay?

There were problems right from the start. The engineer had refused to uncouple the express car after they brought the train to a halt on a small trestle, near Willcox, Wyoming; and no amount of threats would persuade him. Elza Lay finally had to move the train himself, and fortunately he did it just in time. They'd forgotten a charge of dynamite they had placed beneath the trestle, and it blew to smithereens just as Elza Lay had moved the train on to solid ground. When their hearts got back to beating normally after they realized how close they'd come to an abrupt end to their careers, they surrounded the express car and called for the guard to open up. The guard, a man named Woodcock – he'd never forget that ornery old cuss – refused flatly and shouted for them to come and get him. So they placed a charge of dynamite next to the car and scattered.

When it went off the whole side of the express car was blown away, and Woodcock was thrown out unconscious. Kid Curry was mad enough to kill him. Butch remembered how he had stepped in front of the Kid's guns and said, 'Leave him be, Kid, a man with his nerve deserves not to be shot.'

When they blew up the safe, too much dynamite as usual, they had to run up and down the track like wild men, picking up bills that had been scattered by the blast. And not a bad haul, he reflected. $30,000 in money and bonds. And that was the raid that finally brought the Pinkertons in.

Butch had separated from the other three and heard later that they had been cornered by a posse that had been led by

Charlie Siringo and N. K. Boswell. When he met up with them again at the Hole-In-The-Wall, Kid Curry had been 'real proud' about how they had shot their way out of trouble and how he had personally killed Sheriff Joe Hazen when he was foolish enough to lead a frontal attack.

Then there was the train in 1900. He remembered it was 1900 because it was the first robbery he had committed in the new century. That one was with Kid Curry, Deaf Charley Hanks and Bill Carver. Good old Union Pacific Train Number Three, near Tipton, Wyoming. That one had been easy.

They had waited for the train to come to a stop by the water-tower where it was going to fill up. Then they had swooped down out of the low hills and had everybody covered before they knew what time of day it was. When they surrounded the express car and called for the guard to open up, Butch – for the first time in his life – was speechless. By the merest chance, obviously some cosmic joke that he didn't pretend to understand, the guard was old man Woodcock – again. For a few minutes Butch didn't know what to do, then he collared the engineer and told him to tell Woodcock that if he didn't open up the door they'd blow the car sky-high with him in it. The engineer pleaded and Woodcock finally submitted. Butch wiped the sweat off his face with relief, and when they blew the safe – still too much dynamite – there was $50,000 in beautiful new bank notes.

He remembered that train particularly well for another reason. That was the first time that Pinkertons psyched Jonathan De Ford on him. He headed an enormous posse and they had chased them hard, but they escaped again, back to the Hole-In-The-Wall.

Butch shook himself out of his reverie. Nice memories because they got away with a lot of dough, but they didn't apply to this job. Martinette had been explicit, they couldn't stop this train. He got up and made another thorough examination of the area, but found nothing to add to his meagre store of knowledge that he had not already gleaned from his previous inspection.

He accomplished the rest of the trip home without incident,

having to ask directions only six times before he reached Mayfair. He parked the bike in front of the house, thumbed his nose at De Ford and went in for a much needed bath.

10 Come with me, little girl

Butch, Sundance and Reginald arrived in the King's Road a few minutes before the appointed time. They parked the car and strolled down the street, stopping every now and then to look at the paintings that were displayed by the art colony who lived in the area.

They turned into Smith Street and found the pub called the Cheeky Chappie. When they entered they saw Jimmy Trewe standing at the bar in animated conversation with the red-faced publican. He turned as they came in and raised his pint of bitter in salute. They stopped at the bar to get Reginald a pink gin and whiskeys for Butch and Sundance, and then followed Jimmy through to a back room.

They were just seating themselves at a round wooden table when a knock at the door produced Sylvia Jones. Butch and Sundance greeted her effusively as did Reginald with a foolish grin, and Jimmy Trewe with an appraising smile.

He looked inquiringly at Butch. 'Gonna have a bird on the job then, mate?'

Butch was quick to defend the choice. 'Any objection?'

Jimmy shook his head. 'Nah, just asking. I'm not prejudiced. I never worked with one before. I like birds for one thing only. Never found 'em particularly reliable for anythink else.'

'She's gonna get us on the train. Ten thousand pounds, remember?'

Jimmy grinned. 'So she comes.'

Butch unrolled the map of Essex and spread it on the table, and they all crowded round as he pointed out the route the train would take from Harwich. He told them of his scouting expedition and indicated the place on the map where he thought they could lie in wait for the train, and then board it from the car as it slowed down. The bridge wasn't marked on the map and he showed Sylvia approximately where it was, then hesitantly asked her what she thought of his idea about jumping on to the moving train from the top of the bridge.

Jimmy Trewe looked startled and muttered, 'Better you than me, mate.'

Sylvia's reaction was less pronounced. She studied the map in concentration, thought lines deepening, then straightened up and placed her hands on her hips. 'Are you sure there's no other way to get on the train?'

Butch avoided her eyes, apparently finding something very interesting to focus on just above her left shoulder. 'I went up and down the line twice, and I couldn't see any better place. Maybe,' he asked tentatively, 'you have a better idea?'

Sylvia sighed. 'I don't.' She reached across with a smile and patted him on the cheek. 'And I'm sure that if you say that is the best place, then you must be correct.'

Butch swelled a little with the compliment.

'But I'd better see it for myself as soon as possible.'

Butch agreed eagerly. 'Great, we can go out now.'

'Hold on a second, mate,' Jimmy interjected. 'Before you scarper, what about the safe?'

Butch blushed. 'Oh, yeah, I almost forgot about the safe.'

'Almost forgot about the safe,' Jimmy repeated sarcastically. 'Tell me this, mate, what's the point of getting on the train and havin' me along, if you're gonna forget a little thing like that?' He sat down on the edge of the table, all rancour gone and replaced by a whimsical smile. 'Now, I tell you what, let's forget about the birds for a minute, and tell me what I gotta know.' He pointed to himself with a nail-bitten forefinger, and the smile widened. 'I'm an expert, ya know. Ya gotta learn to treat me like one.'

Butch moved hastily to comply. He pulled out a piece of paper from his pocket on which he'd written the information that Martinette had given him. 'It's a German safe,' he read aloud, 'called a *Panzer*, Model Number T 42.'

Jimmy Trewe nodded knowingly. 'That's a tough one, mate. Is it a combination job, or does it also need a key?'

Butch referred to his paper, then looked up. 'It needs a key.'

Jimmy nodded again in sharp, birdlike jerks, his fingers flexing unconsciously as if they were dying to get to the tumblers and probe the secrets of the combination lock. 'I seen 'em before but I never done one of 'em.'

Butch, still anxious to make amends, said, 'I can get you one to practise on.'

Jimmy looked at him thoughtfully. 'That's interesting.' He sniffed. 'You've got better connections than I thought you had, mate – for a Yank. Who's putting up the brass for this lark, anyway?'

Butch's face closed up and he got as far as opening his mouth to tell him it was none of his goddamn business whose money it was, when Reginald cut in, 'I am, Jimmy.'

Jimmy turned a sceptical eye on Reginald. 'Oh, yeah? Last time I heard about you m'Lord, you didn't have two ha'pennies to rub togevver.'

Reginald puffed himself up like a pouter-pigeon. 'It's all changed now, my dear chap. My circumstances are entirely different from our previous association.'

Jimmy still looked unconvinced, but let it pass. He turned back to Butch. 'All right then, when can I get hold of this safe?'

Butch, with a grateful glance at Reginald, replied, 'I'll let you know tomorrow.'

'Will there be anyone else,' Sylvia asked, 'with us on this – job?' She pronounced the word as if it were foreign to her and had a peculiar taste. 'We seem to be such a small band, or is it *gang*?' She giggled.

'Don't know,' Butch answered evasively, preferring not to tell them about the Titan Crusher yet. He was sure that Jimmy Trewe would not approve of the giant Australian. 'I'll decide after I do some more scouting.'

'I always thought that train robbers travelled in bunches, like bananas,' Sylvia persisted.

'That's what we like people to think,' Butch answered, determined to nip this line of conversation in the bud. 'It keeps the field from getting over-crowded.'

Jimmy looked up from the thumbnail he'd been working on and he spat a bit of it on the floor. 'You haven't said how we're going to get into the carriage, and if there's gonna be anybody there to stop us.'

Butch rubbed his chin and smoothed his moustache. 'Ah, yes, well, I'm working on it.'

Jimmy looked at Butch, squinting, as if to see him better, then shifted his gaze to Sundance, who sipped his whiskey and grunted, then to Reginald who was trying his best to look innocent, and then to Sylvia who did look innocent without trying. 'I think you're not tellin' me somethin', mate. Are there going to be lots of calico's around then?'

'That's *calico yard* – guard,' Reginald told Butch, who had obviously not understood.

'Guards, oh yeah. There'll be one or two.'

'And they're going to be carrying Tommy Dodds, I'll bet. That,' he explained, 'is a *rod*, a gun. I want you to know exactly what I mean.'

'Yeah, I guess they will,' Butch confirmed, hoping that he just caught the right note of insouciant boredom. 'But that's what me and the Kid'll be there for. They won't bother you.'

'Stone me,' Jimmy intoned in a mournful voice. 'I never used a gun in me life before. I'm afraid of 'em. We don't 'ave 'em in my line of work. Not even the coppers carry 'em, you know that? Someone might get hurt.'

'Don't worry,' soothed Butch, thinking that it was remarkable that both Martinette and Jimmy Trewe, poles apart socially and professionally, had used almost identical lines about firearms. 'I'm working on something,' he lied. 'And when we get on the train they won't even know you're there. Now, are there any more questions?'

He glanced at Sundance, who had seated himself in a chair and was sipping his whiskey with a contented smirk – the only sign on an otherwise impassive face that he was an interested spectatator – wondering how Butch was going to get out of this one.

'Yeah, I got one,' Jimmy piped up. 'How do we get off the bleedin' train?'

Sundance nodded. 'That's a good question.'

'And I gotta good answer,' Butch said: 'The same way we got on.'

'You mean we jump off?' Jimmy asked in disbelief. He started to look a little queasy.

'Don't worry about it,' Butch assured him. 'It'll be as easy as stepping into your bed at night. Old Reginald here's gonna drive alongside, and I'll personally make sure you get in safely.'

Jimmy took a long pull at his beer. 'I don't bleedin' like it.'

Butch started to say something but Jimmy beat him to it.

'I know, I know, you don't have to remind me. Ten thousand quid.'

Sylvia stared open-mouthed. 'Really?'

Jimmy gave her a sharp look. 'Didn't they tell you, darlin'?'

Sylvia recovered quickly. 'Not the actual amount.'

'How much are you getting then?'

'I don't know,' she replied primly. 'We haven't discussed it.'

'Bleedin' amateurs!' He turned back to Butch who had decided that keeping silent at this moment was better than shooting his mouth off, and busied himself instead with lighting a cigarillo. 'How much time I got with the safe?'

'I reckon you got a clean hour. Will you need that much?'

'Gor blimey,' Jimmy said fervently. 'I hope not, that'll get us too close to London for my liking!'

Butch nodded. 'Any other questions?'

Jimmy Trewe brushed away a lock of ginger hair from his eyes and scratched his head vigorously. 'Apart from wonderin' if I should get my 'ead examined,' he grumbled, 'I can't fink of anything else until after I see the safe.'

'Damned good,' Sundance drawled, standing up. 'Let's go get another drink.'

Butch retrieved his motorcycle from Mayfair and showed Sylvia where to place her inviting bottom. She looked dismayed and hiked up her long skirts experimentally, revealing well-turned ankles and rounded calves, which, although Butch had seen them before when she was in her costume, now seemed infinitely more exciting as he was getting a peek at something he shouldn't. She let her skirts drop. 'I don't think it's very ladylike.'

Butch scratched his head in perplexity. 'Well, I never thought of that. Maybe if you just lift them a little ways,' pointing to the skirts, 'and kinda slide on.'

Sylvia looked around the street. A window-cleaner a few houses away had stopped what he was doing, his sponge poised in mid-air, soapy water dripping from it unheeded on to his crotch. He had seen Sylvia's rehearsal and the glimpse of bare leg rivetted his eyes for the next part of the show.

Sylvia stuck her chin in the air defiantly, hoisted her skirts to thigh level and slid on to the pillion. 'Dirty old man!' she hissed at the window-cleaner. He grinned foolishly and nodded in agreement. Butch turned away from Sylvia to hide his own grin, got on the bike and told her to hold on tight, and they started off for Essex.

She held on a little tighter than she needed to, Butch concluded, and nestled her chin into his back. Butch, who wasn't about to correct her mistake, enjoyed the sensation. It was with an effort that he forced himself to concentrate and improve his erratic driving that almost led him to side-swipe a fruit stall. They reached Colchester without further mishap and drove slowly through town and on to the road to Manningtree. Butch stopped the motorcycle at the spot where he proposed to board the train and pointed out the scanty grove of trees where the car would wait. They walked down the track together to the curve. Exploring fingers reached out tentatively, then held. They looked at each other shyly and smiled.

Everything was as Butch had originally described it and there was no indication that anything short of an earthquake would cause a change, so they returned to the motorcycle hand in hand, remounted and started off for Manningtree.

The subtle change in their relationship was reflected in Sylvia's pressure around his middle. It was now personal, and – Butch felt for a word – comfortable. They passed through the village in a couple of blinks and rode towards the bridge stopping on the Manningtree side. They dismounted and Butch reached for her hand with confidence. They walked to the base of the bridge and stopped.

Sylvia looked at the bridge with an expert eye, noting the arrangement of the girders, the access to the top, the cover, or lack of it and every other minute detail. The lightly travelled road was, as Sylvia looked up and down, devoid of traffic. She disengaged herself from Butch with a smile and quickly scaled the girder to the top with catlike movements. Butch's heart took a fast leap to his throat as she straightened up and walked the six-inch-wide girder in her tiny, buttoned boots as if she were taking a stroll down the esplanade of a seaside resort. She walked down to the far end of the bridge and returned. Butch remained rooted to the spot. She called down, 'I'm sure I can do it, darling, if the train's not moving too fast.'

'Are you gonna come down now?' Butch asked hopefully.

She threw her head back and laughed. Butch flinched, fearing the movement would upset her balance. She descended quickly, hands and feet finding holds as if they had eyes. She took him by the arm and smiled up at him. 'It's really very easy, anyone could do it.'

'Maybe for you,' Butch conceded, 'but I think I'd rather be in the middle of the whole Sioux nation when they're on the warpath.'

She squeezed his arm. 'Silly.'

They crossed over the bridge stepping carefully between the sleepers and continued down the track for a quarter of a mile. Butch stopped her with a gentle pressure, then turned around and, squatting, sighted down the track. The polished rails glinted in the sun and swept towards the bridge in a gentle curve. Butch stood up and shook his head. 'I just don't know if the train will slow down enough for you to jump on when it reaches the bridge.'

'I think it'll have to,' Sylvia said matter-of-factly.

'I'm gonna find out for sure. If there's any chance that you're gonna hurt yourself, we'll find another way. And no arguments,' he said sternly as she started to protest. He took her by the arm and they retraced their steps.

They stopped at a public house in Colchester to buy some beer and sandwiches, then rode slowly out of town until they found a wide expanse of meadowland. Butch rode off the road, stopped the bike and when they dismounted, laid it on its side.

They took the beer and sandwiches and walked on a bit until they found a section of particularly lush ankle-high grass, surrounded by a thin screen of trees. They sprawled on it gratefully, glad to be away from the dusty roads and the bone jarring of the motorcycle. They ate and drank in silence enjoying each other's company.

Butch finished and lay back on the grass, pillowing his head with an arm and staring up into the sky. Sylvia lay down beside him and Butch turned to look at her. He smiled and reached for her slowly and she came to meet him. He kissed her gently at first and she returned it with interest. Their passion did an upward spiral and the dam burst when Butch could no longer take the ache of weeks of enforced celibacy. He fumbled for the buttons and catches of her clothes and she helped his clumsy attempts with sure, quick fingers. Butch tore at his own clothes, grumbling at how much easier it was on the range, and finally he lay on top of her.

'Oh!' she moaned. 'Ride 'em, cowboy.'

They lay for a long time afterwards saying nothing, then with a smile of mutual consent they got up, dressed and made their way back to the motorcycle.

Butch dropped her off at her rooms with a promise that he meant to keep – to see her the next day.

11 The Kaiser at Victoria station

Since his encounter with Butch and Sundance, Jonathan De Ford had become even more convinced that something was up, and as positive that it was illegal. He was still seething from Butch's taunts and his inability to do anything about them, and he was worried about Butch's parting shot that 'we got influence'. Was it just bravado or a genuine appreciation of the situation? He dismissed that line of thinking as negative and resolved to be even more watchful and infinitely more careful about being observed. It took every bit of skill he possessed to tail them without them knowing; and if virtue was its own reward, he was sure he had succeeded. He had followed the three of them when they went to get the motorcycle in Fulham – a curious thing, he thought, for Butch to want – and had trailed them to the outskirts of London, only giving up when Butch had set out on his own as the scant traffic on the road out of London was insufficient for proper cover.

He had followed them also to King's Road, keeping a careful eye on the pub until Butch emerged with a girl, followed a short time later by Reginald and Sundance with a small, ginger-haired man who was a stranger to De Ford. As soon as they were out of sight he went into the pub, ordered a drink and got into conversation with the red-faced proprietor, who fortunately proved to be garrulous.

Was that little man who just left American? he wondered. He looked just like someone he'd known in New York. He was assured that the man was not an American, but was English through and through, and furthermore, he was told in confidence, he was the best safe-cracker in London. Which was all De Ford needed to hear to make another foray into the maze of Scotland Yard, certain that this time they would listen to him, and he wouldn't be treated like just some paranoid Yank with delusions of mayhem.

He demanded to see the chief superintendent, and after an hour of not taking no for an answer was granted a five-minute interview with that lofty personage.

The chief superintendent, as imperturbable as ever, listened without comment or expression and glanced at his silver Hunter with regularity at sixty-second intervals. Yes, he said when De Ford had finished, he had heard of Jimmy Trewe, but guilt by association was not yet a crime in this country. Did De Ford have any evidence that they were up to something *naughty*. De Ford had to admit that no such evidence existed. That was a shame, the chief superintendent concluded, and stood up. When he had some, he continued, guiding De Ford firmly to the door, the Yard would be delighted to hear of it. The door slammed in De Ford's red face.

Martinette answered his telephone with a frown of annoyance. He'd had nothing but a mass of interruptions all day. His face smoothed when he discovered that his friend, the chief superintendent, was on the other end of the line. That damned Yank detective, the peevish voice told him, had just been in again. He was still creating a disturbance about Butch Cassidy and the Sundance Kid, whom he was evidently sticking to like glue, and had informed him that they had been seen with a known safe-cracker. He, the chief superintendent maintained, had sent the damned fellow off with a flea in his ear, but he thought he'd better tell Martinette about it as he had evinced interest in the people concerned. Did he want them picked up for questioning?

Martinette thanked him for the information and assured him that he wanted nothing done at this time, but that he would keep the chief superintendent informed. He said, non-committally, that he had something in mind for Butch and Sundance and if De Ford became too much of a nuisance, he would be the one to be picked up.

The telephone rang again almost at once and Butch identified himself as the caller. He told Martinette about the meeting at the pub and that he now needed the replica safe for Jimmy Trewe. Martinette made notes. And also, Butch wanted to know, did Martinette have access to a German railway carriage like the one on which they were to make the attempt?

'Yes,' Martinette replied, 'I had thought of that. There are exactly similar carriages stored in Victoria station. The German

Government keeps them there for State occasions. The rumour,' he said cynically, 'is that Kaiser Wilhelm would find it beneath him to travel in our royal train.'

'That's real good.' Butch sounded happy. 'That Kaiser guy's gonna help us without knowing it. When can I get to see them?'

'I'll check and let you know about both matters.' Martinette made another note. 'Is there anything else you think you might need?'

'Yeah. A fast, open car that can hold at least five people.'

Martinette's sarcasm was sharp-edged. 'Won't one of Lord Ratlett's many cars do? You seem to have managed admirably with jewellers' shops.'

'That was standing still,' Butch reminded him.

'All right,' Martinette conceded. 'I'll see what I can do.' He made another note.

Butch arrived at Victoria station with Reginald and Sundance flanking him on one side and Sylvia holding on to his arm on the other. Sundance had picked up immediately on the change in their relationship and had cast jealous glances at the pair and had become moody. Butch just smiled and patted him on the shoulder. 'You can't win 'em all Kid. Remember the Savoy.'

Sundance brightened visibly with the memory.

They found the station master's office and identified themselves to the fussy little man who looked at them with suspicious eyes. He grudgingly confirmed that he knew who they were and that high-level permission had been given for them to have free rein in the station. His tone indicated that he did not personally approve or feel they deserved red carpet treatment, and he was slightly mollified only after Reginald stressed that he was Lord Ratlett.

He conducted them past several platforms and into a barn-like structure where locomotives and railway carriages were kept when not in use.

The German carriages were positioned out of the way in one corner. Three of them were coupled together, constructed of oiled teak, with gleaming brass and copper fittings and large gold insignia of the German eagle on the side. They dismissed the station master with thanks and stood peering at the carriages in silence. Butch broke it, his voice echoing in the cavernous building. 'Well, boys, shall we go on board?' He made a deep bow to Sylvia. 'And you too, Princess.'

The first carriage they entered was divided into two sections. One of them contained a double bed over which a purple silk coverlet had been spread, a large emblem of the German eagle woven into the middle with gold thread.

'He sure likes to advertise,' Sundance commented as they passed through the compartment.

The other section was made up as a salon containing everything that a potentate could want in a home away from home, right down to bookshelves, a pipe rack and a glass-fronted cabinet that contained superb crystal. The now familiar eagle crest was everywhere, in bas relief or printed, or etched when neither of the other two processes applied. They stared at the brocaded Louis Quinze furniture that contrasted garishly with the heavy German dining table, the silk curtains in sombre colours, and the gas lamps that had been decorated with miniature gargoyles.

Butch summed it up for everyone. 'Looks like a nice place to visit, but I sure wouldn't wanna live here.' He walked towards the end of the car. 'C'mon, we can't stand around here gawking all day.'

The door that led into the next carriage was secured by a massive iron bolt. Butch slid it back and forth experimentally, then turned the handle to open the door, and stepped out on to the ledge that extended beyond it. He looked up at the space between the cars, searching for an easy way to the roof. It was then that he noticed a series of semi-circular iron rungs that were set into the car to the left of the door and led up to the roof, obviously, he thought, placed there for use by the maintenance crew. He grasped the rungs and climbed up, followed closely by Sundance and Sylvia, with Reginald bringing up the rear. When Reginald's head appeared above the roof line, the first thing he saw was sets of whitened knuckles from holding on for dear life.

Sylvia was standing with one hand on a hip that jutted out provocatively, laughing. 'Come on now boys, you have to stand up. The train isn't even moving! What are you going to do when the train's swaying back and forth?'

'Oh, no. Don't say that,' Butch moaned, lifting his head up to her with eyes that were squeezed tight shut. 'I think I want my mommy.'

Sundance half opened one of his similarly closed eyes. 'Whadda I do now, Butch? I never knew mine.'

Reginald climbed to the top and reached for Sundance. 'Come on now chaps, there's nothing to it.'

Sylvia grabbed hold of Butch and urged him up. 'Reginald is absolutely right, you two big, strong men ought to be ashamed of yourselves.'

Butch clung on to Sylvia and looked at her through half-closed lids. 'OK, so I'm ashamed. Now make me a promise.'

'What?'

'For Christ's sake, don't let go!'

She punched him lightly on the arm and giggled. 'Don't be a baby, open your eyes and look around you. It's great.'

Against his better judgement, Butch did so. He felt giddy, the ground looked a long way down.

'Come with me,' Sylvia commanded. She took a firm hold of Butch and walked him to the far end of the car. Reginald did the same with Sundance. 'You see, it's easy. Now, let's jump over to the other car.'

Butch balked and dug his heels in. He took a glance at what appeared to be a yawning chasm between the cars.

'Don't look down,' Sylvia admonished him. 'Come on!' She grabbed him and jumped across, pulling Butch with her. As he was given no chance to think, it was a question of either going with her, or falling down the hole. He chose the former. After his safe landing he started to tremble, and sweat poured down his face.

'I did it,' he whispered weakly.

'Sure you did,' Sylvia soothed. 'That's a good boy. Now, we'll do it again!' She jumped him back and forth between the cars, Butch protesting all the way, but finally with rote he began to relax and actually started smiling.

'Hey, this isn't so bad after all.'

'I told you so, you silly goose.'

In the meantime Reginald, spurred on by Sylvia's action, forced Sundance into the same routine, ignoring with equanimity the dire things that the Kid threatened to visit upon his person. He too almost began to enjoy it after a while.

Butch now disengaged himself from Sylvia and strolled along the roof with studied nonchalance. He stopped suddenly and clapped himself on the forehead. 'I've just had a terrible thought. What's it going to be like for Jimmy Trewe? We're gonna have to carry him.'

'Just keep reminding him about the money he's gonna get,' Sundance growled.

Butch glanced quickly at Sylvia. 'Yeah, I'll do that. Ten thousand pounds ain't nothin' to sneeze at.'

'That reminds me,' she said, 'you must tell me how much I'm to get.'

'I'll work it out,' Butch promised. 'Now, let's take a closer look at this roof.'

A three-foot-wide strip ran down the middle of the car. It was flat, and extended an inch above the rest of the roof that sloped in a slight incline to both sides. On closer examination, they saw that there were three trap-doors about a foot square, one in the middle of the level strip and one at either end. They were secured by a simple hook and an eye-bolt, and when Butch bent down and unfastened one, he could see into the carriage. 'Inspection hatches, I guess. They're too small to get into.'

'You think they could be useful?' Reginald asked.

Butch shrugged. 'Can't see how right now, but I'll keep them in mind.'

As there was nothing else of interest on the roof they descended and explored the other two carriages. They were very like the first one they'd seen but not nearly as splendid, obviously meant for lesser notables than the Kaiser's retinue.

Butch scratched his head and looked thoughtful. 'Well, I don't know if this has been any great help. Anybody got any bright ideas?'

They shook their heads. 'OK,' Butch said, 'let's go think about it.'

12 Laughing gas

The office of Barry Billington, dentist (Basa to his friends) was two floors up a flight of well-worn stairs of a building in Earl's Court. The red-brick block was one of several buildings in Earl's Court Road that catered for the needs of the district's transient population. On his way up the stairs Butch read signs on doors that proclaimed:

PASSAGE TO AUSTRALIA AND NEW ZEALAND – LOWEST PRICES – TATOOS BY LING FONG. HONG KONG'S FINEST and THE LONDON DIVISION OF THE AUSTRALIAN BEER APPRECIATION SOCIETY

Barry Billington's own sign read: ANYTHING TO DO WITH YOUR TEETH, FIVE SHILLINGS A GO. Butch knocked and went in without waiting for a reply. The Titan Crusher was lounging in his own dentist's chair, a cigar in one hand and a wicked-looking drill in the other. The machine was going full speed, and he was busily drilling holes in a cloud of cigar smoke which issued as a constant stream through pursed lips. Butch shouted over the racket of the generator: 'Practising, Basa?'

The drill shut off with a wheeze and a cough and Basa turned his curly mop around to see who it was. He leaped off the chair with a wide grin and an extended hand. Butch shook it and spent the next few moments counting his fingers.

'Hello, cobber. I was just sitting here thinking about you,' his face clouded, 'and that Baron what's-his-name.'

'Von Clockenspeil.' Butch supplied the name with alacrity, congratulating himself on his remarkable memory.

'Yeah, him. When I get my hands on him for what he's going to do to that poor helpless lady, I'm gonna rip him into little pieces.' He illustrated, his hands making a long tearing motion.

Butch shuddered.

'Now, when do we go, mate?'

'In five days. That's when the train comes over to England.'

'I can hardly wait. I gotta bigger score to settle with him now. Do you know what happened to me last night? I was wrestling my best friend when I thought about the Baron, and it got me so mad that I broke my friend's arm.' The Crusher hung his head and said mournfully, 'And now he won't talk to me.'

'Gee,' Butch commiserated. 'That's a real shame. But maybe you can tell him why you lost your head – after we rescue her.'

The Crusher brightened. 'Do you think he'll understand?'

'Sure he will. I'll bet he'd help out a poor defenceless woman.'

Basa thought it over. 'Yeah, you could be right there, mate.'

Butch looked around at the rest of the office. Alongside the drill there were trays of shiny implements, the ends of which were hooked, barbed or honed to a fine point. On a shelf along the wall a dozen pairs of gleaming false teeth rested, looking like they were ready for action.

'What's that for?' Butch asked, pointing to a bulbous tank that had a rubber hose attached to one end, and a mask at the other.

Basa looked to where he was pointing. 'Oh, that. Come over here and I'll show you.' He picked up the hose and aimed the mask at Butch's face. 'Take a whiff of that.' Basa turned a valve on the tank and the hiss of something could be heard escaping from the mask and straight up Butch's nostrils.

Butch took an involuntary deep breath. 'What the hell is that?' he spluttered, wrinkling his nose, 'What did ya do that for? That was ...' Butch started to giggle. 'That was ...' The giggles turned to guffaws and then gales of laughter. 'Great!' he finally managed wiping away his streaming eyes. He collapsed on the floor, his body racked by wave after wave of laughter. Basa picked him up as if he were a child and set him down gently in the dentist's chair. The laughter finally subsided to giggles and the occasional titter.

'Nitrous oxide,' Barry Billington the dentist answered Butch's question of a few minutes before. 'Most people call it *laughing gas*.'

Butch tittered again. 'I never would have guessed. What do you use it for?'

'Oh,' Basa said diffidently, 'I give it to my patients and they're laughing so hard, they don't feel the pain.'

Butch sat up in the chair with a jerk, eyes wide and staring.

'What's the matter, mate?' Basa said alarmed. 'Did you get too big a whiff? You look like you're about to tickle your tonsils from the inside.' He reached down for a brass spitoon and held it under Butch's chin. 'Do it in here, mate, I just cleaned up the last lot.'

The stench from the spitoon brought Butch back in a hurry from his fixed stare and almost brought up what Basa expected. Butch grimaced and pushed the spitoon hurriedly away. 'No, that's not it, Basa. I just had an idea.'

'Oh, yeah?'

'Yeah. How long will that stuff last?' he indicated the nitrous oxide tank.

'That? Oh, I don't know. Lemme think.' He screwed up his eyes in concentration. 'Yeah, I had a patient once and I had to pull out all his teeth. Yeah, I remember him well,' he added reflectively, ''cause I found out afterwards, he only needed one out. Anyway, it took an hour and a half, and he went away laughing.'

Butch slapped his knee. 'Perfect!' He stood up and went over to the tank and tried to lift it. After a few futile attempts his face fell. 'Oh, hell. I thought we could carry this damned thing.'

'That's no problem, mate, if you really need it.' The Crusher strode over and grabbed the tank by the neck with one hand, lifted it in the air and waggled it. Butch's mouth fell open in admiration.

'How much does that weigh?'

Basa considered the question and jiggled the tank up and down as if to estimate its weight. 'Oh, a hundred, hundred and fifty pounds.'

Butch nodded, happy to discover that he was not a ninety-eight-pound weakling. 'I got this idea, Basa. It's about the train. I didn't tell you, but you know we've gotta get on it while it's moving? That's so we can surprise the Baron, but there's another lit-tle problem.' He held up a thumb and forefinger with a quarter inch gap. 'The Baron's bringing a bunch of bodyguards. Now, what do you think of this? You bring that laughing gas along when we get on the train and pipe it down into the car where the guards are, they start laughing, and they don't bother us when we rescue the girl.'

The giant's face creased into a broad smile. He set the tank down with a bang that splintered a floorboard. 'Yeah, I like it, and all this because I'm a five-shilling dentist. I knew it'd come in handy some day.'

'Will you be able to carry it on?'

'Oh, I'll strap the tank to my back. Now, how many of us are going to help this lady?'

'Oh, there'll be Reginald – he's gonna drive – Sundance and me, and a couple of others,' he added vaguely. 'You'll meet 'em when we do the job – the rescue, I mean.' Butch promised that he'd get in touch with Basa the day before the train came in, and arrange a meeting place.

He left the office and walked down the stairs, whistling.

Butch found the address he sought near Harrods in Knightsbridge, and Jimmy Trewe lurking in a doorway at the same time. He realized how out of place the little man was in this part of town by the actions of the fashionable shoppers strolling by. They took one look at his loud checked suit, sniffed in contempt and quickly turned the other way. Jimmy Trewe was obviously unhappy at being looked upon as a lesser-spotted person, and jumped out of the doorway to greet Butch and pump his hand with enthusiasm. They went into a shop with a curtained window on which *Tinkers* was printed in small letters and no other indication of what lay inside.

An old, white-haired man with gold-rimmed spectacles sat on a stool behind a mahogany counter. A few leather-bound books were stacked neatly to one side; other than that, the shop was devoid of any merchandise. The old man examined them through shrewd eyes. 'Yes sir, can I be of service?'

Butch introduced himself and referred obliquely to himself and Jimmy Trewe being expected.

The old man who introduced himself as Benjamin Tinker, the

proprietor, acknowledged that he had been so informed. He led them through a curtained doorway to a well lit room where a safe stood in the middle of the floor, then he discreetly withdrew.

Butch looked after the man and then turned to Jimmy. 'Do you think he sells much?' he whispered. 'He's got no merchandise.'

'No, no, you got it wrong,' Jimmy explained. 'He sells safes and alarms to the aristocracy. They don't shop like me and you. They look at catalogues and discuss it over cups of tea. Now, let me look at this safe.'

The safe was a three-foot steel cube painted grey. A set of tumblers were exactly halfway down the door and about six inches from the left edge. A key-hole bisected the tumblers and the edge, with a handle to the right of the tumblers and just above them. Jimmy reached for the handle and pulled the door open.

Butch leaned over Jimmy's shoulder and peered at the empty interior. 'Looks solid,' he said, feeling he had to make a comment, even though it was a foolish one.

Jimmy grunted and stood up, wiped the fingertips of his right hand on his trousers and reached for the tumbler knob. He twirled it delicately, cocking his head as if listening for sounds. He shook his head. 'It's a tough one, mate,' repeating the comment he'd made at the pub.

'But can you do it?'

''Course I can. I'm Jimmy Trewe, ain't I?' The smile faded. ''Course, I may have to blow it open.'

Butch remembered his experiences of blowing open safes and had a sudden unpleasant vision of himself and Sundance in handcuffs, being led away by Jonathan De Ford. 'Are you sure you can't just break into it?'

'Dunno, do I? That's what I'm here for, to practise.' He slammed the door and spun the knob to lock it.

Butch reached for a key and a piece of paper that were on top of the safe. He unfolded the paper and glanced at it. 'Here's the combination.'

'I know, I know. Don't tell me.' Jimmy squatted down placing his ear close to the tumblers and slowly turned the knob to the right. 'Now these 'ere German safes are good'uns. Panzer's been making security systems for a long time. This is the new model, and has both the combination and the key lock.' He paused in his exposition and gave a satisfied grunt as something in the tumbler gave a soft click. He turned the knob slowly back the other way. 'They're made of solid steel, these, bent to the right-angles so there's no joins, but they got one weak point. They're still riveted at the bottom.'

'What does that mean?'

'That means that if I couldn't open it any other way, and I had enough time, I could shear off the rivets, hammer 'em through, and the sides would spring open.'

'Do you think you'd have enough time?'

Jimmy looked up. 'On the train? Nah.'

'Then why did ya bring it up?'

'It was something to talk about while I'm listening for the combination.'

'Jesus!' Butch said in exasperation.

For the next five minutes Jimmy turned the tumbler in silence, and uttered a final grunt. He turned the handle and the door swung open. Butch applauded. 'Great, now all you gotta do is open it like that on the train.' A thought struck him and he reached for the key in his pocket. 'The key. You forgot the key.'

Jimmy sat down on top of the safe and folded his arms across his chest. 'I didn't forget nothin'. The bloke guarding the safe will have the key. That's your job to get it from him.'

Butch tossed the key over to Jimmy who caught it deftly. 'The way everybody's got certain jobs around here,' he said testily, 'I might as well be in a goddamn union. I'm going, what you gonna do?'

'Think I'll stay for a while and play with the safe.' He gave it a fond pat.

'OK, I'll call you in a couple of days.' Butch went through to the front of the shop, thanked the old man and told him his colleague would be there for a while, then left.

13 The big game at White's

'I think it's about time you went to work, Kid. Our stake ain't gettin' any bigger, and we sure can't depend on that cheapskate Martinette to come up with some more.'

Sundance flexed the fingers of his dealing hand, and the creases around his mouth and in the corners of his eyes deepened as a lazy smile spread across his face. 'Well, I'm sure ready. Bring on the suckers and let me at 'em.'

'Hey, Reginald,' Butch turned to Lord Ratlett who was sitting on the settee in his crimson smoking jacket reading a newspaper, 'what's the name of that fancy club you told us about, the one where they play cards for big money?'

Reginald lowered the paper to his lap. 'Oh, you mean White's in St James's?'

'Yeah, that's the one. Can you get us in there tonight? The Kid here's got some winning to do.'

'Certainly,' Reginald confirmed. 'I'm a member in good standing; that is, I'm positive I don't owe them any money.'

Butch clapped Sundance on the back. 'Do ya hear that, Kid, tonight we're gonna show them how to do it the good old American way! I'll line up a bunch of these yokels for ya, and you can take 'em to the cleaners.'

'Capital,' Reginald beamed, then his expression changed to puzzlement. 'What does that mean?'

'We're gonna take all their money, Reginald.'

'Oh, good. Most of the gentlemen who go to White's have absolute bags of it.'

Two hours later the trio entered White's of St James's, left their toppers, capes and walking sticks with an ancient porter and entered the main salon. A quiet murmur of conversation greeted their entrance in the richly panelled room. Most of the huge, brown leather chairs that had the look of being lovingly cared for, were occupied by elderly gentlemen who exhibited just the merest curiosity at the new arrivals. They turned back to their drinks and cigars after the brief inspection.

Butch examined the portrait of an old man with prominent jowls and stern expression that hung over the mantelpiece of a fireplace in which a log fire was crackling. 'Who's that?' he asked Reginald.

'That's the founder,' Reginald whispered.

Butch shook his head. 'He reminds me of a judge back in Montana who thought he was having a bad day if he didn't sentence someone to hang before breakfast.'

A waiter approached and asked them deferentially what they wanted to drink. They ordered whiskey and asked for it to be brought into the card room. They walked through to the next room and paused in the doorway to observe. A half dozen green baize tables were occupied with players deeply engaged in their card games. Red, bluc, and white chips were piled in neat stacks. Butch looked slowly around from table to table and then turned to Reginald. 'What game are they playing?' he asked in a low voice.

'The ones closest to us,' Reginald answered in similar tones, 'are playing whist, and the ones just to their right, bezique. The others, I believe, are playing bridge.'

'Then where's the poker game?' Butch demanded in a louder voice. Heads turned in their direction with clear disapproval.

'They don't play poker here,' Reginald said sheepishly.

'Well, that's just dandy! How are we gonna get the Kid into a poker game if they don't play it?'

'I'm sorry, it never occurred to me. Perhaps we can teach some of the chaps. They might find it amusing to learn a new game.'

The waiter arrived with their drinks and Butch snatched at his angrily and downed it in a gulp.

'What you so hot under the collar for, Butch?' Sundance asked, missing the irony of the role reversal. 'I don't mind teachin' a few of these fellas how to play the game.' He laughed softly.

'Yes, I'm sure that would be splendid,' Reginald added, looking anxious to please. 'Look there. That game's breaking up and I know two of the players. I'll go and have a word with them and tell them that I have friends from America who would love to play cards, but only know how to play poker. I'm sure they'd be interested to learn.'

'Well, don't just stand there like a wooden Injun,' Butch grumbled. 'Go ask them, time's awasting.'

Reginald needed no further urging; his mouth twitched in a sickly smile. He shot off and was soon deep in conversation with his two acquaintances. Butch looked on, his hands deep in his pockets and his face resembling a thundercloud looking for somewhere to rain on. Reginald turned around, smiled and beckoned them to come over. 'These are my American friends, Mr Everett and Mr Lynch,' he said to the two men. 'And this is Mr John Buchan,' indicating the man in his middle thirties nearest to him, 'and Mr Godfrey Aldous-Brakespeare.'

The elder of the two men touched his poorly disguised toupee self-consciously and extended a hand that Butch and Sundance took in turn. 'Ratlett tells us that you wish to play poker. I wouldn't mind having a go, be a change from bridge. You'll instruct us in the rules, of course?'

Sundance smiled his slow smile. 'Why, I'd be real happy to.'

'Jolly good. I think a couple of the others might enjoy learning as well. If you'll excuse me a moment, I'll go and have a word.' He left the salon.

Reginald found no difficulty in filling the conversational gap and informed Butch and Sundance that Mr Buchan was a book publisher and as it happened, a very successful novelist as well.

Buchan demurred modestly in a soft Scottish accent that Lord Ratlett was being too kind, and that he was still learning his craft. He felt sure that his best books lay ahead of him. Aldous-Brakespeare returned to the card room with two other gentlemen in tow. They were both about the same size, one muscular and athletic looking, the other with the beginnings of a paunch.

'I've found a couple of chaps who'd be most intrigued to learn this poker game of yours. May I introduce Sir Arthur Conan Doyle,' he indicated a man in his late forties, with alert intelligent eyes, who seemed to observe every detail at a glance. And indicating the other man who was clean shaven, with shaggy brows and a receding hair-line and who managed to make his expensive evening clothes look like they had been tailored for another man, 'This is our distinguished Home Secretary, Mr Winston Churchill.'

'Gosh!' Reginald breathed in awe.

Churchill took the huge cigar he was puffing out of his mouth, his eyes crinkling with amusement at Reginald's discomfort. 'My pleasure, gentlemen,' he said to Butch and Sundance. 'I always enjoy meeting Americans, my mother's American, you know. It might give me an edge in the game we're about to play, eh?'

Sundance, who wasn't entirely sure what a Home Secretary was, remained unimpressed, but cordial. 'I'm sure in a couple of hands or so, you'll be as good as anybody. It's a real simple game.'

'I see sir,' Conan Doyle cut in, 'that you have played a substantial amount of poker, that you're used to winning, you're right handed and you keep a coin for good luck, about which you are superstitious.'

Sundance looked dumbfounded and his mouth fell open in astonishment. 'How,' he croaked, 'did you know all that?'

Churchill laughed heartily, as did the other members of the party. 'We should have told you,' Churchill said. 'Sir Arthur is the author of the Sherlock Holmes stories, and he can't resist doing his little parlour tricks.'

'Oh sure,' Butch exclaimed. 'I've heard of him. He's that guy who wears a funny hat and carries a magnifying glass.'

Conan Doyle smiled and made a slight bow. 'I've never heard of Holmes described in quite that fashion, but, my dear sir, it is entirely accurate.'

'Now, c'mon and tell me how you knew all that,' Sundance persisted.

'Elementary my dear sir. I observed that you have callouses just at the ball of your right thumb and at the first joint of your forefinger, which are entirely consistent with the position they would be in if one was used to dealing cards. I ascertained that you were right handed, again because of the callouses. A right-handed person would use that hand with which to deal while holding the pack in his left. As far as your being used to winning, let us call it an educated guess, one I felt sure would be pretty much on the mark. It would follow that a gentleman who played as much cards as you have done would not continue to do so if he were a constant loser.'

'OK, I got that but how about the superstitious stuff?'

'Oh, that was also simple. That silver dollar you wear on your fob twisted as we approached so that I could see both sides. One side is practically worn smooth from rubbing, one assumes, with your thumb. I deduced that you did so in times of stress, as in the midst of a card game, for luck.'

'Well, I'll be damned,' Sundance exclaimed. 'What's the name of that guy you write about?'

'Holmes. Sherlock Holmes.'

'I think I'll go right out and get me some of them stories.'

'After the card game,' Butch said acidly.

Conan Doyle remained undeterred by the prompting. 'That's very kind of you Mr Lynch. I might also add that it's quite obvious that you have done a great amount of horse riding.'

Sundance looked down at his bow legs self-consciously.

'And to keep the records entirely accurate, one other set of circumstances would explain the callouses on your finger and thumb. A lasting and personal acquaintance with a gun, probably the Colt variety. The callous on your thumb could be explained by continued contact with the hammer, and that on your forefinger with the trigger.' He cocked his head and looked at Sundance shrewdly.

Sundance blushed under his range tan. 'I've had a passing acquaintance with a gun. Comes in handy for shootin' rattlesnakes.'

Conan Doyle's eyes twinkled. 'Oh, yes?'

'I think it's time to sit down and play, gentlemen,' Butch cut in hastily.

'Good idea,' Churchill agreed. He put the cigar back in his mouth and went for a chair, but Sundance beat him to it. It was the one that would allow him to sit with his back to the wall, facing the door and he went to it unerringly from long habit. He always kept in mind what had happened to Wild Bill

Hickok. Everyone found a seat except for Butch who remained standing behind Reginald's chair.

'Aren't you playing, Everett?' Churchill inquired.

Butch grinned. 'Oh, me? No. My friend's playing for both of us. I'll just stand around and watch.'

'Right gentlemen,' Sundance drawled, 'we're gonna play what's called Five Card Draw.' He picked up a deck of cards from the middle of the table, shuffled them expertly and dealt five cards, face up, to each of the players. 'We'll do it this way first, so you can see how easy it is to win at this game. Now look here,' he pointed to Buchan's hand who sat to his immediate left. 'He's got a pair of tens, a deuce, an eight and a queen. Now what he should do if he were playing for real, is keep the tens and ask for three more cards; he'd be trying for three or four of a kind. And now your hand,' he indicated Aldous-Brakespeare. 'You got nothin' that matches, so it's best you get five new cards, or just chuck it in if you don't fancy your chances.'

'Now, Mr Conan Doyle there has a real interestin' hand. A three, four, six, seven and a jack. Now, you should throw away that jack and try for a five. If ya got it, it would be known as filling an inside straight.' Sundance smiled maliciously. 'That's a real good thing to do.'

'Hmm,' Conan Doyle pondered, 'are you sure of that Mr Lynch? The odds would not seem entirely favourable.'

Sundance's smile vanished. 'Yeah, well, if you could do it, it would be real good,' he mumbled.

He turned quickly to Lord Ratlett. 'Now Reginald there's got three kings and a couple of odd cards. If he got another pair it would be a full house, or he might just pull that last king. And Mr Churchill here,' turning to his right, 'should stand pat with his hand. He's got what's known as a *flush,* five cards all of the same suit. Now the way it works, that is what beats what: the lowest is a pair and if more than one player has a pair, the highest one wins; then comes three of a kind, a straight, a dash, five cards in sequence in any suit, like 3, 4, 5, 6 and 7, a full house and then four of a kind, a straight flush, that's five cards in sequence all of the same suit, and finally a royal flush.

That's ace, king, queen, jack and ten of hearts, but you boys don't have to worry about that, it doesn't come up very often.'

'It seems quite easy,' Aldous-Brakespeare remarked. 'How much shall we play for?'

Sundance put his chin in his hand and seemed deep in thought. 'Well,' he said finally, 'let's keep it low in the beginning until you boys get the hang of it. I wouldn't want you to think I'm taking advantage of you. Let's say those white chips are a pound, the red ones five pounds and the blue ten, and let's make it a ten pound limit on any one bet.'

Reginald blanched but said nothing.

Sundance looked around the table. 'Is that OK with everyone?'

They all murmured their assent.

'OK then, I'll deal the first hand, and then it passes to the left.'

'Before you start, my dear chap,' Churchill smiled benignly, 'I believe some liquid refreshment would be in order.' He signalled for a waiter. 'Would anyone care to join me?'

Everyone did except for Aldous-Brakespeare who, with an extremely prudish expression made more ridiculous as his toupee had slipped, expostulated, 'I don't know how you manage it, Winston, you're killing yourself. I neither drink nor smoke and am a hundred per cent fit.'

'And I,' Churchill replied gravely, 'do both and am two hundred per cent fit!'

Everyone broke in to loud laughter, save Aldous-Brakespeare who remained frozen-faced and definitely not amused.

'I think a bottle of champagne is called for,' Churchill announced as the waiter arrived for their order. 'Bring me,' he instructed, 'a bottle of that Bollinger you've put by for me.'

'Do you never drink anything else but champagne?' Buchan asked.

'My dear John, I try not to limit myself. Were it possible I would be delighted to sample fermented banana juice, but champagne is special – in moderation. I have often likened it to war. A single glass of champagne imparts a feeling of exhilaration. The nerves are braced, the imagination is agreeably stirred, the wits become more nimble. A bottle produces a contrary effect. Excess causes a comatose insensibility. So it is with war; and the quality of both is best discovered by sipping.'

'May I quote you?'

A knot of people had gathered round the table to watch the progress of the game and Churchill looked up to see the latest arrival. The short, rotund man with bushy moustache and pale blue eyes, beamed down at Churchill. 'Ah, Wells,' Churchill acknowledged, 'an excellent idea. I should think it would make less dull reading than most of those articles you write on social reform. I've been thinking seriously of appointing a full time chronicler, and you are in the right place at the right time. You shall have the honour of this plum.'

Wells made a deep bow. 'An honour of which I am sure I'm not worthy.'

'Perhaps so, perhaps so,' Churchill mumbled, and then chuckled. 'Do you know everyone?'

Wells said hello to Conan Doyle, Buchan and Aldous-Brakespeare.

'Permit me to introduce you,' Churchill said, 'to Lord Ratlett – this is Mr H. G. Wells – and our two American friends. This is Mr Lynch who is teaching us the game of poker, and that, standing next to you, is Mr Everett, who is engaged in the fine art of observing.'

'How about the game?' Sundance said impatiently, tapping his fingers on the table.

'Ah, the game!' Churchill said. 'Our American friend is becoming impatient to take our money. Deal the cards, Mr Lynch.'

The waiter arrived with the champagne and the other drinks as Sundance dealt the first hand.

'Cheers!' Churchill said, savouring his first sip.

Sundance picked up his cards and edged them over one at a time until the full hand was revealed. He couldn't restrain himself from smiling. Three kings and a pair of sevens, a full house.

Butch, in a position to see everybody's hand and having noticed Sundance's expression, began to experience the warm glow of confidence. The vision of tonight's winnings swelling the coffers was comforting, and he relaxed.

The betting was lively, if cautious, and the pot reached about sixty pounds, which Sundance won with his full house. He raked the chips in and stacked them neatly by colour. Wells leaned over and whispered to Butch, 'It appears that your friend has had some experience at this game.'

Butch shrugged. 'He's played a few hands,' he admitted. 'Sometimes out on the range it's the only thing we can do to pass the time.'

A gleam came in to Wells' eyes. 'You're from the West, then?'

'Well, we've done a lot of travelling, but I guess you could say that.'

'May I inquire what business you're in?'

'Oh, we've done a lot of things,' Butch replied diffidently. 'But I guess you could say that we're in the money business. We're experts in arranging the transfer of funds from banks, and off trains.'

'How fascinating. I don't suppose that any of your work has put you in contact with any of the criminal element, has it?'

Butch attempted and succeeded in attaining his most sincere expression. 'Where there's money, Mr Wells, there are always outlaws. I've come in contact with a few in my time.'

'Marvellous!' Wells said delightedly. 'Would you do me the honour of allowing me to buy you a drink? And perhaps you'd tell me some of your exploits. You see, as Mr Churchill said, I write articles for the newspapers and a first-hand account of the Wild West would have my competitors drooling with envy.'

Butch looked back to the game where Sundance had just taken the second pot and appeared to have matters well in hand. 'Well, sure I'll tell you what I know.'

They went through to the salon and commandeered a couple of chairs. They ordered drinks, and Butch settled himself comfortably and lit a cigarillo. 'Now, what would you like to know, Mr Wells.'

'Have you ever met any of the famous outlaws or lawmen? People like Wyatt Earp, or Bat Materson? Bill Tilghman or Jonathan De Ford?'

Butch reacted sharply to the mention of the name but pretended it was just a crick in his neck. He rubbed at it hard and looked at Wells with a lopsided smile.

'... Or how about Jesse James and Doc Holliday, or even Butch Cassidy and the Sundance Kid?'

The room suddenly seemed very warm for Butch and he pulled out a handkerchief and mopped his perspiring face. 'Hot in here, ain't it?'

'Oh, is it? Hadn't noticed.'

Butch made an exaggerated performance of folding his handkerchief and putting it away, while his mind raced furiously. Did this Wells guy know something and was he teasing him with a tantalizing bit of name dropping? Was he put up to it by Jonathan De Ford to have this 'chance' meeting? Or was he exactly what he appeared to be and it was pure coincidence that he had come up with those names?

'Jesse James,' he ventured cautiously, 'was a little bit before my time, and I never did run into Earp or Holliday.' Butch watched Wells closely for a reaction, but his face remained alive with interest and totally ingenuous. 'Now, I saw Bill Tilghman once, but I never spoke to him, and ... Jonathan De Ford's that Pinkerton guy, ain't he?'

'That's right, he was the one chasing the Wild Bunch.'

'Yeah, I thought so. I had a drink with him once, in Denver. Didn't think much of 'im, real mean *hombre*.'

'Really?'

'Yep. There was a rumour going around that he'd shoot unarmed men. And I hear tell that he hits women and children, and he kicked a dog once.'

'Is that right?'

Butch raised his right hand. 'God's honest truth.'

Wells hurrumphed indignantly. 'My readers will certainly like to hear about that.'

'Now the guys I can really tell you about are Butch Cassidy and the Sundance Kid. I got real friendly with them. Why, Butch and I got so close,' he crossed his fingers and held them up, 'that sometimes we were just like one person. One of the nicest fellas you ever wanna meet.'

'But,' Wells protested, 'certainly he's an outlaw. He's stolen and robbed; and that Sundance Kid is supposed to be a killer.'

'Nah!' Butch pooh-poohed the whole idea expressively by waving his hand from side to side in a negative gesture. 'Mr Wells, I'm surprised at you. You shouldn't believe everything you hear. Why I could tell you some stories about Butch Cassidy that would bring tears to a glass eye. He's the kindest, nicest, sweetest man I ever did meet, and,' he added as an afterthought, 'the most generous.'

'Oh, please tell me, Mr Everett, I'd be most grateful.'

Butch took his drink and leaned back, staring at the ceiling reflectively. 'Well, I suppose that I could tell you about the time that he saved my life, but you don't wanna hear about that, do you?'

'Oh, yes please.'

'Well,' Butch began, making himself comfortable, 'it was like this. I was riding out one day by myself around Diamond Mountain in Colorado. You see, I'd been commissioned by the railroad to see if I could find another good route through the mountains. Well, I'd just found a narrow pass and headed my horse into it to see what was on the other side. The trail took me down between high bluffs and into a gorge that had a river at the bottom. Well, I stopped there and looked for another way out, but couldn't see any, and I was just about to turn my horse around and go back the way I came, when on the horizon right in front of me an Injun popped up. And I wanna tell you, it scared the hell outta me. You see, I could tell by his war-paint and headdress that he was a Gichihumi.' Butch noted Well's blank expression. 'Ya mean you never heard of the Gichihumi?'

Wells shook his head.

'Tsk, tsk, tsk. The Gichihumi are the most savage, ferocious Injuns in the whole entire United States of America. Why, they make the Apaches look like a bunch of boy scouts helping little old ladies cross the road! My heart started going thumpety-thump, but I figured there was only one of 'em and I should be able to make it outta there without too much problem. Just then that Injun gives a blood-curdlin' yell and when I look around, another half dozen have popped up.'

'What did you do then?' Wells asked excitedly.

'Then I started thinking about how my insurance wasn't paid up and about how fond I was of my scalp, and how I didn't want it to wind up in some Injun's wigwam. And then the last thing I thought about was how I wasn't gonna have time to say goodbye to that poor little eight-year-old boy that I'd made friends with in Denver, that only had a year to live.'

Wells dabbed at an eye.

'But I wasn't gonna go down without a fight. I had my good old Winchester with me and I started taking pot shots at them Injuns.'

'Did they shoot back?'

'Sure as hell did! Good thing for me though, they didn't have no guns, but them arrows came whistling down like drops of rain. Got ma horse, Prince. He'd bin with me for six years.'

Wells dabbed at the other eye.

'Well, there came a time that I was thinkin' – Boy, I said, you come to the end of the road. I shot two of them Injuns but I was down to my last bullet and had arrows sticking out of both shoulders, and one in my side. I was just gonna turn that rifle round and use it on m'self when . . .' he paused dramatically, 'you'll never guess what happened.'

'No, no, tell me.'

'That Injun in front of me shot an arrow in my heart, and I *died*.'

Wells' face fell and he turned ghastly pale.

Butch laughed and leaned over and patted him on the knee. 'That was just a little joke, Mr Wells. I have to do that when the memory becomes too painful.'

Wells looked relieved and the colour returned to his face.

'Now, what really happened was that all of a sudden shooting broke out from both sides of the canyon and those Injuns started droppin' like hot turds from a donkey with diarrhoea. Well, I just stood there and thanked the good Lord. Pretty soon two men came riding down the mountain and jumped off their horses when they reached me. "Howdy Pardner" the first one says, (he was the real handsome one) "my name is Butch Cassidy and this is my *amigo*, the Sundance Kid. We just happened along and it looked like you needed some help. Hope you didn't mind us bustin' into your party." Thank you for saving my life, was all I could say. I wanted to shake his hand but the arrow was still in my shoulder. Well, they took me with them and nursed me back to health, and that's how come I'm sittin' here today tellin' you all about it. So, when you say "Butch Cassidy and the Sundance Kid" around *me*, you'd better smile.'

Wells, who was busily scribbling notes, ran out of paper and completed them on his cuff. He looked up and, as Butch suggested, smiled. 'Mr Everett, that is one of the most exciting stories it has ever been my privilege to hear. I myself write adventure books and many of my readers have been kind enough to think of them as exciting. I don't suppose you've read *The Time Machine* and *War of the Worlds*?'

'Sorry,' Butch said, 'I haven't.'

'No matter. They were futuristic in concept and certainly don't compare to your real-life adventure. I hope you will allow me to share this with my readers in a series of articles.'

Butch spread his hands. 'Feel free.'

They walked back into the card room to see how the game was progressing. Butch lit up with a glow of pleasure; the stack in front of Sundance had multiplied significantly – untidy stacks of red, blue and white chips leaning on each other for support. Butch gave Sundance a broad wink and was answered by an almost imperceptible lowering of one eyelid. Not a muscle quivered in Sundance's poker face to show that anything had passed between them. Besides Sundance, Churchill looked to be a big winner and, surprisingly, Reginald not far behind.

'Ah, Everett,' Churchill greeted Butch as he approached. 'Lynch here has proved to be an exemplary instructor of this rather interesting game. As you can see,' he pointed to his stack of chips with a fresh cigar, 'it has been a highly rewarding evening. As I have always derived great satisfaction from good companionship and stimulating conversation, I'm pleased to discover that if one plays one's cards right,' he chuckled, 'there is an additional bonus to be gained. We are currently discussing politics, a subject, my detractors will tell you, upon which I need very little prompting to debate. Have you ever been engaged in politics in your own country, Everett?'

Butch, visions of dollar-signs dancing before his eyes, mumbled a reply. 'I thought of running for sheriff once, but I didn't think my friends would speak to me if I won.'

Churchill laughed heartily. 'You have a very droll sense of humour. Now, Buchan here is interested in law enforcement, he sees spies everywhere and advocates a much closer scrutiny of foreigners in this country. Says he's going to write a book about it.'

'That's correct,' Buchan confirmed. 'Can you deny that there's a large increase in activity in the German embassy staff, for example. I'm sorry to say that war seems to be the inevitable terminus at the end of the line. You're in a position to know, Churchill. Don't you think so?'

'My dear Buchan, at the present time I don't think war is nearly so dangerous as politics. *That* is a veritable jungle, filled with sabre-toothed tigers. At least in war one can only be killed once. In politics it can happen many times.'

'Why did you change parties four years ago?' Conan Doyle asked. 'It was never made clear.'

'Ah! That is a question whose profundity would keep us occupied here until the middle of next week. Suffice it to say that some men change their party for the sake of their principles, others their principles for the sake of their party.' Churchill extracted his pocket watch and looked at the time. 'Gentlemen, I suggest we play one more hand and then, as much as I regret it, terminate the activities for this evening. I have an early morning meeting with the Prime Minister and would like to be just this side of *compos mentis* in case he fires off any unexpected broadsides.'

It was Aldous-Brakespeare's turn to deal and he did so quickly, setting the pack down near him when he finished. They all picked up their hands and examined the cards. Reginald glanced up now and then at Sundance's poker face and made a conscious effort to mimic it, but Sundance was too intent on his own hand to notice. He'd fanned his five cards just enough to expose a corner. With slow deliberation he chose the middle card, extracted it and placed it face down, in front of him. He folded the remaining cards and slipped them under a stack of chips, then reached into his breast pocket for a thin cigar. He flicked a match to life with his thumbnail and, while making a show of lighting the cigar, he observed what everyone else was doing through the cloud of smoke. Churchill and Buchan had each drawn two cards, Conan Doyle three, and Aldous-Brakespeare had exchanged his for a complete new hand. Sundance drew his one card and looked at Reginald, who had done the same. Reginald flushed and grinned sheepishly.

The betting began slowly, an initial five-pound bet seen by everyone and raised by Churchill with an additional ten. They all stayed in for that one, but Sundance decided it was time to push a little. He raised fifteen pounds.

'Too rich for me,' Conan Doyle exclaimed, 'with what I have. 'I'm out.' A disgruntled Aldous-Brakespeare decided to join him.

Sundance surveyed the remaining players. 'Well, gentlemen,' he drawled, 'it's up to you.'

'I'm feeling lucky,' Churchill bellowed. Heads turned at the other tables to see what was going on, and several of the men came over to watch. 'I'll match your fifteen pounds and raise you another twenty-five. How about you, Buchan? Going to stay in?'

Buchan looked at his cards again. 'I think one more wee bet might be in order.'

Churchill turned to Reginald, 'And you, Ratlett?'

Reginald looked confused momentarily. 'Ah, yes sir, I think I will stay in.' He pushed twenty-five pounds worth of chips into the centre of the table.

'Well, hot damn!' Sundance's teeth flashed in the briefest of smiles. 'Got somethin' real good there, huh? Well, let's just see what you boys are made of. I'll see ya, and raise you one hundred more.'

Butch edged around the table and peered over Sundance's shoulder. His nerves had started jumping when he saw Sundance betting like a Texas cowhand who'd just come off two months on the trail. His relief was visible when he saw the four nines that Sundance held in his hand. Butch chided himself for doubting Sundance; after all, the Kid was a pro and wouldn't make those kind of mistakes – with their money.

'Ah-ha!' Churchill's eyes crinkled with amusement. 'Methinks Mr Lynch is trying to tell us something.' Churchill fingered the chips in front of him. 'Let's see, now,' he muttered thoughtfully. He counted out chips, 'One hundred ... and two hundred more.'

The crowd gasped and Reginald gulped. Buchan folded his hand and threw it on the table; he inclined his head towards Churchill. 'That, my dear sir, will do it for me.'

'I'll call you,' Sundance drawled. He pushed over two hundred pounds worth of chips that left him with half a dozen whites, a couple of reds and a lonely blue.

Reginald looked around the table with an earnest expression, and licked his lips. 'I'd like to join in as well ...' He hesitated. 'But as you see I don't have enough chips left. Would you mind taking my IOU?'

Sundance glowered at him and was about to explain the meaning of table stakes, when Churchill cut in. 'Certainly, Ratlett, we're all friends here and, some might even suggest, gentlemen. I have no objections; you, Lynch?'

Sundance bit off a reply and just shook his head. Reginald smiled at Churchill in gratitude, took out his notepad, wrote out the IOU and tearing off the sheet put it with the rest of the pot. Butch felt himself going hot at Reginald's actions. He grimaced at Wells.

'Exciting, isn't it?' Wells whispered.

Churchill rested his half-smoked cigar on the edge of the crystal ashtray, smiled jubilantly and slammed his hand down on the table face up, fanning the cards for all to see. 'A full house,' he chortled. 'Three aces and a pair of treys.'

Sundance allowed his poker face to crack, a chuckle started way back in his throat, then he swiped at his moustache with the back of his hand as if to stifle it. 'Well, I'll tell you, Mr Churchill, that's not quite good enough.' He laid his cards down one at a time. 'Read 'em and weep. Four nines are a little bit too much for ya.' Sundance started to reach for the pile of chips.

'Ah-hmm, excuse me,' Reginald said in a small voice. 'I believe, uh,' he cleared his throat again and the rest of the words came out in a rush, 'I believe this beats you.' He laid his hand out.

Sundance looked at the cards in disbelief. 'Well, I'll be a son-of-a-bitch,' he muttered. 'Jee-sus Christ, a goddamn royal flush!'

'Well done, Ratlett,' Churchill exclaimed; he clapped Reginald on the back.

Reginald beamed, circled the chips with both arms, and shovelled them in. He started assembling them by colour, and then counted his winnings. 'How splendid!' he announced. 'Eleven-hundred and fifty-five pounds, minus my IOU, of course.' He ripped it up with some ceremony and deposited the scraps in the ashtray. He shoved the chips over to Conan Doyle who had been acting as the banker, and received bank notes in exchange.

Churchill cashed in his winnings. 'Not bad,' he commented. 'I'm still £125 to the good.' The two big losers, Sundance and Aldous-Brakespeare, sat disconsolately with identically sulky expressions.

Everyone stood and went through the amenities of saying goodbye with promises to do it again in the near future.

'Don't forget to watch for my article,' Wells said to Butch.

'I'll sure keep an eye out,' he promised.

Butch, Sundance and Reginald walked out, retrieved their hats, capes and walking sticks and stepped out on to the pavement.

Sundance held out a hand to Reginald, palm up. 'Give.'

'But Sundance,' Reginald protested, 'I won the money.'

'And who lost twenty-five hundred bucks aboard that boat?' Sundance said with menace.

'Oh, yes,' Reginald tittered. 'I almost forgot.'

'Well I didn't. Give.'

Butch placed a hand on each of their shoulders. 'C'mon now boys, this ain't nothin' to fight about. We're staying in Reginald's house rent free, ain't we?' he said to Sundance. 'And Reginald owes us money, so let's split it three ways. You gotta look on the bright side, Kid. It was a good thing he was in the game.'

14 Shootin' practice

With only a few days left to go, Butch began a period of frenzied activity, mainly to fill in the time. He took to getting on his motorcycle and riding just anywhere. He convinced himself that he should take advantage of being in a new country and act like any other tourist who came to visit. He explored the country roads and villages of Berkshire, Hertfordshire and Sussex, stopping to watch the early season cricket matches that were played on the village greens. Or he would stop to examine a building like a student architect, marvelling at spires and eaves and cornices. Once he even went in to a medieval church and poked around its musty corners.

On the days when Sylvia could get away from the circus, Butch commandeered the Itala and they would drive off into the country seeking out wide stretches of commonland where the spring flowers were in full bloom. They would frolic like children between pale yellow primroses and the deeper yellow buttercups and the different blues of bluebells, forget-me-nots and periwinkle that dotted the landscape. They would follow paths into deserted woods where the trees had a new mantle of fresh, green leaves and find resting places when the mood took them, and make gentle love.

Butch, for the first time he could remember, reviewed his forty years as if he were looking at them through the wrong end of a telescope. He'd suffered hardship, deprivation, the constant fear of being caught. He wasn't dismissing the good times, but paused to examine the bad ones and what the future might hold for him. He wondered if it was too late for him to settle down like a normal human being with a wife, and raise a family and become a respected member of the community.

And then there was Sylvia. Could she be the girl he could settle down with? She was fifteen years younger – not too much of a gap, he decided – and would she want to marry him anyway? He was sure that she had a deep affection for him, maybe even love. And his feelings about her? He still wasn't sure what it meant to fall in love with a woman. He didn't know whether or not his feelings had been too blunted by experience to feel that poignant emotion. If she asked him, he would say he was in love with her. He'd said it before to countless women but then it had been a meaningless phrase, something you were expected to say in the right situation, like 'thanks for dinner', or 'here's lookin' at ya', or 'pardon me' when you burped. But he sure as hell wasn't sure about love. In fact he wasn't sure of anything until this job was over.

They made one more trip in to Essex, pushing the Itala to its maximum, until they reached Colchester, and then slowed to a crawl until they reached the bridge the other side of Manningtree.

Sylvia had wanted one more look at it and he couldn't blame her. Secretly he was glad it was her jumping off the bridge, and not him. He was aware of his selfishness and instantly ashamed of it, but still glad it was her. Sylvia also wanted to know the details of the robbery as was her right as a member of the gang. She wanted to know if anyone else was coming, and how they were going to get past the guards. Good, solid, intelligent questions, and ones that you'd expect to ask if you had any interest in your own safety and any intention of returning to something approaching normality in one piece. For reasons that he couldn't completely explain other than the most obvious one, that he was embarrassed to tell her how sketchy his plans were, he decided that she, like Jimmy Trewe, had better learn about the Titan Crusher on the night of the robbery when it was too late to object. How do you tell someone that you are going to subdue guards with a licence to kill (Martinette had said they were killers, and he'd believed him) with something as nebulous as a canister of laughing gas? It was so crazy that, like the gas, it was almost laughable, except in this game you could wind up dead. So he fended off her questions with a lot of jokes that didn't sound funny even to him, and a few times with – 'don't worry 'cause I'll be there,' that sounded like an empty promise. Of course he'd be there. What else did he have to do in the small hours of a May English morning? Sylvia had become moody over this obvious subterfuge. She sulked for long periods, her hazel eyes dark with accusation; but Butch wouldn't budge and in the end she resigned herself to getting no more out of him.

Butch stopped the car by the bridge and they got out.

Jonathan De Ford had become extremely adept at following Butch without his knowledge, even in a motorcar – a feat he was sure would one day become an exact science. His professional pride insisted that he make notes of the operation, because some day he might be called upon to instruct new Pinkerton recruits in the embryo art of tailing a suspect.

He was unable to keep pace with the Itala as it sped out of London, and soon the only thing that remained of the car was its dust cloud. But he continued on at the best speed he could make, hoping that he would come upon Butch further down the road, and he was rewarded when he reached Colchester.

He spotted Butch on the road out of town, now going at a snail's pace. De Ford slowed his own car to keep his distance. After they passed through Manningtree he saw Butch come to a halt, and stopped his car, pulling off the side of the road. This time he had come prepared. He took out his binoculars and focused them on the distant scene. Butch and the girl had stopped where the road ran alongside a railway bridge. They seemed to find the bridge, which looked very ordinary, extremely interesting.

De Ford started to feel excitement. Butch and railroads, the proximity alone meant something was going to happen, and he was damned sure it was crooked. He saw Butch and the girl get back into the car and start to turn around. De Ford got back into his own in a hurry and made for a cart track he had seen a few yards further on that led down into a shallow depression. It would be enough cover.

The Itala went by without slackening speed or giving any appearance of Butch having noticed De Ford's car. De Ford backed out on to the road and made for the bridge. It was as insignificant close up as it had looked through the binoculars, but it was a railway bridge and he would have to find out about the trains that ran on it.

When De Ford got back to town he found his way to Liverpool Street station and located the station master's office. De Ford represented himself to the man as a reporter-cum-train-fancier, and that he was combining his job and his avocation with a series of articles for a New York paper. The station master was only too pleased to tell him about the Great Eastern's operation, in such a wealth of detail that De Ford got lost after the first set of couplings. He finally managed to inquire if the line ever handled any special trains and was told that occasionally a royal train or one from the Continent graced the Great Eastern's tracks. In fact, the station master looked around conspiratorially as if prying ears were poised to hear every word, there was a train coming in during the next thirty-six hours. It was a secret, but he was sure that De Ford, with his bluff honest face, was trustworthy. De Ford's pulse quickened. A train of German origin containing a high-ranking official, was scheduled to land at Harwich and make a nonstop run to London in the wee hours of the morning.

Almost unable to contain his excitement, De Ford asked if the train was carrying anything valuable. The station master with the smug egotism of a petty-official who knows something you don't, and wants to make sure you realize how important he is, told De Ford that he'd heard a rumour to the effect that the train was carrying a vast amount of money that was destined for the German embassy.

De Ford thanked him profusely and left in a state of light-headed euphoria.

Sundance and Reginald had started their day early: the Kid by choice, in an effort to work off his nervous energy, and

Reginald, protesting to no avail, as he was rousted out of bed at the crack of dawn.

'Where are we going this time of the morning? The servants aren't even up yet.'

Sundance raised himself on his tiptoes and glared down at Reginald, who was attempting in vain to hide himself under the bedclothes. 'Gotta practise my shootin'. We got this job coming up and I haven't practised in so long that I could get beaten to the draw by a seventy-five-year-old squaw with a broken arm.' Sundance poked Reginald with a forefinger, 'And you wouldn't like it if you had your hide ventilated and I couldn't do nothin' about it.'

Reginald squirmed to get away from the probing finger and stuck his head out from under the cover. 'All right, all right!' he said petulantly. 'Leave me alone. I'll get up, I promise.'

Sundance addressed a spot on the wall as if he hadn't heard. 'I wanna find a good place to shoot, somewhere where no one'll bother me; and I don't wanna take all day gettin' there.'

'You don't want much,' Reginald grumbled. 'What are you going to shoot at?'

'Well, tin cans, of course, unless you're volunteerin'. I wouldn't mind trying my hand at a moving target.'

'Very amusing,' Reginald said frigidly, and sat up. 'And where am I supposed to find you tin cans?'

'Well how the hell should I know! This is your town.'

Reginald sighed. 'I suppose I can ask Cook.' He reached up a skinny arm, grasped the velvet bell-pull and gave it a tug, as Sundance started for the door. But by the time Reginald got up, washed and dressed, breakfasted and instituted a search by the staff of the storerooms, pantries and rubbish bins for empty tins, it was nine o'clock. There was not a tin to be found, and Sundance fumed and paced, muttering oaths as he went. Finally in exasperation, Reginald said, 'We'll go to Harrods; they must have empty tins.'

''Bout time you had a bright idea; and where do we go to afterwards?'

Reginald hesitated and finally did have a bright idea. 'Ah, just the thing! We'll go to Richmond Park, hire horses and ride to an isolated spot. I must change—' and he dashed back to his rooms. He emerged in a few minutes with one arm through a black hacking jacket while vainly searching for the other sleeve; Sundance found the armhole for him. Reginald bent to tuck his breeches into high black boots, then straightened up, adjusted his tie and set the silk topper on his head at a rakish angle. 'Ready, Sundance. How do I look?'

'Reginald, old buddy, you're as perdy as a goddamn picture. You're what every momma in this town is prayin' to find for her virgin daughter.'

They took the Rolls to Knightsbridge and parked in front of Harrods. 'I'm leaving this vehicle in your charge,' Reginald said to the uniformed doorman. 'Take good care of her, there's a good chap.' The doorman bowed and touched his hat.

Reginald led the way into the building, down the main aisle to the food hall. They stopped inside the entrance and were approached by a frock-coated assistant.

'Good morning, m'Lord, can I be of service?'

Reginald flushed with pride at being recognized. 'Good morning, my good man. Yes, you can be of help. My friend and I are in need of various items.'

The assistant eyed Sundance with just a bare flicker of disdain. Unlike Reginald's fashionable riding attire, Sundance had on his faded Levis, an open-necked shirt and fringed buckskin jacket.

'Certainly, m'Lord, how may I be of help to you and ... the American gentleman?'

'We'd like some empty tins.'

The assistant blinked. 'Empty tins, m'Lord?'

'Yes, yes, anything you have in stock will do.'

The assistant blinked again and cleared his throat. 'I believe there might be a slight problem, m'Lord. I'm sorry to inform you that it is Harrods' policy only to sell tins that are filled. I'm terribly sorry.'

'Yes, yes, I know all that. Quite admirable, but certainly you must have some empty ones somewhere.'

The assistant looked at Reginald blankly for a long moment. 'I will make inquiries, m'Lord.' He made a stiff little bow and hurried away.

Sundance leaned against a counter and lit up a cigarillo, while Reginald paced back and forth, hands behind his back, whistling tunelessly between his teeth. The assistant returned after a short interval with a look of trepidation on a normally expressionless face.

'I'm very sorry, m'Lord, we seem to be out of stock.'

'Out!' Reginald said in disbelief. 'What's Harrods coming to? You're supposed to have everything!'

'Ah, yes ... might I suggest that you purchase full tins, and empty them?'

Reginald thought about the suggestion, 'Capital idea. I'll take two dozen.'

'Do you have any particular size in mind, m'Lord? You see, we have a large variety.'

'Oh, let's see, six of the *foie gras*, some soup tins, three or four of the Yorkshire ham, oh, yes, and I particularly like those ones containing the Mayfair ox tongues, and perhaps a couple of biscuit tins, I think the Huntley and Palmer ones will do.'

'Very good, m'Lord. If you'll just follow me.' The assistant assembled the order on a counter, then produced a tin-opener and looked inquiringly at Reginald. Lord Ratlett smiled and nodded in approval. Solemnly and with the gravity befitting the situation, the assistant opened each of the tins and emptied the contents into a rubbish bin. 'Would you like them delivered, m'Lord?'

'No, we'll take them with us. Put them in a hamper.' Reginald thanked the man and swept out of the food hall with Sundance trailing; a small boy lugging the hamper brought up the rear.

They arrived at Richmond Park and drove around the east side and entered by way of the Robin Hood Gate. Sundance took his holstered Colt and ammunition from under the seat, put them in the hamper and closed the lid. Reginald manoeuvred the car along the winding path to the riding stable and stopped in the courtyard. A stableboy appeared instantly to open the doors. A grizzled old man with red-veined cheeks ambled out and doffed his cloth cap. Reginald told him that they wished to hire two good riding horses, and the stableboy was duly dispatched to bring them. Sundance, who was no mean judge of horseflesh, eyed them critically. They were a black and a roan and stood about fifteen hands. Sundance grunted his approval. The stableboy started to saddle them and Sundance went over to get a closer look at the contraption.

'Not much to these saddles, is there?' he said to Reginald. 'I mean, there ain't even a saddlehorn. Hey, boy, lower them stirrups, I can't ride with 'em up to my chest.' Sundance grabbed the reins and swung himself up.

'You're not supposed to do it that way,' Reginald protested.

'You tryin' to teach me how to ride a horse?' Sundance spluttered. 'I was breaking broncs while you was still wet behind the ears. I didn't get these bow legs from sitting around no tea parties.'

The stableboy looked away and stifled a giggle.

'And what's with these damn reins?' Sundance continued his tirade. 'Jee-sus Christ, don't you limeys know nothin' about riding?'

'My dear Sundance,' Reginald said with massive dignity, 'we English were riding before there was an America.'

'Yeah, and you haven't learned nothin' since. Gimme that hamper.'

The stableboy handed it up and Sundance balanced the basket on his lap. Reginald hurrumphed his way over to his mount and was given a leg-up, English style. Sundance led the way out of the stableyard and Reginald trotted after him.

'Which way?' Sundance said in a belligerent tone.

'I'll show you,' Reginald returned curtly and cantered off. Sundance followed a stiff-necked Reginald as he led the way in a north-westerly direction. In ten minutes they were climbing Spankers Hill and reined in at the fringe of the wood. They tethered the horses to a convenient birch tree and marched into the wood, following the vague outlines of a footpath. They came to a clearing in about five minutes; Sundance stopped and put down the hamper. The clearing was long and narrow, pinched in the middle like an hourglass. The sunlight filtered through the leaves and lit the ground in patches. Sundance lifted the hamper lid and took out the holstered gun. He strapped the belt around his waist and adjusted the holster until it was in the right position. He tied the two rawhide thongs that hung down from the bottom of the holster around his thigh, made final adjustments and grunted with satisfaction. He took out the Colt, thumbed back the hammer, spun the barrel slowly to check the loads and replaced the hammer on the one empty chamber. Reginald watched with a mixture of keen curiosity and excitement.

'I always keep one chamber empty,' Sundance replied to the unspoken question. 'That's just in case you get banged around and the gun goes off by accident. I knew a guy once who didn't do that and his gun got turned a funny way when his horse spooked and know what he did?' Sundance nodded solemnly. 'Yep, shot his balls off.'

Reginald's eyes widened. 'My goodness!'

'Yep, you listen to the Kid, here, and you won't hurt yourself. Now, take that hamper and count out twenty-five paces, then set about five of them cans on top of the hamper.'

Reginald did as he was instructed and returned to Sundance's side.

'Now, Reginald,' Sundance began his lecture, 'shootin' is an art. It takes a lot of hard work and a lot o' practice, and, a big chunk o' talent. Now, looky here,' Sundance put the Colt back in the holster and let his arm hang relaxed alongside it. In a blink, the gun seemed to have magically appeared in his hand, hammer cocked.

'Gosh,' Reginald exclaimed, 'that's incredible!'

'Ah, it's nothin' much, I'm gettin' slow.'

'Slow? I couldn't even follow it.'

'A lot of guys can do that; it's what you do with it afterwards that counts, watch this.' He put the revolver back in the holster again, set himself in a slight crouch, and then the gun was in his hand once more, shooting five times with almost no gap between shots. The tins jumped off the hamper.

'My God,' Reginald shouted, 'I wouldn't have believed it if I hadn't seen it with my own eyes.'

'Well,' Sundance admitted grudgingly, 'it weren't too bad considerin' I ain't had no practice for a long time.'

Sundance exhausted his ammunition, filling the Harrods' tins full of holes, and resisted Reginald's exhortations to let him have a go with, 'You do the drivin' and I'll do the shootin'.'

They stopped at a pub for lunch. Sundance couldn't help smiling when he looked up from his steak-and-kidney pie to see Reginald regard him with awe and, wonder of wonders, remain speechless.

'I'll be damned glad when this thing is over,' Butch mumbled as he was hanging on to the commuter strap of the underground train that was on its way to Trafalgar Square.

The man with muttonchop whiskers who hung on next to him absorbed in his newspaper looked at Butch sharply and then edged away. The girl in the seat in front of Butch, who had been enjoying the pressure of his knee, moved her legs quickly to one side and averted her eyes. Butch coloured with embarrassment. He hadn't realized he was talking to himself in front of strangers.

The train pulled into the station and the doors opened. Gratefully, Butch left the train and his fellow passengers behind. He made his way by the now familiar path through Whitehall and into the Foreign Office, stopping outside Geoffrey Martinette's door. The door opened before he had a chance to knock, and a stern-looking Geoffrey Martinette greeted him with watch in hand.

'Do you realize you're three minutes and forty-five seconds late? That sort of bad time-keeping could ruin this entire operation.'

'So, sue me,' Butch flared. He poked Martinette in the chest and backed him into the room. 'I'm getting tired of you, you little squirt. "Do this! Do that! Be on time here!" What the hell do you think I am? An *animal*, and you're my keeper?'

'That's precisely what I think,' Martinette replied coldly, pushing Butch's finger up so that he looked like the Statue of Liberty. 'And *I* am getting tired of *you*, your complaints, your whining, your belligerence and your loosely constructed ways of doing things, which you insist upon calling *American*. You're not only a burden in your own country, you're becoming tedious in mine.'

Butch moved in, braced his feet and stuck his face close enough to Martinette's so that their noses almost touched. 'I want you to believe something,' he growled. 'The only way I'd like to see you again is laid out in a wooden box. Boot Hill is loaded with guys like you, smart-ass punks who pushed their luck and wound up with a lung full of lead for their trouble. And I'm real tempted to make sure you wind up the same way.' Butch cocked a finger and pulled an imaginary trigger. 'Bang, bang,' he said.

Martinette flinched involuntarily as the invisible bullets passed through his body, but the victim made a complete recovery. 'You still have a job to do for me, and I still have Jonathan De Ford.'

Butch placed his hands on his hips and gave Martinette a contemptuous look. 'And that's all you got, you keep him hanging over my head like a rawhide noose. But I'm getting tired of waiting for the trap-door to drop, and pretty soon I just won't give a damn. If you don't like the way I do things, fire me. I think I'll just manage to live with the shame.'

'That won't be possible. It's too late to get anyone else.'

'That's what I thought, so you're gonna have to put up with me and all my funny little ways whether you like it or not – you dumb shit-head.'

Martinette's lips compressed into a thin, white line. 'You are going too far, Cassidy,' he annunciated slowly between clenched teeth. 'I could step on you like the loathsome bug you are, and no one would be sorry about it.'

'The hell you can, you need me.'

Martinette fought for control and managed it with effort. 'That is an unfortunate truism with which I have to live – for a little while yet. But don't push your luck any further than you already have. When this operation is over I can still change my mind about what to do with you.'

Butch shook his head emphatically. 'Uh, uh, my runty little *amigo*, that was sure the wrong thing to say. You blackmailed me into this in the first place. One job, that's it, or else.'

'What's that supposed to mean?'

Butch was beginning to enjoy himself, and smiled. 'That

means I ain't gonna stand by like a whipped dog while you put the spurs in. I got to know a few people while I bin here. A few nights ago I met a man called *Wells*, H. G. Wells. I checked up and found he's a very well-known writer. We had ourselves a nice little talk about lots of things and I told him a few stories that he's gonna write about. I think he'd love to know about you.'

'You wouldn't dare.'

'Just try me. I also met another guy I got real friendly with. Reginald tells me he's your boss. His name was Winston Churchill.'

Martinette was aghast: 'You met Churchill? What did you tell him?'

'I didn't tell him nothin' – yet. But I might tell him how his boy runs things when his back is turned. I don't think he'd be too happy about that. Where I come from we'd call what we got goin' a *Mexican stand-off*. That means – so you don't get it wrong – you got loaded guns, and so do I. If I go down, I'm takin' you with me!'

Martinette moved past Butch and sat down behind his desk. 'I suggest we put aside all talk of what might be and concentrate on what is going to happen. As we are not going to operate on the basis of mutual trust, let's make it on the basis of something we both understand – self-interest. I want those papers, and you your freedom. Deliver them to me and I guarantee that you get it.'

Butch laughed mirthlessly. 'I wouldn't trust you as far as I could throw Buckingham Palace, but if that's the way it's gotta be, let's get on with it. You're supposed to have a car for me.'

'I do. I've managed to get an American car, called an Oldsmobile. It's an open car, will hold about six people and can do about eighty miles an hour. The owner would be most grateful to get it back in one piece.'

'We'll sho'nuff do our darn'dest!' Butch mocked in his most exaggerated southern drawl.

Martinette took out his note book and consulted it. 'Is everything else planned for?'

'Planned for?' Butch repeated in disgust. 'There's so many

ifs in this job I don't know whether I'm comin' or goin'. If any one of them goes wrong you might as well kiss the whole thing goodbye. I told you before I never tried to get on a moving train, and you didn't exactly go out of your way to make it easy for me. You want a professional job and the only pro in the whole damned thing besides Sundance and me is the safe guy, and he gets seasick when he steps off the kerb. You know what you are, Martinette? You're an amateur. If the American secret service wanted to do this, they sure would have done it a lot better. I only hope those Germans are as dumb as you are.'

'I'm sure,' Martinette said in tones frigid enough to freeze Butch where he stood, 'that you would be capable of doing a much better job. It's too bad you think so little of the British Government, and this department, but I shall try to live with it. Perhaps next time you see your friend Mr Churchill, you'll ask him to appoint you to my job.'

'Yeah, maybe I'll do that.'

'Now, I ask you for the second time, is there anything else?'

'Nothing. We'll leave around ten in the evening tomorrow to get in position. Where will you be during this whole thing?'

'I'm not entirely sure yet, but close by.'

'That's real comfortin'.'

Butch and Sylvia called back at Hill Street to find Sundance sitting around smoking and drinking, patiently waiting for the evening when he would make another of his periodic trips to the Savoy.

Reginald had gone down to the country to visit his mother and was due back the following morning.

Butch said goodbye to Sundance, and he and Sylvia went off to spend their last evening together before the job.

15 'What the hell are we doing here?'

Butch took several deep breaths to calm his nerves, but it wasn't having any effect on his heart that was beating at the same fifty-mile-an-hour speed that he figured the train would be going. For the fifth time in as many minutes he checked himself in the mirror, reknotted his bandana and wiped his sweating hands on the sides of the faded jeans that he considered his lucky pair. He'd worn them on lots of other jobs and he was still in one piece. He hoped fervently that the talisman had enough magic left in it for one more safe operation.

He fumbled with his Colt, swearing under his breath as he tried to push a bullet into the chamber with trembling fingers. He finally loaded five of them leaving the hammer at rest on an empty chamber. He pulled back a corner of his buckskin jacket and tucked the gun in his belt, then adjusted the jacket so that it was hidden. He looked in the mirror again and was satisfied. One thing left to do. He took the Derringer out of its case, loaded it with two .45 slugs, then placed the gun in its holster and strapped it on to his right calf. He hoped he was just being careful – a backup gun as a precaution for an emergency that might never arise, if he was lucky.

He sat down on the chintz-covered chair in blue and white stripes that reminded him of prison bars, and watched Sundance at work on the other side of the room. They had not spoken for the last ten minutes while they were making their final preparations, and the Kid was still deep in concentration examining his pistol with a critical eye. He caressed it lovingly, tucked it away in his belt and looked up at Butch with a mirthless smile.

'I'm ready,' he drawled. 'How you feelin', Butch? You look a little green around the gills.'

Butch rubbed at the scar below his eye, an unconscious gesture that was a tip-off he was under stress. 'Great, Kid, great. But I still can't help thinkin', what the hell are we doing here?'

Sundance leaned up against the dresser and crossed one leg over the other. 'This sure ain't like any of our other jobs, and I sure don't like the idea of havin' nowhere to run ... just in case.'

'Like the Hole-In-The-Wall.'

Sundance nodded, 'Like the Hole-In-The-Wall.'

'Shit!' Butch banged a fist into his hand, stood up and started pacing. 'Government, politics, spies. I don't know how we got mixed up with them. Do ya know what my dad told me when I was a kid? He said, son, whatever you do when you grow up, do it real good. But just remember one thing, stay away from politics and politicians. They're the meanest, 'orneriest critters in all God's creation. You'd do a lot better cosying up to a rattle-snake than to put your trust in them fellas.' He stopped pacing and pointed a finger at Sundance. 'And I took his advice didn't I? You're a witness. I became a good honest-to-God, straight bank robber and train robber, and I did it real good.' He dropped his arm in disgust. 'Roll me a cigarette, will you?'

Sundance took out his tobacco pouch, spread the tobacco on a paper, licked it closed and handed it to Butch. He rolled a second one for himself, scratched a match on the sole of his boot and lit both of them. 'We coulda gotten outta here, Butch.'

'Oh yeah? Where to? With De Ford doggin' our trail, America's out.'

'How about France?'

'We got enough trouble speakin' the lingo here.' Butch turned at the sound of a knock and when the door opened Reginald bounded in enthusiastically. He stopped in the middle of the floor with a toothy grin on his long face.

'How's this, chaps?' He made a clumsy pirouette. With the probability that Reginald had consulted the 'Who's Who of Crooks and Robbers', he was attired in what the well-dressed highwayman should wear when out for a night of jollity; black rollneck sweater, black drainpipe trousers that accentuated the length of his legs, black hacking jacket and black boots. Perched jauntily on top of his sandy hair was a black homburg. He strode over to the mirror, pulled the hat down to his eyebrows and practised a snarl. He examined his bared teeth and knitted brow, gave the mirror one final scowl, then turned to Butch with a grin.

Sundance, who had gone into a coughing fit at the first sight of Reginald, turned away.

'Reginald,' Butch said poker-faced, 'I just don't know who you're gonna scare more, them or us.'

'Oh,' Reginald said with immediate concern. 'I'm saving that for those German villains.'

'Yeah, you do that. Ready to go, Kid?'

They stopped in the hallway and Butch motioned them to silence. He opened the door a crack and peeked out. The sun had set a half hour before and the last vestige of twilight was merging into night. Along the street a lamp-lighter was on his appointed rounds lighting the last lamp in line with a long pole. A handful of pedestrians were strolling along towards their destination; a hansom cab clip-clopped towards Park Lane; a chauffeur was polishing a black limousine.

Jonathan De Ford was not in sight at his usual post around the corner. Butch opened the door wider and the three men stepped into the street. They turned right at South Audley Street and right again at the next corner into Mount Street. The gleaming Oldsmobile was parked about twenty yards down the road and was unique enough to have attracted a little knot of admirers. Like the Red Sea they parted and allowed the threesome through.

'Look Mummy, cowboys,' a little girl pointed at Butch and Sundance.

'Shhhh,' her mother whispered. 'I'm sure the gentlemen are just going to a fancy-dress party.'

'How fast will she go, sir?' a little boy of about eight asked Reginald, who climbed into the driver's seat.

'Oh, very fast, perhaps about eighty miles an hour.'

'Gosh!' the little boy breathed in awe. 'Are you going to do that now?'

'Possibly, my dear little chap. We're off to rob a train, you see,' Reginald giggled, and the group of people guffawed loudly at the joke.

'Very funny,' Butch grumbled in an undertone. 'Why don't you tell everybody where we're going?'

Sundance turned the crank and Reginald started the car.

'Oh, they'll just think I'm joking, Butch.'

Butch bit his lip and stared straight ahead and Sundance climbed into the back seat. Reginald put the car into first gear and started off, waving to the crowd. 'Have a good trip!' they shouted.

They motored into Berkeley Square and started around it to get to Berkeley Street. 'Uh-oh,' Sundance said. He was half turned on the seat looking through the narrow slot that served as a rear window. 'That bastard De Ford must have been hiding 'cause he snuck outta somewhere, and he's followin' us.'

Butch turned around to look. 'OK, Reginald, here's your chance to show us some fancy driving. Lose him.'

Lord Ratlett needed no further urging. He put his foot down and the car shot forward. He screeched around the corner into Berkeley Street, swerving at the last moment to miss a four-wheeler; the horse shied and the driver divided his time between controlling the horse and shouting curses at the fast retreating car. A few moments later a second car with a grim-faced De Ford at the wheel, barrelled past, again just narrowly missing the four-wheeler. The elderly female passenger promptly fainted.

Reginald took the right turn into Piccadilly on at least two wheels. He was concentrating hard on what he was doing, a fixed smile on his face and the tip of his tongue protruding from the corner of his mouth. Sundance's shout, as he slid violently from one side of the seat to the other, registered only as a faint background noise. The speedometer hit sixty as they started the turn into Hyde Park Corner, the rear end sliding as Reginald touched the brake.

'I'll lose him in Belgravia,' Reginald shouted and pointed the nose of the car into Grosvenor Crescent, scattering pigeons and people before him as he went.

'For Christ's sake, slow down!' Butch screamed.

'But you wanted me to lose him,' Reginald protested peevishly.

'Yeah, and I wanna live to tell about it.'

Reginald slammed on the brakes as they entered Belgrave Square, throwing Butch forward so that he banged his head on the windscreen. He stomped hard on the accelerator almost at once and Butch shot back into the seat with a thud. The Oldsmobile zoomed three-quarters of the way round Belgrave Square and took a sharp left into West Halkin Street.

By the time Jonathan De Ford reached Belgrave Square it was once again the peaceful place it was meant to be, and there was no telling which way out of it the three of them had taken. De Ford pounded the wheel in frustration. He was sure they were going to rob that train tonight, and now he'd lost them. The only clue he felt he had for sure was the bridge where he'd spied on Butch and the girl. He could drive out there and see what developed, but what could he do on his own? He pondered. Then it might be too late anyway. With the deepest resignation he'd felt since becoming a lawman, he started off for Scotland Yard.

Sundance pounded the back of the seat and chortled, 'Ya done it, Reggie old boy! We lost 'im.'

Reginald did his best to look nonchalant, as if dodging in and out of streets at breakneck speed was a daily occurrence, and he almost succeeded. He turned the car into Knightsbridge and proceeded at a more sedate pace towards Kensington. They turned off the High Street and stopped at a red-brick Victorian building. Sylvia came out of the doorway where she'd been standing and got into the back seat of the car.

Butch looked at her approvingly. She had her long hair tucked up inside a flat cap and was dressed in dark sweater and trousers. If he didn't know better she could have passed for a boy. They exchanged terse greetings, wanting to say more but afraid that additional conversation would reveal how nervous they both were. Butch had another more prosaic reason – he didn't want Sylvia to see his teeth chattering.

Reginald started the car down the road, took a left and a right and stopped in front of the pub where Jimmy Trewe said he would wait for them. Reginald went in to get him and emerged a few moments later with Jimmy following close behind.

He grinned at them when he reached the car. 'Whatcha mate,' he said breathing the whiskey fumes of courage all over them. He held up the satchel he was carrying and addressed Butch, 'Got my April Fools here, mate. Oh, I forgot, you don't understand English. That's *tools.* Let's get on wiv it before I change my mind.'

Sylvia moved over to make room for him and he climbed in.

'That's it, then, huh?' he slurred. 'All our happy little band's togevver again to rob this bleedin' train?'

Butch had been trying for days to work out how to spring the Titan Crusher on them and still had not come up with a satisfactory method. 'Not exactly,' he said. Sylvia gave him a sharp look but Jimmy voiced the question.

'What does that mean?'

'Well, you see there's this other guy that I kinda thought might help out. I haven't told you about him before 'cause he's kinda peculiar.'

Sundance slapped his knee and guffawed. 'I wouldn't let him hear you say that, Butch.'

'I'm intrigued,' Sylvia said. 'What do you mean by *peculiar*, and how's he going to help?'

Butch fiddled with his neckerchief, smoothed his hair, twirled the tip of his moustache into a point and channelled his discomforture at Lord Ratlett. 'Well, don't just sit there Reginald, get going.'

Reginald obediently put the car into gear and they started off.

'Well, it's like this,' Butch drawled. 'We met this Australian guy, a friend of Reginald's,' he added, giving himself the option of where to shift the blame. 'His name is Barry Billington.'

'And you'd better smile when you say that, pard,' Sundance interjected, 'and he's *Basa* to his friends.'

'Yeah, that's right,' Butch agreed, 'and it's a good idea to be his friend. He's six-six, weighs 280 pounds, and I sure as hell wouldn't wanna be his enemy!'

'Oh,' Sylvia said in a small voice, 'he's coming along to protect us, I suppose.'

Jimmy tittered nervously. 'Sounds good to me, mate.'

Butch seized on Jimmy's comment. 'Yeah, I thought so too,

but there's a little problem. He's,' he blurted it out in a rush, 'a real law-abidin' citizen and I couldn't tell him we were robbin' a train, or else he wouldn't a come.'

'What did you tell him?' Sylvia asked.

Butch looked embarrassed. 'Well, I kinda made up a little story. I told him that this German baron kidnapped a young girl and was bringing her to England to force her to marry him against her will, and we were gonna rescue her.'

'And he believed you?' Sylvia said incredulously.

'Well, he ain't too bright.'

'Then why do we need him? He might muck up the whole thing.'

'Oh, there's another reason,' Butch said matter-of-factly, hoping that he sounded more confident than he felt. 'He's the guy that's gonna take care of all them guards.'

'May I ask how?' Sylvia said.

'Laughing gas.'

'Laughing gas,' she repeated.

'Yep, that's right. He's bringing along this tank of laughing gas and he's gonna spray it on all them guards and pretty soon they'll be laughing so hard, they'll be helpless.'

'Butch, that's the craziest thing I ever heard.'

Sundance, who'd been laughing uproariously during the exposition without the benefit of nitrous oxide, wiped his eyes and said between giggles, 'Yeah, I think so too.'

Sylvia looked at both of them in amazement. 'I think you're all round the bend.'

'Well, that's it anyway,' Butch stated with defiance. 'Nobody else came up with any better ideas, so he's coming, and that's the way we're gonna do it. And I'm warning you, don't let on what we're really doing.' Butch faced forward in the seat and stared straight ahead, mouth clamped tightly shut. The conversation died as if a tap had been shut off.

They turned into the Earl's Court Road and Butch pointed out the Titan Crusher's building. Reginald pulled up outside the entrance. Three men stood in front of the door having a fierce argument in loud voices. They had just reached the stage of pushing and pulling at each other, and punches could be confidently expected at any moment. Basa, who was leaning in the doorway, saw the car and waved at them. He picked up the tank, slung it under one arm as if it were a loaf of bread, and strode out on to the pavement.

'Sorry fellas,' he said to the men blocking his path as he pushed through, scattering them like ninepins.

'Why, you dirty ...' one of them screamed, and then thought better about completing the sentence when he took a good look at Basa.

Basa poked his head into the car and grinned at Butch. 'Hi there, cobber.' He nodded at Reginald and Sundance and looked questioningly at Sylvia and Jimmy. He turned back to Butch: 'Are these the other folks who are gonna help us rescue that poor lady?'

'Yeah, that's right Basa, that's Jimmy and that's Sylvia.'

Basa looked hard at Sylvia. 'Well, I'll be a wallaby's winkle! Sorry Ma'am, I thought you was a boy. I just wanna tell you, I think it's a real decent thing you're doing, helping out that poor lady. And you too,' he said to Jimmy.

Butch jumped in quickly before they could answer. 'Yeah, Sylvia's gonna get us on the train. She does a trapeze act and she'll be able to swing on to it; and Jimmy's a lock expert.'

'Oh good, I'll just stow my tank of laughing gas, and we'll get going.' Basa pushed the canister into the car and lodged it between the front and back seats. Butch sized up the space left in the back seat, looked at the Titan Crusher, opened the door and got out.

'You'd better sit in front, Basa. You're not gonna fit in there.'

The giant settled himself cautiously on to the seat and Butch climbed into the back. 'Tally Ho!' Reginald said, and they took off down the road.

Once they reached the country the traffic eased to a trickle, and Reginald was able to put on some more speed. They raced through Easthorpe and Stanway, slowed for Colchester so as not to attract any attention, and covered the last twenty-five miles to Harwich at a leisurely pace.

A steam engine in the now familiar blue of the Great Eastern line chugged past them heading for London as they entered the town. They counted fifteen cars and a guard's van and they watched its swinging red lantern in silence until it winked out of sight in the distance.

'Eleven-twenty-five,' Reginald said, looking at his watch. 'That should be the last scheduled train on the line tonight.'

'That's just over two-and-a-half hours to wait for our train,' Butch muttered. 'Reginald, drive over to where the ferries come in. We'll park near the dock and keep an eye out for the boat. Damn it, I hate this waiting,' he said to nobody in particular.

Jonathan De Ford was having his usual success at Scotland Yard, which meant that he was having none at all. He'd been shunted back and forth between sergeants and junior inspectors without so far even ascending to the next level. By this time, of course, he was a well-known face around Scotland Yard. 'That crazy Yank detective' was whispered behind his back, but not so low that he couldn't hear.

De Ford had pounded a new dent into the desk with his demand to see a senior officer, and so far the only thing he had accomplished was bruised knuckles. The inspector eyed him stolidly from across the desk. 'That's very interesting, sir. A train robbery, you say?'

De Ford was white around the lips. 'I've been saying it for three hours. When are you going to get it through your thick skull that there are some American desperadoes out there who are gonna rob a train?'

'Now now, sir, no need to be rude. Perhaps you can give me the details of this alleged robbery.'

'I can't give you the details, damn it, it hasn't happened yet.'

'Well sir, that does present a small problem. If no such robbery has occurred, I don't see how we can help you.'

'Let me speak to your superior officer,' De Ford shouted.

'I'm afraid that's impossible sir. He's at his club and cannot be disturbed.'

'Then who's running this place?'

'I am sir.'

'That must be a comfort to the crooks in this town.'

The inspector retained his bored expression. He took a pipe

from his pocket, filled it slowly and lit it with care. The silence hung between them like the Great Wall of China. The inspector puffed on his pipe and sighed, 'I do believe, sir, it has been said that sarcasm is the lowest form of wit.'

Sundance pointed at the harbour. 'There's the ferry and it looks like the right one. I can see a train on it.'

Reginald looked at his watch. 'Two minutes to one, it must be the right one.'

From their vantage point just outside the dock they could see a group of men walking to the quayside and positioning themselves to tie up the boat.

At the near end of the track that led down to the quay a solitary locomotive stood stationary, its engine turning over slowly, wheezing like an asthmatic fighting for breath. Puffs of white smoke curled lazily from the shiny brass chimney cap. On a siding that led off the main track another engine waited ready to push a guard's van into its position at the end of the special train.

The ferryboat edged into its space and was secured port and starboard to the accompaniment of much shouting from the crew, and cajoling from the foreman. The bow section flap was lowered and joined on to the dock. The engine at the back of the boat fired up and started pushing the three carriages on to the dock.

A small group of officials walked out from the station building and stopped at the entrance to the boat. They formed themselves into a pecking order, the most officious-looking one at the head, the others forming a loose 'V' behind him. In a few moments a German officer, resplendent in ceremonial uniform, disembarked, surrounded by a troop of soldiers. He stopped in front of the official and they bowed to each other, and then shook hands.

'Is that the Baron?' Basa asked.

'The Baron?' Jimmy inquired.

'Oh yeah, mate,' Basa said. 'Didn't Butch tell you about the Baron Von Glockenspeil?'

'Sure I did, Jimmy,' Butch cut in, 'you remember.'

'Oh yeah, yeah, the naughty ol' Baron.'

Basa hardly heard the reply as he was looking intently at the scene in the docks. 'I don't see the lady, Butch.'

'They wouldn't bring her out here in front of everybody, Basa. They've probably got her hidden away in that boat, or maybe even tied her up on the train.'

Basa wrinkled his forehead in concentration. 'Yeah, I didn't think about that.'

Reginald chipped in. 'From what I can see from here, he looks like a colonel. Beastly looking chap. Can you see the way he's scowling at everyone? Too imperious by half. Nasty piece of work.'

The formalities seemingly completed, the party on the dock split into two groups, the colonel and his soldiers going to inspect the train as it was being readied for its journey, and the British officials back to the station buildings.

'Hadn't we better think of gettin' outta here?' Sundance said.

Butch took a long look at the train that was being trundled into position. 'We gotta while yet, Kid. I reckon it'll be another half hour before they stick that train together.'

They watched in silence as the locomotive backed up to the stationary carriages and was coupled on to them by a pair of railroad men. When this operation was completed one of them waved to the engineer in the other locomotive and in a few moments the sound of the engine could be heard reverberating around the yard. Slowly the guard's van was pushed from the siding on to the main line and then ahead, until it touched the last carriage with a gentle tap.

The colonel shouted orders to his men and they divided into two equal groups and boarded the first and third carriages.

'Time to go,' Butch said. They piled into the Oldsmobile and Reginald set the car on the road for their first stop at the bridge. They had the road to themselves as they sped through the countryside and reached the bridge in about fifteen minutes. Reginald pulled off the road and stopped on the Harwich side of the bridge. Sylvia stepped out of the car and surveyed the structure that was outlined by a three-quarter moon. Aside from the headlamps that cut twin holes in the night, everything else was pitch black.

Butch stepped out and handed Sylvia the rope-ladder that she had borrowed from the carnival. She accepted it without a word and looped it around her shoulder.

'Nervous?' he asked in a low voice.

'A little. Aren't you?'

'I guess so. Are you sure you're gonna be able to do it?'

'It's a bit late to worry about that now.' She leaned over and gave him a quick impulsive kiss on the cheek. 'See you down the line, darling.'

She turned away and quickly ascended the girders that led to the top of the bridge. When she reached it she planted her feet firmly and stood up. She blew Butch a kiss, her hand like a pale butterfly in the moonlight.

'Good luck,' he whispered hoarsely. He got back in the car and Reginald started off for their rendezvous point.

Martinette was concealed in the deep shadow that the customs building at the extreme north edge of the railway yard provided, and from his vantage point had a restricted view of the train where his line of sight was cut off by the wall. The side of the yard he was on was in semi-darkness shading into black, unused at this time of night, as all the scheduled trains were long gone. Martinette looked around him and judged that he could afford to move closer without any risk of discovery. The last thing in the world he wanted was to be seen lurking in the shadows and so put the Germans on their guard. He decided that the glare of the arc lamps was bright enough so that no one could see past the veil of light and into his corner.

He edged around the side of the building, eyes intent on the scene ahead, and he swore under his breath as he tripped over something that was soft and yielding. He bent down to see what it was and stifled an explosive epitaph. The body was stretched full length, the head resting against the wall. Martinette touched a shoulder and the man who had been quiet responded with shallow stertorous breaths. Martinette turned the man's head gently. The hair was matted with blood where he'd been struck on the back of the head and a small pool of it, deep purple in the dim light, was congealing on the ground. Martinette straightened up and stared fixedly at the train. This was a development that he had not expected, and even more serious, one that in his careful planning, he had completely omitted as a possibility. Somehow, the Germans had discovered that he was placing an agent on the train and had nullified the man's use with ruthless efficiency. Martinette tried to think how they could have found out; someone had slipped up badly. He was sure that he hadn't given anything away. His moves as usual had been planned and precise. So that left Butch or one of his party. The misgivings he had had all along about using those undisciplined ruffians rose like a high tide. What had seemed like a good idea initially, was turning into a nightmare. He vowed that if he were still in charge of his department after what he was now positive was going to be a fiasco, he would use only professionals, and British ones at that. He sealed off that compartment of his mind. That was non-productive thinking. There was an operation to run and a possibility, if only remote, that it still might come off. He stooped to examine the man again – he was breathing in quick, shallow breaths, but regular. He loosened the man's collar and tried to make him more comfortable. He stood up, stepped over the man and slid along the wall of the building.

The locomotive that was to push the guard's van into line was, he estimated, about fifty yards from his position. He glanced over at the German train. The three carriages were just emerging from the boat on to the dock, and the engine to which they would be attached was preparing to back up for the coupling. He made his decision quickly and darted from the building, keeping as much as he could to the shadows, and worked his way behind the second locomotive. It would bring him into the edge of the light, but that could not be helped and he guessed that there would be enough activity so he could reach his destination unnoticed. He went down the side of the engine away from the driver, who was standing talking to the fireman on the other side, and reached the steps to the guard's van without being seen. He felt foolish and exposed, but ploughed ahead doggedly and soft-footed his way up the steps, although the clamour from the train being shunted into line would have covered the noise of a regiment of banshees on heat. He slid the door of the van open just wide enough for him to squeeze through and shut it behind him.

The click of the lock in the sudden silence was loud enough to startle him. He pressed himself against the side of the car and looked around quickly. Still empty. He had to assume that the Germans would put their own man on board, so as not to cause any suspicion when the train pulled out. The impostor had not yet arrived and Martinette sought out a place to hide. Two, he thought viciously, could play the game of eliminating unwanted personnel. A partition ran across the last quarter of the car behind which, when Martinette looked, were a couple of stools and a spare uniform hanging on a peg. He would hide there hoping that the surrogate guard would not inspect the entire car immediately, and if he did, that would be too bad for him. It would be too bad for him in any case, but that way it would happen more quickly.

Martinette searched for a weapon. He was not in the habit of carrying a gun and in any event he did not want to kill anyone, yet. He found an open tool-box stowed in the corner and, right at the top, a hammer that would do nicely. He hid himself and waited for events to take place in their proper order.

Reginald slowed the Oldsmobile down as they approached the stand of trees where they were to hide until the train came. He stopped the car and then backed it in between a row of elms that formed a sort of corridor. Reginald jumped out of the car and started undoing the canvas top. He folded it neatly into the well provided in the rear. The others remained seated, watching him work.

'Oh, I see,' Basa said. 'I was wondering how we were gonna jump on the train with the top up.'

'Yeah, Basa,' Butch said, 'we think of everything. Now, listen, have you checked out that tank of gas. Is it working OK?'

'Oh yeah, I tested it right before we left. You wanna whiff?'

'That's OK, I'll take your word for it.'

Jimmy Trewe shook his head wonderingly at the exchange and mumbled something unintelligible.

Reginald was reaching to shut off the engine when Butch stopped him. 'Keep it running, Reginald,' he instructed. 'When that train comes, I'd like to know this thing's ready to go. We're only going to get one chance.'

Sylvia walked with practised ease down the narrow girder until she reached the London side of the bridge. She paused on the edge and looked over, then, counting as she went, paced off five steps backwards. She rehearsed her run to the edge with quick, lithe steps, confidently placing each foot squarely in the middle of the girder. A half a dozen times she backed up and then ran forward until she was satisfied that her last step landed at precisely the same place each time. She sat down on the girder dangling her legs over the edge and looked back down the line. She could not see anything yet, but far off in the distance there was the faintest rumble of a train approaching. The mournful sound of a train whistle cut through the stillness that surrounded her and confirmed it.

Although it had not been more than twenty minutes since Martinette had hidden himself, he checked his watch constantly. It seemed like an eternity before anything happened. At last the guard's van was being pushed on to the main line to be joined to the back of the train. Martinette felt the soft thump as the two cars met, heard the rasping of the couplings as they were fastened and the wheeze of the locomotive as it backed away. Martinette tensed as the door slid open and someone stepped inside. He could hear the sound of a match as it was struck and the rattle of a glass guard that he identified as that belonging to a lantern. A few moments later the guard snapped shut and the lantern was noisily hung on a bracket.

The engineer pulled on the steam whistle twice, filling the dock area with an eerie sound. Doors banged on the carriages and the engine chugged slowly out of the yard. In a few moments the train was out of Parkstone Quay and on its way to London.

The light that had filtered through the cracks and into the cubby-hole where Martinette was hiding, faded completely. Martinette groped for the wall to reassure himself and took a firmer hold on the hammer. The train was picking up speed and the guard's van rattled over the sleepers, swaying from side to side. Martinette opened the flimsy door to the partition a crack and peeked out. A man with a guard's uniform stood with his back to him on the outside platform, the lantern glow bathing his body in ruby tints. He held on to the rail and seemed fascinated by the retreating landscape.

Martinette stepped out of the cubby-hole quickly and advanced on his unsuspecting quarry. He held the hammer ready and picked out a spot on the back of the man's head. He got within five feet and hesitated. Another first in his life, he thought wryly, to knock someone out without killing him. He'd never done either before and he viewed the prospect with some distaste; but if he was going to salvage anything out of this botched up operation, it was a necessity. Some sixth sense warned the man at the last moment and he half turned as Martinette struck, so that the hammer clipped him behind the ear, probably saving his life. He fell like a stone, without a whimper, his peaked hat rolling all the way across the carriage. Martinette dropped the hammer and bent to examine his handiwork. Gingerly he turned the man's blond head over to one side. A purplish lump was already visible through the short hairs at the back of the scalp. Martinette felt relief, the man was still breathing. He grabbed him under both arms and dragged him into the car, then went rooting around until he found some twine stuffed in the drawer of a battered table. He tied the man's hands and feet, satisfied himself that the knots would hold and rolled the unconscious form against the side of the carriage. He retrieved the hat from where it lay and tried it on. At least two sizes too big. He wadded some newspaper that he found on the floor into a ball and stuffed it into the hat and tried it on again. Not perfect, but it would have to do.

He went into the cubby-hole and took the uniform jacket off the peg and exchanged it for his own. It too was large but the shiny buttons made it official-looking, and in the dark he thought it would pass if someone came to check on him. And that gave him a thought: if someone did come in he might have to defend himself and he was sure the hammer would be inadequate. He bent down over the unconscious man again and went through his pockets. As he should have guessed, a pistol was in the first one he tried. He took it out and examined it, a gun of German make of course, a Luger. He put it away in his waistband, then went past the partition leading to the door into the next carriage. He lifted the shade that covered the window and looked through. The blinds were down on the other side also and nothing could be seen. Just as well, he thought.

Jonathan De Ford had finally left Scotland Yard at one o'clock in the morning in complete disgust, but only after the inspector had eventually tired of the 'ridiculous Yank' and had excused himself for yet another cup of tea, and sent back in his place a constable who had been in the Force for two weeks. De Ford, through a film of rage that clouded his judgement, did recognize the insult for what it was.

He flagged down a passing hansom and bellowed at the driver to take him to the nearest police station to the Liverpool Street railway terminal. He marched into the station by Tower Bridge and demanded that the sleepy-eyed constable direct him to whomever was in charge. The constable decided that it was too early in the morning to argue and sent De Ford up a flight of worn wooden stairs to where he would find the inspector on duty.

The reception De Ford got this time was unique in his experience. The inspector actually seemed interested in what he was saying and, wonder of wonders, even excited at the prospect of a train robbery that had not even happened. In truth the inspector, who had been in that position for more than a month, was excited. He saw a chance to make a name for himself quickly, and all of a sudden the route to becoming a chief superintendent did not seem as convoluted, or the goal as distant. De Ford was a little stunned by the rapidity with which the inspector issued crisp orders to a group of constables sitting in the common room. It was just after two a.m. when the brand new Wolseley, crammed to capacity with De Ford, the inspector and four constables, headed into the Essex countryside, its shiny bell clanging merrily.

Sylvia swung her legs on to the girder and stood up in one motion. The single yellow eye of the locomotive was visible in the distance and growing larger every moment. Sylvia measured off the right amount of paces to the edge of the bridge and then crouched down, like a runner in starting blocks preparing for the hundred-yards dash. She could hear the train slowing down for the curve that would sweep it across the bridge, the noise of the engine now drowning out all the other small night sounds. Now the locomotive was just starting across the bridge. It slipped by underneath her, enveloping her in a cloud of smoke. She stood up quickly. The first carriage had just gone by, the second carriage, the third. She started her run, stepped into space and landed right in the middle of the guard's van with catlike grace.

She remained exactly where she was, crouched on all fours, and waited for her heart to return to normal. She was more than a little surprised that she had made it, just the way it had been rehearsed. For her, this was the riskiest part of the whole operation.

She crawled along the top of the carriage and found the iron ring just where she had been told to expect it. She unwound the rope-ladder from her shoulder and tied the ends on to the ring with expert knots that she had learned in the circus. She straightened out the rest of the rope-ladder and let it drop over the side. The train was just passing through Manningtree and everything was on schedule. The next part was up to Reginald's driving skill and Butch's ability to get everyone on board safely. She hoped sincerely that he would do it well; after all, she had a vested interest in things going well.

'Here comes the train,' Butch said unnecessarily. 'Are you ready, Reginald?'

Lord Ratlett set the homburg squarely on his head and pulled down on the brim until he was satisfied that it would take a force nine gale to dislodge it. He revved the engine. 'OK, pard,' he rasped, 'I'm ready to get them varmints!'

As ridiculous as he sounded, Butch could not muster the energy to laugh, his stomach was doing flip-flops.

'Hey, that's pretty good,' the Titan Crusher said with admiration. 'Wish I could talk like that, then I could play at being a real gunslinger.'

Reginald waved a hand. 'It's nothing, old boy. I've been practising.'

'God's struth!' Jimmy said.

The train approached, slowing down all the while and when the locomotive came abreast of the car, the speed was down to about ten miles an hour. Reginald tensed at the wheel and watched the carriages and the guard's van roll past.

'Now!' Butch said. Reginald let out the clutch with a jerk and the car surged forward, emerging out of the tree-lined corridor like an errant champagne cork. They sped after the train and caught it up in seconds. Reginald eased off the accelerator as they pulled alongside the guard's van. Butch looked up and saw the pale oval of Sylvia's face on top of the carriage. She waved and pointed to the rope-ladder that dangled down the side. Reginald started the tricky manoeuvre to bring the Oldsmobile as close to the side of the carriage as possible, his eyes darting to the side to estimate the distance. He edged the car over inch by inch, and the gap narrowed until there was about a foot of space between the two vehicles.

Butch clapped Sundance on the back. 'Go, Kid.'

Sundance jammed his hat on his head, grabbed for the rope-ladder and pulled himself up, hand over hand, his feet scrabbling until they found holes. Sylvia reached out a hand and helped him over the top.

'Now you, Jimmy.'

Jimmy's eyes were wide and staring, stark terror written all over his face. 'I can't do it!' he wailed.

Basa stood up and slung the tank of nitrous oxide over his shoulder. 'That's all right, little fella. I'll carry you.' He reached over and plucked Jimmy Trewe from the seat, then lifted him like a rag doll and slammed him over his left shoulder in a fireman's carry. The whoosh as Jimmy's breath was knocked out of him was audible. The car was drifting dangerously close to the carriage and Reginald jerked it back the other way, widening the gap. The Titan Crusher seemed as unconcerned as if he were stepping into a bathtub. He stepped up on to the door frame, reached out a long arm and took hold of the rope-ladder and swung himself over. He climbed quickly to the top, unimpeded by his twin burdens and paying as little attention to them as if it were only epaulettes that adorned his shoulders. Butch looked up at him in open-mouthed wonder. The train was just coming out of the curve and starting to pick up speed; and Reginald, in an effort to compensate, applied a little too much accelerator and shot past the rope-ladder. He realized his mistake immediately and let the car slow by itself. Butch waited for the ladder to swing into range, then jumped for it. 'Keep close!' he shouted over his shoulder. Butch climbed to the top and was helped over the side by Sundance. 'We did it,' Butch said breathlessly.

Basa grinned at him and patted Jimmy Trewe on the head. 'I think the little fella's passed out.'

Jimmy moaned and opened one eye. 'Where am I?' Then, with sudden realization, 'No don't answer that, just tell me I'm dreaming.'

'It'll be all right,' Sylvia soothed. 'Basa will look after you, won't you Basa?'

'Sure will, Ma'am. Don't you worry little fella. You'll be as safe as a joey in his mama's pouch.'

'Let's move out,' Butch said and started crawling on hands and knees towards the next carriage.

The train was picking up speed all the while, and by the time Butch reached the end of the guard's van and surveyed the three-foot gap to the next carriage, the wind was whipping at his face with great velocity, and the soot particles that pitted his skin were stinging barbs. He narrowed his streaming eyes, raised himself and jumped for the next carriage, landing on all fours. He sat down, turning his back to the wind. Sylvia and Sundance traversed the gap in quick succession and the Titan Crusher brought up the rear carrying Jimmy under one arm, and taking the long stride between the carriages with nonchalant ease.

'I'm gonna scout at the other end!' Butch shouted over the noise of the wind. He scuttled down to the other end of the carriage in apelike fashion and leaned over the edge to look down. He pulled his head back with a jerk. A German soldier was standing guard on the platform between the carriages and Butch had looked down on the middle of his spiked helmet. He retreated from the edge and motioned the others over, and then put a finger to his lips in the classic gesture for them to do it *pianissimo*. When Sundance reached him he told him about the guard.

'So, whadda you wanna do?' Sundance asked.

'I think we'll stand by while Basa goes to work with the laughing gas, then when we get his buddies out of the way, we'll jump him.' He motioned Basa over and pointed at the inspection-hatch in the middle of the car. 'Leave Jimmy here, and start feedin' them that gas.'

Basa grinned in assent, pushed Jimmy over where Butch could grab him and then took himself over to the inspection-hatch. He detached the hose nozzle from the tank, unlatched the trap-door and lifted it just enough to insert the nozzle. He turned the valve on full and the gas hissed out. Butch went over to the other hatch, unlatched it, raised it a crack and bent his face down so he could peek in. Several soldiers were in the compartment, three of them were playing cards, the others staring vacantly out the windows. Two of them looked to be asleep. The train was swaying from side to side and Butch was getting a cramp from bending down and also acutely aware of a pain in his knee where a bolt was pressing in it. For what seemed like an eternity, nothing happened. Then one of the card players giggled, and one of the others questioned him in German, which Butch interpreted as meaning *What's so damned funny?* Before he could get an answer to the question, he too started giggling. In another minute the whole of the contingent was engaged in uproarious laughter, the card players holding their sides, the loungers wiping their eyes and the sleepers in the throes of hysterical dreams.

Butch slammed the hatch and locked it, and waved at Basa

giving him a cut off motion. Basa shut off the gas, extracted the nozzle and relatched the trap-door. Basa reslung the tank on his shoulder and came over to Butch.

'Good going,' Butch said. 'Me and the Kid'll take care of this guard now.'

'How you gonna do that?'

Butch opened his mouth and shut it again. 'Don't know,' he confessed. 'Jump him, I guess.'

'Aw, let me do it, Butch. I haven't had so much fun since I went shark wrestling off the Barrier Reef back home.'

Butch spread his hands. 'Hell, Basa, go ahead then. I don't want you to think that I'm the guy who spoils your fun.'

'Gee, thanks Butch. Just watch this for a minute.' He unhooked the nitrous oxide tank and put it where Butch could stop it from rolling off the train. Sylvia crawled up to Butch.

'What's he going to do?' she whispered.

'Take care of the guard.'

They watched the Titan Crusher as he strode on top of the carriage, seemingly unaffected by the wind streaming past him. He straddled the two cars, poised for a second, then jumped on the German's shoulders, crushing him to the ground with his weight; the cigarette the man had been smoking dropped on the platform and rolled over the side. Basa picked him up by his shirt and examined him. He was already out cold. He opened the door to the guards' carriage and threw him in, shutting the door again. His head popped over the edge of the carriage. 'OK, Butch, all done. What do you want to do now?'

In a voice filled with awe Butch said, 'Do you think you could go down to the next carriage to see if there's a guard there?'

'Sure, what do you want me to do if there is?'

'Make sure he doesn't bother us, I guess. That other carriage is full of Germans, too, you know.'

'Better take ma tank then. I'll give them a little whiff of laughing gas.'

'Good idea,' Butch agreed.

'And when I've finished,' Basa continued, 'I'll come in and settle that dirty old Baron.'

'That's all right, Basa,' Butch said quickly. 'You leave that to us. You better keep watch on top here to see nobody bothers us.'

'Aw, Butch,' the giant hung his head. 'Can't I come in and help you take care of that guy?'

'Not now, Basa,' Butch said firmly. 'You wanna help us rescue that poor lady, don't you? Well, you gotta make sure we ain't interfered with.'

He relented. 'Oh, all right.' Basa leaped on to the carriage, lifted the nitrous oxide tank into position, then strode across the roof towards the front of the train.

Martinette discovered that by stepping on the rail that surrounded the end of the guard's van and leaning forward against the car, he could just peek over the top. He admitted grudgingly to himself that the girl was good. He had not even heard her land on top of the carriage, although he knew exactly when she was going to do it. He watched her now as she helped Sundance over the side, followed closely by the huge Australian carrying Jimmy Trewe, and finally by Butch. He tried to shift to a more comfortable position and ease his aching back, as he watched the Australian feed laughing gas into the guards' carriage. And he noted with reluctant admiration that the crazy thing must have worked. He saw Basa jump down between carriages and reappear a few moments later waving his success – another guard out of the way.

Martinette stepped down as the Australian went on to the next carriage and the other four lowered themselves to the passage that led to where the envoy was. Unbelievable, but Phase One seemed to be a complete success. Martinette stood irresolute on the platform. He was dithering, and fretted because of it. Should he go through now and take personal charge, or wait as his agent was supposed to, until the party came back to the guard's van, where the papers could be checked for their authenticity?

He looked behind him. Reginald had dropped back in the Oldsmobile and was keeping pace with the train about fifty feet away. Martinette decided to wait for a while and see what developed. He would do anything he could to avoid being seen by the opposition.

Jimmy kissed the side of the carriage. The comforting walls closed about him and gave him some semblance of security. He thought about the return trip he would have to make and was racked with a spasm of shudders. Butch was talking to him and it finally registered.

'Jimmy, you gotta open the door.'

Jimmy tried to concentrate and get the tide that had his limbs awash with fear, to back off. 'Yeah,' he mumbled and bent down to look at the lock. He jiggled the handle just for something to do and was amazed when the door opened. He looked at Butch and shrugged.

Butch drew his gun, Sundance already had his out. 'Go ahead, Kid.'

Sundance opened the door softly, darted in in a crouch and flattened himself against the wall. Butch followed close behind and flattened himself on the other side. Sylvia and Jimmy hung back. Butch and Sundance were in the narrow passage that led to the salon. The door was closed. The door at the side of the passage, they knew from their previous examination of the German carriages, led into the bedroom. It was also closed. Sundance lifted his neckerchief so that it covered his nose and mouth. Butch did the same and motioned to Sundance, who padded along to the bedroom door, tested the handle, flung it open and jumped inside. He reappeared in a moment and shook his head.

Butch nodded and they advanced on the door to the salon. Sundance turned the handle slowly and pushed the door open a little at a time. He looked back over his shoulder and nodded. Butch responded by giving him a go-ahead motion with his gun. Sundance entered the salon stealthily, Butch right at his heels.

The colonel was sitting with his back to them. He had replaced his uniform jacket with a vermilion smoking-jacket, and seemed engrossed in a book he held in his lap. He was smoking a cigarette in an ivory holder, one manicured hand reaching absently for an onyx ashtray to flick the ash.

Butch stepped forward and cleared his throat. 'Put your hands up buddy, and don't make any sudden moves! We got you covered.'

The colonel turned slowly in his chair, a slight narrowing of the eyes the only sign that he acknowledged this intrusion of his privacy. 'What are you, and what is the meaning of this?' The voice was authoritative, the English clipped and precise, with only a bare hint of a German accent.

'Shut up, we're asking the questions,' Sundance growled. 'You got something we want.'

'I am not a moron. Zat is obviously vhy you are here holding guns on me.'

'He's got a point there, Kid,' Butch admitted.

The colonel, evidently impatient with the speed at which things were moving, took the initiative. 'Vhat is it you vant?'

'Hey, *hombre*,' Sundance said with menace, 'you just hold your horses. We'll tell you when we're good and ready.'

Butch, who was used to the Kid's perversity, ignored it. 'You got some papers you're bringing to your ambassador. We wan' 'em.'

'Ach, zo.' The Colonel favoured them with a thin-lipped smile. He took his hands down slowly and puffed on his cigarette. 'It is ze papers you are after,' he mocked. 'Why not? You shall have zem. Zey will not do you any good, anyvay.' He smiled, giving Butch an uncomfortable feeling that the man knew something he didn't. 'But first, tell me, did you haff trouble getting on ze train?'

Butch was surprised at the question. He looked to Sundance for a reaction and didn't get one. 'As a matter of fact, it was goddamn easy.'

The colonel nodded once. 'Goot. I would be distressed to zink you vere put to any great difficulty.' He took the cigarette from the holder and stubbed it out in the ashtray. 'I vill get ze papers for you.'

'Just tell me where they are, and I'll get 'em.' Butch said.

The colonel gave an indifferent shrug and pointed at a leather pouch that had been thrown carelessly on to an overstuffed chair.

'Watch him,' Butch said. He pocketed his gun, picked up

the pouch, undid the clasps and extracted a rolled-up sheaf of papers. He smoothed them out and looked at them. 'They're in German,' he accused.

'Vhat did you expect, you dolt. Ve are German.'

'That's a good point, Butch,' Sundance said.

'Kid,' Butch said in a low voice, 'something stinks around here and I don't like it. This is all too easy.'

Sundance kept his eyes on the colonel and shrugged without replying.

Butch looked around the carriage and then back at the colonel. 'Where's the safe?'

The German's eyes narrowed for the second time but the mockery had been replaced by something that approached concern. 'Vhat safe? You haff vhat you came for.' His eyes flicked involuntarily to a boxlike structure covered with an embroidered cloth depicting the German eagle. Butch caught the glance and went over to it and whisked off the cloth. 'Thanks, colonel.'

'You vill not get any help from me in opening the safe.'

Butch smiled. 'I don't need your help. I got some of my own.' He went to the door to the passage that had been left ajar and beckoned to Jimmy, who was waiting expectantly. He trotted in with relief on his face, followed by Sylvia. Butch pointed to the safe. 'There it is, let's see how quick you can open it.'

Jimmy went over to the safe and gave it a tender caress. He muttered under his breath and bent to examine it, then looked up at Butch. 'I need the key, or else I'm gonna 'ave to blow it, and that could be messy.'

'You heard the man, colonel, let's have the key,' Butch said, 'and without any arguments. I don't wanna get rough. But then again, I won't have to. My *compadre* here,' he indicated Sundance, 'has got a very short temper, ain't that right, Kid?'

Sundance kept his unwavering stare on the colonel and grunted a confirmation. 'Just say the word, Butch, and I'll show this guy a few Apache tricks.'

The colonel paled a little, his lips compressed into a hard line, the tendons in his face pulling his cheeks taught with the strain. He looked at the four people in the carriage without moving his head, his eyes flicking from one to the other with the rapidity of a serpent's tongue.

'It don't look like he's gonna co-operate, Butch,' Sundance drawled conversationally. 'Which piece of him do you want me to take off first?'

'Now, just hang on a minute, Kid. I don't wanna get his blood on my clothes. Let's think. Where would you hide a key you wanted to keep safe, and where you could get to it easily?'

'Try round his neck,' Jimmy piped up without looking round, his ear pressed close to the tumblers and his fingers manipulating them with the delicacy of a surgeon's. 'These berks always keep keys around their necks, they think that's the last place you'll look.'

From the way the pupils dilated in the grey eyes, Butch knew that Jimmy had hit the bull's-eye first time. Butch held out a hand. 'Let's have it, colonel.'

The German did nothing at first. His fingers twitched spasmodically and he stared at Butch with an unreadable expression. Two pinpoints of colour appeared high on his cheekbones. With great reluctance he raised a hand to his neck, fumbled inside his collar and drew out a cord with a key attached to it. He lifted the cord over his head and threw the key contemptuously at Butch's feet.

Butch stooped to pick it up with a humourless grin and when he spoke his tone was dry and matter-of-fact. 'If we had just a little more time, you bastard, I'd make you pick that up with your teeth.' Butch handed the key to Jimmy. 'How long will you be?'

'Dunno mate, do I? This ain't as easy as cracking a walnut. I'm workin' as fast as I can. I don't want ta stay here one second longer than I 'ave to.' Then Jimmy thought of the return trip on top of the swaying cars and broke into a sweat.

Martinette made up his mind. He felt as useless as a teat on a bull staying in the guard's van wondering how the operation was going, or if it still was. As unwise as it seemed to reveal himself, the need for action was overpowering and the adrenalin coursed through his veins. He levered himself on top of the carriage and started to crawl forward. The wind whipped the oversized hat from his head and sent it spinning across the Essex countryside. Martinette brushed the hair from his eyes and continued to crawl to the edge of the carriage roof. With his heart in his mouth he made a staggering leap to the next car, landing awkwardly and bruising his shin. He suppressed a howl of pain and rubbed at the spot until the hurt subsided to a dull ache, and he could move on. He clambered down the side of the guards' carriage and tried to peer into the window of the closed door to the envoy's car. All he could see was a crack of light where the door at the other end of the corridor was slightly ajar. He tested the handle, found the door open and went into the carriage, shutting the door softly behind him. He crept along the passageway, reached the open door and took great care not to show himself as he looked into the carriage.

Butch satisfied himself that everything was going as well as could be expected. Sundance had his gun levelled on the German who was doing a fair imitation of a statue, its perfection marred only by the tiny pulse that throbbed on his temple.

Jimmy was totally involved in the working of the tumblers and seemed completely oblivious to anything else.

Sylvia was leaning against a silk covered wall, arms folded across her chest, a small, secret smile on her lips.

Butch was holding the papers he had taken from the pouch and started to riffle through them idly in an attempt to pick out a word or two he would understand. The last page was titled with a string of unpronounceable words and seemed to contain a list of names. He started to read them. They were in alphabetical order and began with the surname ADLER, and the first name, Heinrich. It was followed by APPLETON, George. He looked at the third name on the list and froze.

For a moment it seemed that the blood flowing through his arteries had reversed its circuitous route; the nerves deadened beyond recall, his limbs stiff and locked in place, the world turned topsy-turvy. The name read BERTOLUCCI, Louisa – Sylvia Jones.

Butch turned a stricken face to Sylvia, and Martinette picked that moment to walk into the carriage. He had eyes only for the papers that Butch held in his hand and so did not see the .32 calibre revolver that Sylvia now held in hers.

'I think this farce has gone on long enough,' she said coldly. 'Sundance drop your gun, or I'll kill you. I warn you, I'm a crack shot.'

Sundance reacted as if he had been stung by a bee. He turned to Sylvia with jerky, puppet-like movements, and stared at her in open-mouthed amazement. His head revolved with an effort as if it were seated on a bed of rusty bearings. 'Whadda we do now, Butch?' he croaked.

16 'Always leave 'em laughing'

Butch stared at Sylvia as if he were seeing her for the first time, and maybe he was. The face of the girl he thought he loved had changed from the soft, yielding lines he'd always seen before to harsh, masculine contours that would brook no nonsense. The eyebrows that had once been gracefully arched were knitted together in an almost unbroken line. The hazel eyes had darkened to the colour of Rio Grande mud-flats and regarded him with the warmth of a polar bear in search of its next meal. 'Like the lady says, Kid, you drop your gun.'

Sundance opened reluctant fingers and the gun fell to the carpeted floor with a soft thump.

'Who's this?' Sylvia said to the German. She jerked her head to Martinette.

The colonel beamed expansively, ignoring the question for the moment. 'I will take those papers, Herr Cassidy, and your gun. You vill not need them anymore.' He dropped the papers casually on the chair, took the revolver from Butch's belt and, having retrieved Sundance's gun, held it on him with the air of a man who knows exactly what he is doing with firearms.

'Now, take those ridiculous masks from your faces. You see, I knew who you were despite the childish attempt to disguise yourselves.' Butch and Sundance complied with reluctance.

'That, *Fraulein*, is Geoffrey Martinette, the deputy head of the British Secret Service department called MI5, and I would say he is looking somewhat ill at the moment!' He laughed harshly. 'Are you not feeling vell, Herr Martinette? Is it because all your childish schemes are tumbling about you? You British are such fools that for years I have had the trouble to convince the Kaiser that you are not putting on an act. He cannot believe that you are as stupid as you really are. He thinks you are playing some subtle game that we do not understand. I am afraid he has a soft spot for your country because of his relationship to your royal family. He refuses to understand that you will always engage amateurs to do a professional's job.'

Martinette's sallow complexion had gone chalky but he had recovered enough of his composure to set his face into an expressionless mask. He perceived everything about him with the clarity of heightened awareness brought on by the danger of the situation. Out of the corner of his eye he saw that Jimmy Trewe had finished working the tumblers, had inserted the key in the lock and was now sitting on his haunches watching the proceedings liks a spectator at a tennis match. Butch seemed stunned to immobility, his arms hanging loosely at his sides. He addressed the German in a voice that he was glad to hear sounded calm in his ears. 'Congratulations, Herr Colonel. I assume you had this all set up in advance? A fine piece of work, you seem to have caught us napping.'

The colonel acknowledged the compliment with a slight bow.

'And now,' Martinette continued, 'that you have closed the doors of your trap, so to speak, what do you intend doing with us?'

The colonel looked sorrowful without managing to convey the impression that he expected Martinette to burst into tears. '*Ach*, Herr Martinette, that is a very distressing question, but what *am* I to do?' He spread his hands in a gesture of complete helplessness. 'I'm faced wiz a quite untenable situation; common burglars attack ze private train of ze special German envoy in ze pursuit of his peaceful duties, and threaten his life if zey do not get their way, their object to steal jewels and money to ze value of hundreds of thousands of marks.' He smiled condescendingly at Martinette. 'Yes, *mein Herr*, we've learned also about ze story you were to put out. But, to return to my sad little tale. Ve vere forced to defend ourselves and the aftermath of the unfortunate mêlée vill be the discovery zat ze burglars have not survived. A pity, ve vill say, but one zat vas unavoidable.'

'You're going to kill us in cold blood?' Martinette said stoically. 'How will you explain my death? I don't think I could be classed as a common criminal.'

'Your Government,' the German retorted, 'vould classify you as Jack ze Ripper if it suited them, and if it were able to avoid an international incident.'

Martinette declined to comment as he knew this was true.

'But now,' the German said, 'let's put that talk aside. It distresses me to continue it and my curiosity gets ze better of me. How did you get past the guards?'

'They immobilized them with laughing gas,' Sylvia said from the corner. 'They enlisted some Australian oaf to administer it.'

The colonel laughed heartily. 'Laughing gas, *ya*, that is good, very original. Whose idea was that?'

Sylvia pointed to Butch with the barrel of her gun. The German inclined his head at Butch. 'Excellent, Herr Cassidy. It's a shame your talents were not more profitably channelled. But you did not have to go to such lengths. The guards vere instructed to let you pass unmolested.' He turned to Sylvia. 'Where's zis Australian now?' he demanded in a voice from which all mirth had disappeared.

'He's out in the carriages attending to the guards. He won't bother us.'

'Ve shall have to deal wiz him, also.'

Sylvia accepted the order with a nod.

'Will you satisfy my curiosity now, Herr Colonel?' Martinette asked.

The colonel took a fob watch from his pocket and consulted

it. 'Vhy not? Ve have another forty minutes until ve reach the station. Time enough to do what has to be done. Vhat do you vant to know?'

'I suppose those papers were all fakes,' Martinette said, 'and that you had no intention of bringing anything authentic with you, after you learned that we would attempt to steal them? And that you continued with the trip expressly to embarrass the British Government? An excellent opportunity for you to manufacture a crisis.'

'On ze contrary, my dear Martinette, ze papers are exactly vhat your agents reported zem to be. Ve used zem as one would attract a bear to honey, and when it was revealed that British spies – ve vill plant documents to prove zat – accosted the representative of the German Government, ze insult vill be so great it cannot be overlooked, and ve at last vill be able to start zis war, instead of just chattering like house*fraus*.'

'And you kept them in plain sight?' Martinette said in amazement, 'not even trying to conceal them? What if we'd taken them, pouch and all, and thrown them out of the window, to be picked up later?'

'That was not the plan,' the German said, 'as ve knew from Fraulein Bertolucci. And I must confess it amused me to use the real papers. It added a certain piquancy. After all, one does not stand and admire a great painting in the same way, when one knows it is only a reproduction, and knowing the conclusion as I did, I wished all the elements to be genuine. It is not my style to use *ersatz*. And by the way, Herr Martinette, how did you get on the train and so get caught in my net? I had no expectations of bagging you along with ze others. In my experience, the generals do not put themselves in the front line. I can only assume from ze ill-fitting jacket you're vearing, zat you have disposed of my man.'

'He's still alive,' Martinette said grimly. 'Just tied up and unconscious, and I might add in much better shape than my agent.'

'*Ach*, zo you found him.'

'I did stumble across him,' Martinette said sardonically.

Butch found his voice at last. 'Sylvia ...' he hesitated, trying to think what to say next. 'How did you – get into this? You bin playing me for a sucker all along? Didn't nothing we do mean anything?'

Sylvia smiled sweetly but appeared unable to assimilate herself back into the character she'd played, like something that had slipped from memory and was irretrievable. It was a pale ghost of the warm smiles she had for Butch during their hours of love-making. 'You are a fool, Butch. You know nothing of security. Any woman could have her way with you. I've been a German agent since I was eighteen,' she said with pride. 'I was recruited when I went with the circus to Germany. They showed me the only true way to live, the German way. And how did I get into this, as you put it? It was so easy it was laughable. You have him to thank for that,' she pointed at Sundance.

'Me?' Sundance croaked in astonishment.

'Of course, you. And the unbeatable combination of your weakness for women and your big mouth when you're making love to them.'

Sundance stared at Sylvia in complete bewilderment.

'You still don't know, do you?' she mocked. 'In that case, I'll remind you. Do you remember the evening at the Savoy when you met Mata Hari? You made love to her that night ... and several other nights,' she said. 'You couldn't stop trying to impress her with your big plans for a train robbery, could you?'

'Oh, no!' Butch moaned. 'You didn't tell that woman what we were doin', did ya Kid?'

Sundance flushed to the tips of his moustache and looked so guilty that no answer was necessary. 'Well,' he mumbled, 'I might have done a little braggin'. I don't rightly remember. She kept fillin' up ma glass with whiskey.'

'Mata Hari is one of the most remarkable women of our time,' Sylvia declared with reverence and perhaps something more. 'She is held in the highest esteem by the German Government and will one day take her rightful place in history, just as soon as Germany wins the coming war.'

'Crap!' Butch said with disgust. 'Do you really believe that shit? You're sick, lady; and I must have been blind.'

'How did you make contact,' Martinette asked, breaking through the emotional outburst.

'With great ease,' Sylvia said dryly. 'When Mata Hari told me that that imbecile Reginald Ratlett was with the party, I simply wrote to him and told him I was dying to see him. I knew he'd come running. He also thought he was in love with me,' she shot Butch with a vicious glance. 'And then I thought I would be able to work my way into the scheme by just being around. But I needn't have bothered. They approached me with an invitation to join them at the first meeting. I was so surprised that I was almost caught off my guard. Didn't you wonder why I accepted so readily?' she accused Butch.

'No, damn it, I didn't. I just thought . . . I don't know what I thought.'

'Enough talk,' the colonel said. 'Ve have less than half an hour until ve reach ze station and ve have things to do, do we not, my dear?'

Sylvia smiled demurely.

The train lurched going over some sleepers and Martinette shifted his weight to keep his balance. He noted the exaggerated movement Jimmy Trewe had made from his seat on the floor. He had thrown his arms back to save himself from falling and as he righted himself, one hand had slipped into a back pocket.

'I regret,' the colonel was continuing, 'that we must end zis meeting after such a brief acquaintance, but it is ze fortunes of war, eh Martinette?'

The door behind the colonel crashed open. 'Where's that dirty old Baron!' yelled Barry Billington (Basa to his friends). Everything seemed to happen at once. The German jerked around and snapped off a shot at the Titan Crusher. The bullet hit the nitrous oxide tank with a metallic ping and went ricochetting off through the carriage.

Butch dived for his Derringer, pulled it and shot almost before it had cleared the holster that was strapped to his calf. Butch was not known for his accuracy and he would admit, if pressed, that it was a lucky shot. The bullet banged into the second pistol the German held, and spun it out of his hand.

'Hey, that's not nice. You could hurt someone like that,' Basa said and threw the tank at the colonel. The colonel flung his arms out to protect himself and he caught the hundred pounds of projectile neatly, its momentum banging him into the wall of the carriage hard enough to dent it. Sylvia hesitated for a precious few seconds trying to decide where the greatest danger lay and finally pointed the gun at Basa. Jimmy Trewe whipped his hand out from behind his back with the speed of a striking cobra and smashed Sylvia's gun hand with the cosh he had pulled from his pocket. She screamed in agony and dropped the gun, staring dumbly at her broken wrist that hung limp and useless.

Martinette, who knew what his priorities were, and seeing that matters were well in hand, went for the papers that the German had dropped back on to the chair. He folded them hurriedly and put them away in an inside pocket.

'Where'd you come from, Basa? I thought you were watching the guards?' Butch asked.

'Oh, ma tank of gas ran out and those guards were all laughing harder than an Aussie with a dozen kegs of beer, so I came to find the Baron.'

'Sure glad you did,' Butch said with gratitude.

'Hey!' Basa exclaimed looking at Sylvia, who had now collapsed on the floor. 'Why was she trying to shoot me? I thought she was gonna help us rescue that poor lady.'

'Things have changed,' Butch said in a grim flat voice. 'She was with the dirty old Baron.'

Martinette had straightened up from the chair and was staring at Butch in total non-comprehension.

'Not now,' Butch said out of the corner of his mouth, 'I'll tell you later.'

'Where's the lady?' Basa insisted. 'We gotta save her.'

'Basa,' Butch reached up and put a hand on his shoulder. 'I got some bad news for you. We've been tricked. They somehow got wind of us rescuing her and they're bringing her into the country by boat.'

'No kidding ... then how're we gonna help her?'

Butch turned around and pointed at Martinette. 'You see that guy over there? He's with the British Government and he's promised to make sure she's safe. Ain't that right, Martinette?'

Martinette looked bemused and at a total loss for words.

'Oh yeah?' Basa said. He strode across the unconscious German and stuck out a hand that Martinette reciprocated automatically, and started pumping it with a grip like a bear trap. 'That's real good of ya. You're a real nice fellow.'

'Thank you,' Martinette got out between teeth that rattled together as he was jostled by the giant's exuberance. 'Please, may I have my hand back?'

'Oh yeah, sorry. I forgot myself. Didn't hurt ya, did I?'

Martinette shook his numbed fingers, trying to get the circulation working again. 'Let's get out of here,' he said peremptorily.

'What about them?' Sundance asked, indicating the German and Sylvia, who had fainted.

'Leave them. They're not going anywhere.'

'Aren't you gonna arrest her as a spy?' Sundance persisted.

'Certainly not. Her effectiveness is completely nullified. And besides, the repercussions would be too great. Let's go!'

Sundance retrieved the two Colts and handed Butch his.

'I'll be with you in a second, I'll just take ma tank,' Basa said.

Butch tried not to sound exasperated. 'Leave it, Basa. I'll buy you a new one.'

Basa stopped in mid-stride. 'Oh yeah? I guess that'll be all right then.'

Martinette was already in the passageway sprinting for the outside door. Butch paused for a last look at Sylvia who, in repose, had once again taken on the innocence and beauty he had fallen for. He shook his head to clear it and hurried after Martinette, who led the way up the side of the carriage. It was only after he had reached the top and had turned around to help the others up, that he noticed Jimmy Trewe was missing. 'Where's Jimmy?' he shouted above the wind.

'I'll get him,' Basa volunteered and went back in the carriage. He reappeared a few moments later, dragging Jimmy who was clutching his satchel of tools. He lifted the little Cockney to his shoulder and climbed to the top of the car.

Butch squatted by the open trap-door and peered in. He slammed the door shut and raised his voice to be heard. 'They're still finding things pretty funny down there. My pappy'd be proud of me, he used to say – *Always leave 'em laughing.*'

The five of them made their cautious way across the coach and lowered themselves to the space between it and the guard's van. They went into the car.

Martinette shook off the uniform jacket, put his own back on and transferred the papers. He then led the way to the other end of the van, snatching the lantern from the bracket on the fly. They could see Reginald in the Oldsmobile off to their left, where he had had to diverge from the track to follow the road. Martinette waved the lantern at him and he acknowledged by turning the head lamps on for a brief instant. He speeded up and searched for a path on the uneven ground off the road, that would bring him next to the train.

17 Exit at eighty

Jonathan De Ford and the squad of coppers bounced and rattled over the pitted country road at a breakneck forty miles an hour, seriously testing the Wolseley's capacity to hold together. They had not seen another living thing since they had left the lights of London far behind; and what worried De Ford more as the minutes passed was that there was no sign of the train they were to intercept. De Ford was aware that his credibility rating was dropping by the second, as he received more and more doubtful glances from the eager inspector, who was beginning to wish he'd never seen this Yank. It was the unknown engine driver who saved De Ford from further embarrassment. He had evidently decided that driving through the night was too lonely an occupation, and pulled on the whistle for reassurance. The plaintive cry echoed through the empty countryside.

De Ford became animated in an instant. 'Did you hear that?'

The inspector breathed a sigh of relief. 'Yes sir, it appears to be a train.'

De Ford pointed through the windscreen. 'I can see the light,' he shouted. 'Can't you get this tin can to go faster?'

'Not with six persons in here,' the driver grumbled. The constable turned to the inspector. 'Do you want me to try to stop the train, sir?'

The inspector considered the question. He had not really thought about what they would do when they found the train. He decided that he had already exceeded his authority by going well outside his own patch. He was beginning to have misgivings because, if this thing went very wrong, he was in no doubt that he would be shat upon from a great height.

'No, don't try to stop the train. Just drive close enough to see if we can observe anything out of the ordinary.' The constable nodded obediently and gripped the juddering wheel harder.

The train's beam was now completely visible and growing larger every moment. Reginald had manoeuvred the Oldsmobile next to the train and allowed his speed to slacken just enough to bring him even with the rail of the guard's van. Martinette was already standing on the rail supporting himself with one hand on the carriage, and when the car drifted into range he jumped into the back seat.

'Go ahead,' Basa shouted to Butch and Sundance. 'I'll come after you and bring the little fella with me.'

Butch jumped on to the rail, waiting for his chance and stepped into the car. Sundance tumbled in after him.

'Look!' Reginald shouted and pointed ahead of him. 'There's a car approaching, and I do believe it's the police. I can hear the bell.'

Butch saw the car and heard the faint clanging of the bell at the same time. 'Oh no, that's all we need! C'mon Basa,' he yelled urgently.

'Tell him to bring the car closer!' Basa shouted. Reginald had allowed the Oldsmobile to drift with his absorbtion in the approaching of the police car. Butch pounded him on the back. 'Get closer, Reginald.'

Reginald woke from his reverie and jerked the wheel over.

'Thanks, cobber,' said the Titan Crusher and stepped into the car.

Reginald checked to see that everyone was in safely and did a double take. 'Where's Sylvia?' he asked in alarm. 'Is she hurt? And what's he doing here?' he nodded at Martinette.

'She's not coming,' Butch informed him. He felt a lump in his throat.

'Why not?'

'She's a German agent.'

'You're joking,' Reginald stated in disbelief.

Butch said tiredly, 'I'll tell you about it later, and Martinette's here 'cause he loves us. He couldn't stay away.'

Martinette ignored the barb. He was too furious for it to register. He had an extremely good idea of who had persuaded the police to come out, and let loose a string of oaths that he never used in polite society. He swore on the head of his sainted mother that if they evaded the police and made a clean getaway, Jonathan De Ford would be on the first boat out of the country – and if he had his way it would be a leaky canoe without a paddle! They wouldn't spoil this operation now. Somehow, against all odds, this band of misfits had produced what he wanted, and he had no intention of making long explanations to Scotland Yard. He leaned forward and tapped Reginald on the shoulder none too gently. 'You'll have to lose them, we must get away.'

'Don't worry my dear chap,' Reginald yelled with glee. 'I'll scorch past them so quickly, they won't even see my dust.' Reginald swung the car away from the train and on to the road.

De Ford pounded the back of the seat. 'Look – a car! It's them! I told you they were going to rob the train.'

The inspector, whose expectations of promotion had lifted again, smiled happily. 'After them, constable.'

The two automobiles were on a collision course, converging on each other at speed.

'It's time for evasive manoeuvres,' Reginald announced. 'Hold on, everyone.' He swung the car due west, crossing over the lane the police car was using, slid into a shallow ditch at the side of the road and flew off the other end, landing in a meadow with a bump.

'Whoo-ee!' Butch expelled his breath with a whoosh as he landed hard in the seat from three feet up.

Reginald, with his head-lamps blazing, zig-zagged across the field avoiding pot-holes, trees, and a rabbit that was mesmerized by the light. Its ears twitched in gratitude.

The constable slanted into the ditch at a forty-five-degree angle. He had not warned anybody to hold on and when the car did its flying act, everybody, including him, hit their heads on the roof. De Ford bit his tongue and blasphemed in true Western fashion. The inspector's first thought was to demote the irresponsible driver, but he gave up when he couldn't think how to go lower than constable. 'After them!' he shouted. 'And watch where the bloody hell you're going!'

The meadow was a dark, desolate mass that tilted upwards in a gentle slope and gave everyone in the racing Oldsmobile the impression that they were drifting in the middle of a sinister sea. The head-lamps pierced the blackness for only short distances, and at the speed they were going they were almost on top of obstructions before Reginald could see them. He swerved in and out of trees that stood stark in the waning moonlight, imagination turning the benign limbs into grotesque shapes that seemed to snatch at them as they rushed past. Reginald saw the faint glimmer of a brook just before they reached it. 'Hold on,' he yelled, 'a stream!' He stepped on the gas. The car spanned the channel and almost made it to the other side, the back wheels just catching the far bank. The car pitched and bucked, the rear wheels scrabbling for purchase, the front end lifting. The noisome smell of burning rubber drifted in tendrils on the air; they wrinkled their noses.

The rear wheels strained and pushed the Olds on to solid ground with a crunch that shook the car so hard, the metal sang and bottomed the undercarriage on a boulder.

They went on at reduced speed, with a rattle that foretold this car would not die of old age.

The police car did not fare quite as well. At the speed it was going and with the six heavy bodies inside, it travelled about halfway across the brook, landing with a jarring plop that splashed water high above the windows and thoroughly saturated the occupants. 'You stupid berk!' the inspector screamed. 'I'll have you walking the beat for the rest of your natural life.' He wiped away the water that streamed down his face and fumbled with the handle of the car door. He jumped out and sank to his waist, and uttered a string of surprised curses. He peered into the gloom and saw the Oldsmobile slowing down. 'After them, lads!' he commanded and scrambled for the bank.

The Oldsmobile was sounding its death-knell, the rattles and bangs reaching a crescendo in a discordant symphony of metal on metal. 'Son-of-a-bitch,' Butch muttered and gained little satisfaction from it.

'Look,' Sundance said, 'there's a light up ahead.' They all looked at where he was pointing, and through the screen of trees the glow from a trio of lamps indicated that someone was up at this time of night.

Butch jumped out of the car with sudden resolution. 'Let's go,' he said and raced off.

'Hey!' Basa shouted at his retreating back. 'Why are we running away from the police? I thought they were on our side.'

Butch yelled back over his shoulder. 'They're only pretending, Basa! They're really more Germans. C'mon!' The urgency in his voice prompted everyone to action and they ran after him. Butch burst through the last of the scrub and thinly spaced trees and pulled up short. He could see clearly ahead of him now, and the lights formed the perimeter inside which was a balloon, straining at its ropes. Butch could see a man fussing around the gondola and another packing items in a basket that was next to a stack of hydrogen cannisters.

The rest of the party caught up with him and stopped and stared.

'Whaddya think, Kid?' Butch asked.

Sundance looked back the way they had come; faint shouts of the pursuing police could be heard in the distance, coming closer. Sundance shrugged. 'Never flew in one of 'em before, but this sure looks like a good time to start.'

'Sounds good to me,' Butch agreed. 'Let's go.'

They took off for the balloon without giving the others a chance to argue and left them with no option but to follow.

The man nearest the balloon looked up curiously as they ran up. He was kitted out in aviators' costume with goggles perched on his forehead. He started to voice a greeting but was prevented from uttering such civilities by Butch, who swept him aside and rushed to the gondola.

'Sorry *amigo*, but we're in a hurry. I got no time to explain, but we're taking your balloon.'

'But,' the man spluttered, 'you can't do that.'

Sundance drew his Colt. 'This says we can.'

'In you go boys,' Butch said.

Martinette, who thought his authority was slipping away beyond recall decided that his best course of action was to drift along with the strong current. He could always assert himself later, if there was to be a later. He looked up at the balloon through the eyes of a man who has suffered for years from vertigo.

'Hey, that looks like fun,' Basa said. He lifted Jimmy Trewe with one hand and dumped him into the gondola, and then grabbed Martinette, who was hesitating, by the collar and tossed him in. Reginald, Butch and Sundance were already climbing over the side and Basa vaulted in after them. They crowded into the confined space of the gondola in a manner that would have done credit to a tin of sardines.

'Your knife, Kid.'

'Damn it, I'm gettin' it out Butch. Give me a chance.' Sundance unfolded his clasped knife and started sawing away at the restraining ropes.

The balloonist's helper, who had remained where he was in dumbfounded silence, found his voice and the use of his limbs at the same instant. 'Stop thieves!' he shouted wildly as he ran towards them.

Butch pulled out his gun and shot into the air. The man stopped as if he had been pole-axed. 'Don't be a hero,' Butch pleaded. 'We just wanna get outta here.'

The last restraining rope parted with a 'ping!' but nothing

happened. For a beat in time they all stared at each other without saying anying.

'Too much weight,' Martinette groaned.

'Dump the sandbags,' Butch ordered. A dozen of them were attached round the edge of the gondola, and feverishly they started to rip them off.

The police had just appeared through the trees and were only fifty yards off. The last sandbag dropped to the ground and very, very slowly the balloon started to rise, trailing the ropes where Sundance had cut them.

'Stop!' the inspector yelled. 'I'm arresting you in the name of the law!'

De Ford had saved his breath and determinedly led the race for the balloon. He was well out in front of the pack of policemen when he jumped for the rope drifting over his head and clung to it with desperation.

Basa leaned down over the gondola to get a better look at him. 'I don't know who you are, cobber, but we don't want you along on this trip!' He slapped De Ford's hands as if he were administering punishment to a naughty child. The crack sounded loud in the still night air. De Ford yelped with pain and let go, falling five feet to the ground and landing in a heap.

The balloon was drifting slowly higher and further away as the police arrived. 'Stop!' the inspector yelled again. 'Come back here immediately!' He stamped the ground with frustration. 'Get them, lads!' he shouted to his constables. The constables dutifully pulled out their truncheons as one man and waved them at the retreating balloon. Then one of them had the bright idea of throwing his truncheon. The others followed suit and their aim was excellent, as all four truncheons bounced harmlessly off the bottom of the gondola. They threw their helmets without any better success.

Butch waved at the little crowd of furious policemen. '*Adios, amigos.*'

'You won't get away with this!' De Ford roared.

'But we are!' Butch countered. The balloon drifted higher and higher and the yells diminished in volume, until they were lost to hearing.

'Where are we going?' Basa asked.

'Now that, my friend,' Butch replied, 'is a very good question. Anybody know how to fly these things?'

'I remember seeing one at a fair once,' Reginald recalled.

'And that,' Butch concluded, 'means you don't.' It seemed that balloons fell outside everyone's expertise.

'Nice view from up here,' Sundance commented.

Now, as it happened, that night the prevailing winds were east north-east and were stronger at higher altitudes; so that, as the balloon rose, it was pushed along at a fair clip. Jimmy came out of his doze and sniffed the air. 'What's that smell, then?'

Butch's eyes snapped open with sudden realization. 'Sweet Jesus, salt water! We're getting near the sea.' He jumped up, rocking the gondola, and looked over. Pale tints of dawn in the east illuminated the vast expanse of the English Channel less than a mile off. Butch sounded scared. 'We gotta get down from here.'

'How do we do that?' Basa asked.

Martinette supplied the answer with chilling accuracy. 'Short of shooting a hole in that gas-bag, we don't. We'll be swept out to sea.'

Butch looked up at the bag. It hung above them, blotting out the sky. 'Maybe it wouldn't be so bad with a slow leak,' he mused. 'Still got ya knife, Kid?'

Sundance grunted.

'Think you could climb up there and cut a small hole?'

Sundance looked up at the bag fifteen feet away. 'Why me? I'm no goddam monkey.'

'I don't mind going,' Basa said.

'How about me?' Reginald volunteered.

'All right,' Sundance grumbled. 'I'll go.' He took the clasped knife out, opened it and placed it carefully between his teeth. He stepped up on the rim of the gondola and started climbing the rope, hand over hand. He stopped when he came within pricking distance, wrapped his legs and one arm around the rope and took the knife from his mouth with the other hand. He worked the tip of the knife into the fabric of the balloon with careful deliberation. The hiss of the air was audible when he punctured the last layer of the fabric.

'Make the hole bigger, Kid!' Butch shouted up at him. 'That hole ain't big enough to stop us short of France!'

Sundance worked at it dutifully and soon there was a nice, large rent in the balloon and the gas rushing out made the ragged edges sing. They started to drop as they passed the coast. 'We're gonna land in the water, and I've already 'ad my bath this month!' Jimmy wailed.

Butch pointed ahead of them. 'Look, there's some islands coming up!'

The balloon plunged lower and lower as the gas-bag deflated. In a few minutes it deposited them with a soft splash about ten yards off-shore from a small island. The depleted gas-bag covered them all with its folds. They struggled out from under the fabric, waded into the water and on to dry land.

The 'island' was a barren chunk of rock devoid of plant-life, that poked its spiny head all of three feet above the water – no place to be in rough weather. Martinette informed them that this oasis formed part of a chain of islands called *The Naze*, and they had been blown very near to where they boarded the train.

They wondered how they were going to get back to the mainland; but just as they reached the depths of the doldrums they spotted a fisherman in a paint-scarred boat, weaving a course through the inlets. They shouted and waved and eventually managed to attract his attention. An astounding feat, it transpired, as he was three-quarters deaf and had forgotten his glasses that morning. They conveyed their desire for passage with much shouting, and at last made a breakthrough. The compensation they settled on to persuade the fisherman to give up his daily catch could, considering where they were, have been classified as piracy on the high seas.

They landed wet and bedraggled, and made their weary way to a railway station.

Martinette cautioned them that there would probably be an all-points bulletin out for them and they should stay out of sight until he had a chance to make a telephone call. Martinette went into the small station alone, found the station master, showed him his credentials and commandeered his telephone. In a few minutes he had reached his friend, the chief superintendent, told him of their dilemma and that the project was to remain hush-hush. The chief superintendent promised to get the search called off immediately and, although Martinette owed him a more detailed explanation, agreed to let him off until he saw him in person. They made a strange sight boarding the train, and were avoided by the gentlefolk riding into London.

When they disembarked at Liverpool Street the first thing that attracted their attention was a news-vendor calling loudly to potential customers: 'Daring train robbery! The Kaiser's personal envoy is robbed of millions!' Reginald went up and procured copies of all the daily papers and rejoined the others. They huddled in a corner and read the accounts of their exploits, of which no two matched.

Jimmy gave a nervous laugh. 'Look, it says 'ere we got away with a fortune in jewels and money. Can you imagine that? That's a laugh, ain't it?'

Butch looked at him speculatively and went back to reading his own paper.

'Thank God,' Martinette declared with relief, 'no one is mentioned by name, and the descriptions are vague enough to fit thousands of people.'

'Yeah, I'm a little surprised at that,' Butch admitted. 'I sure thought De Ford would go hot-foot for the papers, and blab to them about everything.'

'It appears,' Martinette commented dryly, 'that my telephone call was made in the nick of time. Count yourself lucky.'

'And you,' Butch retorted. 'The Kid and me decided that if we were going down, sure as a bear shits in the woods, you were comin' with us.'

Martinette remained impassive. 'Perhaps it's a good thing it wasn't put to the test.'

As they left Liverpool Street station, Martinette told Butch and Sundance that he wanted to see them in his office, he hoped for the last time, so that he could get all the details from start to finish for his report. He said he would call with a time and left without a backward glance.

They bid the Titan Crusher farewell, assuring him that Martinette would rescue the 'poor lady' and that they would see him soon and let him know how it came out. Basa grinned, told them he'd be available for any other little capers as he'd really enjoyed himself, gave them each a parting bearhug that left them breathless, and strode off.

Jimmy was about to walk away when Butch collared him. 'I think we got some talking to do, my little Cockney friend.'

'What do ya mean?' Jimmy asked guiltily. Butch pointed to the satchel without a word. 'Oh, that,' Jimmy said. 'I was going to tell you about it, honest.'

'Sure you were. How much did you get?'

'Dunno mate, do I? Didn't exactly have time to sit around and count it.'

'In that case it'll be right pleasurable to sit around and count it together. You come with us. We're going back to Reginald's house in Mayfair.'

The four men entered the drawing room and shut the heavy door behind them. Sundance made a beeline for the liquor cabinet. Butch drew the heavy velvet curtains together, shutting out the sunlight that slanted into the room. Reginald lit the gas lamps and turned them up high so that the shadows retreated to the distant corners. Sundance handed around the drinks and they imbibed in silence, and with gratitude.

Jimmy still clutched his satchel as if his fingers were glued to it and showed his reluctance when Butch prised it away from him with a glare of gamecock belligerence. It died a-borning and his chirpy cockney face became morose.

Butch opened the satchel, turned it upside down and dumped the contents on the carpet. Multi-faceted and many-coloured gems cascaded down and rolled under chairs. A jewelled tiara, several strings of pearls and a dozen signet rings fell into a heap. Stacks of bank notes, neatly packaged, tumbled out and formed a rough pyramid.

'By God!' Reginald exclaimed wide eyed. 'A king's ransom, we're rich!'

Butch stared at the collection in a daze. 'Looks like there's enough there for me to buy Basa a new tank of laughing gas.'

Sundance guffawed and slapped Butch on the back. 'You're right, *amigo*. Maybe even a whole factory!'

Reginald clapped his hands together. 'I can pay off my father's debts and still have enough left over to provide a dowry for my sister!'

Butch looked meaningfully at Sundance. 'And we don't have to pull off any more jobs.'

'I think I'll buy a pub,' Jimmy chipped in.

Reginald had a sudden thought that creased his brow with concern. 'What if the Germans make an official complaint? Martinette will never let us keep it.'

'To hell with Martinette!' Butch spat out vehemently. 'He was with us the whole time, and there ain't no way he can say we got away with all this.'

'We gotta get rid of these jewels,' Jimmy murmured, deep in thought.

'I understand Holland is an excellent place for that,' said Reginald. 'Perhaps we can arrange for a trip to the Continent, a small holiday, you know, as far as anyone's concerned.'

'That,' Butch decided, 'is what we'll do.'

18 Sylvia who?

Butch took a cigarette from a packet he found lying around, called *Snake Charmer*. He lit it without enthusiasm, blew a wobbly smoke-ring and slumped into a chair. His thoughts were on Sylvia and, now that the commotion had died down, he discovered that he had plenty of time to think about her. 'Damn woman!' he muttered to the empty room. He'd trusted that bitch, and yes, he admitted to himself with a flash of honesty, he had been in love with her. And she'd turned out to be the most scheming, deceitful woman he'd ever met, whose only purpose had been to use him to further her own nefarious plots. Never again, he swore, would he get involved with another woman, at least, in that way. Prostitutes were the only ones you could trust. You hired one to do a specific job, paid the asking price and got on with it. At the end, you parted without recriminations and with the knowledge that you'd probably never see each other again. And no heartache, no pain, no emotional outbursts. That damned Martinette had set him off so that he was sitting here now, smoking, biting his lip, and so tense that he had a backache, when he'd called to arrange a time for Butch and Sundance to come to the Foreign Office. He had made a laconic comment that when the train had reached its destination, Sylvia, along with the colonel, had been whisked off to the German embassy, and that his information was that she'd be leaving the country at once, doubtless to carry on her work where she was not as well known. Or perhaps, Martinette put in the spur, to join Mata Hari who had already left the country. Didn't Butch think they made a perfect couple?

The door to the drawing room opened and Sundance popped his head in. 'Reginald's just come back from the country – this you gotta see.'

'See what?' Butch asked in annoyance. 'I don't wanna see nothin'. Just leave me alone.'

'Butch, are you in there?' Reginald called from the hall. 'I want you to meet someone.'

Sundance opened the door wide and Reginald came through. Butch was about to utter as nasty a remark as he could at short notice when Reginald stepped aside; and Butch stared, his mouth open wide.

'May I introduce my sister, Samantha,' Reginald said with pride.

Samantha Ratlett was the most beautiful girl Butch had ever seen, so totally unlike her brother that Butch's first thought was about whether there had been a mix up of babies at the hospital. Long, golden hair that fell to her shoulders framed a perfect oval face. Cornflower blue eyes under blonde lashes looked at him with innocence, intelligence and a hint of mischief. The full-lipped smile was ravishing. Butch drew in a deep breath, all thoughts of Sylvia What's-her-name gone.

19 'Whadda we do now, Butch?'

Butch and Sundance arrived at the Foreign Office bathed, brushed and attired in new suits, impeccably fitted bowlers perched on their heads, and they each carried ebony-handled walking sticks. They had taken meticulous care to prepare for what they hoped was the final meeting with Martinette. Neither one had voiced his feelings of apprehension for what might actually lie in store for him. They trod the now familiar path to Martinette's door, and Butch knocked. Martinette opened it and stared at them without expression.

'The Home Secretary wants to see you. Follow me.' He made it a curt command. Martinette led the way through Whitehall to the Home Office and entered the building. A feeling of gloom had descended like a dark cloud on Butch and Sundance. They were held up in the anteroom for only a minute while the private secretary informed the minister of their arrival, and they were ushered into the office.

Winston Churchill came to greet them, hands extended, a smile creasing his pudgy face into myriad lines.

'Mr Cassidy and ... what is your real name? I can hardly call you *Mr Kid*.'

'Harry Longbaugh,' Sundance murmured in embarrassment, 'but I'd be obliged if you'd call me *Sundance*. All ma friends do.'

Churchill looked at him up from under heavy lids in the way for which he'd already become known. 'As you wish, *Sundance* it is!'

'And call me *Butch*,' Butch volunteered.

Churchill nodded. 'Please sit down, gentlemen.'

They dropped into buttoned leather chairs arranged in a semi-circle around a massive mahogany desk. Churchill sat down behind the desk and rocked gently in his swivel chair. On the wall behind Churchill's head were a group of pictures of him as a young officer in the 4th Hussars and another group from when he was part of the Nile Expeditionary Force, where the camera had caught him posing with local sheiks – and in one picture looking as inscrutable as the sphynx that was photographed in the background. Trophies from his military campaigns and his years as a correspondent elbowed each other for room on the other walls, assegais vied for prominence with ivory tusks and hubble-bubble pipes. His desk was an untidy mess of papers and folders and held a globe of the world and a shell-casing that was used as an ashtray, filled with cigar-butts.

Churchill reached for a thick folder on the desk and tapped it with a fingernail. 'These are the translations of the papers which you – liberated. I don't speak German,' he added with a smile. 'Barbaric language. I'll never learn it and won't even try until the Kaiser marches on London.' His impish grin dismissed any thought of that as a possibility. 'They make exceedingly interesting reading. I'll place a copy of this before the King today. I feel sure that when His Majesty has time to digest it the diplomatic couriers will be leaving for Berlin in droves. You see, I feared the Kaiser's expansionist policies would start hostilities between our two countries, perhaps as early as next year. With this material I have every confidence that we shall now be able to delay the inevitable, with luck for another three or four years. It will allow us a breathing space, and will give us time to prepare: time, gentlemen, that we sorely need. We must educate our own politicians as well as forge bonds of friendship and a policy for mutual protection with our potential allies. I must tell you, gentlemen, that there is only one thing worse than fighting with allies, and that is fighting without them. In war you don't have to be nice, you only have to be right!'

Churchill's sonorous voice mesmerized Butch and Sundance; they were overwhelmed by his presence.

'Did we do all that?' Sundance asked in a small voice.

'My dear chap, you have done Britain and the free world an immense service and I, on behalf of this country, offer profound thanks. Now, as to your rewards. I, of course, know of your past history and what I prefer to call your *indiscretions*; but you are still young men and have useful lives ahead of you. I have always believed that a young man cannot expect to get very far in life without getting some good smacks in the eye. Let's assume that you have now received enough of them, and will henceforth continue on clear-sighted.' Churchill stood up and walked over to the window. He beckoned to Butch and Sundance. 'Come over here. There's something I want you to see; something that, if I'm any judge, will gladden your hearts.'

Butch and Sundance went over dutifully and stared down at the pavement where Churchill was pointing. Jonathan De Ford was standing next to a car, a burly uniformed constable at each elbow. He was red in the face and protesting vehemently, his mouth opening and closing in furious bursts. Churchill turned with an impudent grin. 'I thought you'd be pleased to know that your old friend De Ford is being deported. I felt his removal, although his course of action was entirely altruistic, was warranted in view of the services you've performed for us.'

'Well, I'll be damned!' Butch exclaimed.

'Probably, sir, probably. And I shall doubtless keep you company.' Churchill waved at an officer who was looking up at the window. The officer saluted and issued orders to his men, who bustled De Ford into the waiting car. Churchill returned to his seat and indicated that the others do the same. 'Now, for a more tangible reward. Unfortunately, because of the delicacy of the situation, we will be unable to give you the public accolades you so richly deserve.'

Butch hung his head and flushed. 'Aw, that's all right,' he muttered.

'So, instead, I've decided to make use of my special fund created for such purposes, and issue you each with a bank draft for one thousand pounds. And I also think that once the King hears of the part you have played, he will want to reward you in his own way.'

'You mean a *medal*?' Sundance said impressed. 'I never had a medal before.'

Churchill's eyes twinkled. 'Entirely possible, Sundance. Now, just one last thing. I would deem it a personal favour if, were another situation to arise where your type of resourcefulness was required, I could call upon you again.'

Martinette jerked his gaze away from the pigeon that peered in at him through the window and stared at Churchill with incredulity. 'But sir, are you aware of what you are saying? The difficulties . . . !'

'Don't argue about the difficulties, Martinette; the difficulties will argue for themselves.'

'Yeah, Martinette,' Butch agreed hotly. 'If Mr Churchill wants us to do a job for him, it's between him and us.'

Churchill slammed his fist on the desk. 'Well said, Butch! I'm glad I can count on you. And you too, Sundance. In fact I'd appreciate it if you'd come back to see me in a fortnight. I think I have something that may require your talents. And I'm looking forward to our next poker game.'

Sundance thought of the fleecing he had taken, and coloured. 'Sure, Mr Churchill, any time.'

Martinette slumped dejectedly in his seat. When one had friends in Court . . .

Back in the street, Butch and Sundance nodded a curt goodbye to Martinette and strode off.

'How about that!' Sundance enthused, then stopped abruptly. Butch also stopped and they looked at each other for a long moment. 'Are you thinking what I'm thinking?' Sundance asked.

'I think so, Kid. We just got conned into being spies for the British Government.'

'Whadda we do now, Butch?' Sundance asked mournfully.

Leslie Thomas
Bare Nell 90p

Little Nell Luscombe, paddling naked in her native Devon streams, was the delight of the local GIs. She grew up into Bare Nell, learning that there was a good living to be made from her substantial charms. From servicing the Weymouth fishermen, she progressed to the pinnacle of her profession . . . running a high class establishment – within earshot of the division bells at Westminster . . .

'A most disarming heroine, guileless and open-hearted, innocent and lascivious . . . it is all good fun. And Nelly's a love!'
DAILY TELEGRAPH

Stephen Vizinczey
In Praise of Older Women 80p

'A cool, comic survey of the sexual education of a young Hungarian, from his first encounter, as a twelve-year-old refugee with the American forces, to his unsatisfactory liaison with a reporter's wife in Canada at "the belated end of his youth", when he was twenty-three . . . elegantly erotic, with masses of that indefinable quality, style . . . this has the real stuff of immortality' PUNCH

'. . . a writer of originality and grace . . . his novel is a delight' GUARDIAN

James Stephens
The Crock of Gold 70p

Part fantasy, part fairy tale, part polemic in the Irish war of the sexes, to explain the story of this remarkable book would be as difficult and pointless as to explain Lear's nonsense rhymes or Lewis Carrol's *Alice* stories. To read it for yourself is the only answer, the only way to discover whose was the crock of gold and where and why it was buried.

Bryan Forbes
International Velvet 60p

The splendid sequal to *National Velvet* the classic story that became the memorable film.

Sarah is the niece of Velvet Brown, the heroine of *National Velvet*, who's now grown up. Orphaned by a road crash, Sarah comes unhappily to England to live with her aunt. Her sadness fades only when she discovers her talent for riding and Sarah finds her horse and her ambition – to ride for Britain and win Olympic gold . . .

Geoff Pike

Henry Golightly 75p

From East of Suez to the grey drizzle of Liverpool, in company with Baggy Rinkle, Willy the Wog and the *Indie* boys, Henry sets out on life with one eye for the distances and the other for the talent on the dockside . . .

'A born storyteller' LESLIE THOMAS

Golightly Adrift 75p

The further adventures of Henry Golightly, fiction's bawdiest sailor of fortune. Tales of dusky maidens and legendary houses of pleasure beckon Henry from the scruffy bed of a Scouser tart and he's off to sample the pleasures of the sunlit southern seas on board the *Caribbean Hunter* . . .

Piers Paul Read

Monk Dawson 80p

'A Voltairean journey through contemporary panaceas . . . we follow Dawson from his Roman Catholic public school through every stage . . . His success, sexual, social, religious and professional, is due to his conviction that he has found the meaning of life, in a world always uncertain of it . . .' SUNDAY TELEGRAPH

'A remarkable novel . . . profoundly moving' GRAHAM GREENE

The Junkers 80p

'A young Englishman in the Foreign Service is posted to Berlin in 1963. He pursues and beds Suzi, who is related to the von Rummelsbergs, a family of expropriated refugee Junkers from Pomerania. One of his tasks turns out to be an investigation of the Rummelsbergs' activities in the Nazi era. The absorbing and contrasting back-history of the three von Rummelsberg brothers is gradually teased out . . .' PUNCH

'Full of cold wit, coldly compelling realism and sentences so stylish they're a joy . . . one of the most promising writers of his generation' GUARDIAN

Hank Searls
Jaws 2 80p

It's two years since the Long Island resort of Amity was terrorized by the monster killer shark . . . the nightmare story that thrilled the world as *Jaws*. Out in the deep water there is a new and even more terrible predator . . . the pregnant mate of the great shark who is even larger – and deadlier – than the male.

Jackie Collins
Lovers and Gamblers £1.50

Al King – rock/soul superstar and legendary superstud; Dallas – smouldering beauty with big ambitions and a sordid past. From London to New York, Hollywood to Rio, they gambled with life. Their story will shock you.

'Erotic . . . glitter and glamour . . . riots, bomb scares, orgies and drug trips . . . a real blockbuster' EVENING STANDARD

Ernest Lehman
The French Atlantic Affair 95p

170 people with nothing to lose and everything to gain from the biggest hijack ever attempted. Their target – the *Marseilles*, their ultimatum – the liner, its passengers and crew will be destroyed in forty-eight hours unless the demand is met. Just thirty-five million dollars and a safe getaway . . .

'A first-class ticket to a voyage of suspense . . . Ernest Lehman is a superb writer' SIDNEY SHELDON

Ian Kennedy Martin
Rekill 75p

Two men, veterans of the same war, their destinies bound together in a manhunt to the death . . .
Van Dhoc, former Vietcong captain, striking across two continents, sworn to take revenge on the US personnel who committed the massacre of Da Loc . . .
And Leeming, US Army Colonel, with a military record peppered with question marks, sent by US Army Intelligence after Van Dhoc, a pursuit leading finally to the Albanian citadel of Scutari.

'For sheer horror, I've rarely read anything to touch it' DAILY EXPRESS

James Herriot
Vet in a Spin 80p

Strapped into the cockpit of a Tiger Moth trainer, James Herriot has swapped his wellingtons and breeches for sheepskin boots and baggy flying suit. The disappointments, triumphs and frustrations of his RAF career remind him repeatedly of incidents in his veterinary practice.

'Marks the emergence of Herriot as a mature writer, with a smooth flowing style, good dialogue and a clutch of new characters like Gertrude, the beer-swilling pig, and Roddy Travers, the travelling man who carried his huge lurcher dog in a pram' YORKSHIRE POST

Colin Dexter
The Silent World of Nicholas Quinn 75p

The newly appointed member of the Oxford Examinations Syndicate was deaf, provincial and gifted. Now he's dead. The trail leads Inspector Morse into a murder puzzle where the clues include an assortment of unsavoury academics, the Arab connections who provide the Syndicates and two tasty ladies . . . And then there's the second murder at the Syndicate . . .

'. . . superior, meticulously-plotted classical detective story' GUARDIAN

Arthur Herzog
Heat 70p

The latest terrifyingly prophetic bestseller from the author of *The Swarm.*

In a secret laboratory, engineer Lawrence Pick and a team of scientists piece together a nightmare prediction of catastrophe . . . the long-feared 'greenhouse effect', which can swiftly put an end to all higher life forms and turn our planet into a self-generating inferno . . .

'Gruesome and alarming' EVENING NEWS

George Markstein
Chance Awakening 80p

The chilling new espionage bestseller from the author of *The Cooler.* A catalogue of second-hand books in the post one morning, one page marked in red ink . . . For Michael Golly, London businessman, it was the code he'd been expecting, even fearing, for years . . . How could he trust anybody, for a minute, for the rest of his life?

'Clever and diabolical' LISTENER